The Iron Widow

Kate Warne, Civil War Spy Series, Book 4

Peg A. Lamphier

Writing Wench Press

Lytle Creek CA

Iron Widow
Kate Warne Civil War Spy Series, Book 4

Copyright © 2019 by Peg Lamphier

Cover Art by Daniel Aley, www.flutterspace.com

Author photo by Marvelle Thompson

Writing Wench Press publishes this edition.

PO Box 113

Lytle Creek, California 92358

Visit the press online at www.peglamphier.com

ISBN: 978-1-947278-09-7

For
Anna Scrum

You never know how strong you are
until being strong is your only choice.
Bob Marley

Also by Peg A. Lamphier

Kate Chase and William Sprague:
Politics and Gender in a Civil War Marriage
❈
Spur Up Your Pegasus:
Family Letters of Salmon, Kate and Nettie Chase,
1844-73
(with James P. McClure and Erika M. Kreger)
❈
Women in American History:
A Social, Political and Cultural Encyclopedia with Document Collection [4
volumes] (with Rosanne Welch)
❈
The Lincoln Special

Kate Warne Civil War Spy Series, Book 1

❈

The Great Show
Kate Warne Civil War Spy Series, Book 2

❈

Deadly Delights
The Perils of Petronella Crabtree, Journal 1

❈

Soldier, Diplomat, Archeologist:
The Bold Life of Louis Palma di Cesnola

❈

Little By Little We Won: Angela Bambace and the Fight for Worker's
Rights

❈

Rebel Belles
Kate Warne, Civil War Spy Series, Book 3

❈

Technical Innovation in American History
An Encyclopedia of Science and Technology
[in 4 volumes (with Rosanne Welch)]

Chapter 1

1855

Kalamazoo Michigan

*L*ily froze, her hands gripping a bean mid-snap. When Pa got in one of his moods, it was best he not notice her.

He stomped across the kitchen, his boots thumping on the floor. "I tole you a hunnerd times woman. I lak my dinner on the table when I come in." Pa advanced on Ma, fist raised. Lily watched his face transform from rage to a kind of eager expectation. He wasn't a big man, but he was big enough.

They'd all been out haying all day, her, Polly, Ma and Pa, so there was no way Mama could have dinner ready. And he knew that. Not that it mattered. It never did. Lily braced herself for what she knew would come next. What always came next.

Pa swung his arm back and brought it forward. His fist met Ma's cheek with a meaty thwack.

Ma's head spun, her body following in a slow pirouette. She twirled, like a leaf caught in the wind, and flew into the corner between the table and the stove. Lily watched Ma catch against the wall before sliding to the floor. The soft thump she made seemed to echo in the violent air.

Pa stalked across the room and leaned over Ma. Lily let the bean drop into her lap. Ma pulled her arms over her head, whimpering in small pants.

"Cow, stop that noise." Pa's voice was low and menacing. He never yelled, never lost control. Joseph Nettleton thought himself a hard man, but a fair one. He required only what was a man's due: strict obedience from his wife and children. His neighbors, stoic Norwegians and Swedes, saw only his neat and prosperous farm. His wife and children knew the real man.

Lily watched as Pa drew back his black booted foot and kicked her mother in the abdomen. Ma squealed and writhed in her corner, but she didn't fight back. If she'd ever fought back, it was so long ago that Lily could not remember.

Pa's face glowed with suppressed excitement. He enjoyed it when his family suffered. He enjoyed all kinds of suffering, from wringing chicken necks to drowning the rats he caught in traps. A grim little smile found his face as Ma pushed herself to her feet. She wavered, caught the table and stayed upright.

"Now you lazy cow, git my dinner on the table." Pa cast his eye upon Lily. "What you lookin' at girl?"

She shook her head and stared down at the green beans cradled in her apron between her legs. She reached for another bean and held her breath. As she snapped the bean into three parts, she sensed his movement. He grabbed her arm, his fingers digging into her flesh like hooks into the blocks of ice they cut from the pond each winter.

"You're no better than your damn worthless mother." His fingers dug into her even harder, and then released her. He grabbed her chin and forced it up. His pale blue eyes reminded Lily of a wolf she'd seen last winter, hungry and pitiless. He gave her one swift, short nod. An understanding passed between them. He dropped his hand and left the kitchen. Lily listened as his great black boots stomped echoes up the stairs.

Lily looked at Ma but didn't move. Once she would have leaped up to help her, but not anymore. There was nothing she could do because Ma wouldn't do nothing for herself. Lily used to pity her, but not anymore. It was one thing for Ma not to defend herself. But she wouldn't defend her daughters either. By the time Lily's body changed from child to the lumpy and messy realities of womanhood, she'd grown to hate her mother almost as much as she hated her father. *Almost.*

A bright red bruise had bloomed on the left side of Ma's face. Ma shuffled over to the stove and pulled the big black iron skillet off the shelf onto the stove. With her right hand, she stirred up the fire, while her left hand probed her cheek. Then she got a chunk of fatback, cut it into bits and laid them in the smoking skillet. The whole time Lily sat watching. Neither of them spoke.

Once the fat sizzled Ma turned and faced Lily. The two women appraised each other. They'd quit saying much to each other. Unspoken sins piled up between them, creating a wall that grew higher with every beating, every horror Pa visited on his family. No one talked anymore, not even little Polly, who escaped most of Pa's violence. So far.

Lily stood, stepped toward the stove, her shoulder brushing Ma's as she did. She dropped her apron full of beans in the skillet and walked out of the house. She paused in the yard, scanning for Pa even though she knew he'd gone upstairs. Years of habit were hard to break. She skirted the barn, a neat two-story affair sporting a fresh coat of whitewash. Pa didn't like sloppiness or half-done tasks. Every building, from the chicken coop to the wood shed, looked new built. Fence posts stood straight, as if they feared slumping in Farmer Nettleton's presence. Though made of logs instead of the fancier board houses found in town, their house had curtained windows and a wide front porch, looking for all the world as if a happy family lived inside.

Before she stepped behind the barn Lily turned and glanced around. No one. The farm might appear perfect, but it wasn't. It reminded her of an apple she'd once filched out of the barrel in the cellar, picking it because it had been the reddest and smoothest. But when she bit into it she found a dark rotten core, part crusty, part oozy. Worst of all, there'd been a worm in the apple's black heart. Well, to be honest, half a worm. She'd spat out the wormy bite but not before she felt the creature wiggling in her mouth. These days she was a lot more careful about biting into fruit. She nibbled around the outside, working her way toward the center a little bite at a time. The farm was like that apple and Lily lived there like she ate apples.

Behind the barn she found her favorite tree stump and sat. It was a little higher than other stumps and had a seat cut in it. When she was younger she liked to pretend the stump was a throne and she the queen. She tried to recapture that feeling of being an unrecognized queen, one sitting on a golden throne masquerading as a tree stump. She kept hearing her father's fist hit Ma's face. Pretending got harder and harder to do.

No one in Kalamazoo Michigan ever got out. No one ever became rich or famous. How could they? Not from Kalama-

4

zoo. If I could only get to Detroit. Or Chicago. Great things could happen in cities like that. But not Kalamazoo.

When she was younger, she thought if she did well at the little school in town, Pa would let her go away for teacher training. Kalamazoo College didn't take women, but there was a teachers college in Detroit that did. She used to dream she would go there. That dream should have died years ago, but she hadn't given up on it. At least not until yesterday.

Farmer Gosford had come courting yesterday. He came after church like he'd been doing for months, pretending he was there to talk to Pa. He was a big lump of a man, like God forgot to finish him. His hands were as big as dinner plates and his ears stuck straight out. Every time the wind blew Lily feared Farmer Gosford's ears would catch the wind like a sheet blowing on the clothesline and sail him away. Worst was his eyes, which followed Lily every move like she was a tender rabbit he wanted to boil in his stew pot.

Once Farmer Gosford had been just a farm hand, the awkward son of a family too poor to do anything more than work other people's farms for wages so small they never quit being poor. Then word came of the gold strike in California and Bob up and traveled west. He returned a little over a year ago, his skin tanned a soft nut brown that made his mouse brown hair seem almost blond and arms bulging from working the gold fields. Like most of the Forty-Niners, he didn't get rich in California, but he made enough money to buy the farm outside Kalamazoo near where Lily's family lived.

That he once escaped Kalamazoo and returned made it clear he was a fool. He was also a fool for her, which made her wonder even more about his mental acuity. Not that Lily undervalued herself. Her thick black hair, which reached nearly

5

to her knees when undone, coupled with eyes so blue they were almost purple. Her hair and eyes fascinated men less than her chest. Lily grew breasts back when the other girls her age still looked like children. By the time she was fifteen she commanded a prodigious bosom and had begun to under-stand its power over men, young and old, good and bad. She was the belle of Kalamazoo, for whatever good that did her. Being pretty didn't buy a girl a train ticket away from this aw-ful place. Farmer Gosford probably imagined Pa would leave her the farm when he died and but Lily didn't think so. He probably wasn't going to leave his daughters anything.

Sunday afternoons he, her parents and she would sit in the house's front room. The men talked about cows and goats, how and when to plow in spring. They spoke of reapers and mules and the money Pa made in oats and corn.

Ma darned socks and mended shirts, but never said a word unless asked to. And she wasn't asked to. Lily spent most of these visits pretending she didn't notice Farmer Gosford's greedy fascination with her chest. As winter turned to spring, they'd moved to the front porch. Lily felt even more exposed outside the parlor's gloom. Still, her parents pretended not to notice Gosford's unseemly interest in Lily's body. He never asked about her nor spoke to her. He never asked her to take a walk, nor showed any interest in her thoughts. He never spoke of ideas and as far as Lily could tell, he'd never read a book. In short, Farmer Gosford was the dullest man she'd ever had the misfortune to meet, not that she'd met that many men.

But he had a solid farm with a neat little white house. Could I? Would it be worth it to escape Pa and Ma? It was all she thought about these days. *Could I? Should I? And what about the school in Detroit?*

Yesterday her dreams of teachers college died. They'd been out on the porch, the July afternoon hot and muggy, everyone's shirtsleeves rolled up. Pa was holding forth about education and how it was foolish and useless. Once a man could read a little and do enough arithmetic to keep his books, he didn't need any more schooling. Pa figured education was something lazy men used to avoid hard work. Farmer Gosford agreed with Pa. Farmer Gosford always agreed with Pa. Both men also agreed that however foolish education was for men it was more foolish to educate women.

Lily listened to them congratulate themselves on their shared belief that God abhorred an educated woman. Her heart beating in her chest like a wild thing, she thrust herself into a gap in their conversation. "But Pa, don't you agree that someone has to teach boys to read and do their sums? And if women are teachers, then men can do more important work?" Lily had been working on this argument. They needed teachers everywhere. She could go anywhere if she were a teacher. She could buy books and read and read and read. She could be someone. She could escape Pa.

Pa and Farmer Gosford both stared at her as if she was a talking goat. Pa rocked back in his chair and looked down his sharp nose at her. "Well, that may be Lily girl, but it ain't natural. An educated woman is an abomination."

Farmer Gosford wagged his head up and down, his dirty blond hair flopping against his forehead.

Pa thumped his chair forward. "No gal o' mine would ever suffer such a fate."

"But Pa," she started. She wanted to argue that as a teacher she would make wages, which she could send to him. Pa liked money. More than he liked people for sure. It was an argument that might work.

He was having none of it, not with Farmer Gosford watching. "Don't argue with me Lily girl. I've raised you to be a decent woman and a farmer's wife. No daughter of mine will run around the city besmirching her character and acting unnatural." He shook his head. "You'll be a wife and mother." Then he said the worst thing he'd ever said to her. "Just like your Ma."

Lily sighed and pushed herself off her stump. She needed to set the table and make sure Polly's hands and face were clean. Pa hated it when his daughters weren't perfect. Ma might not protect her daughters, but Lily did what she could to keep Pa's eye off her little sister.

Pa came to her room that night. After he returned to the room he shared with Ma, Lily packed a bag, kissed her sleeping sister and left the house. She would return only once more.

Chapter 2

January 5, 1862
Washington City

*K*ate's bedroom door closed with a soft snick. She rolled over, throwing her arm up over her eyes against the morning light, then peeked out just a little. Hazzard stood in front of the bed, a breakfast tray held before him. He wore the deep blue velvet-dressing robe she'd given him for Christmas. And that was all. A devastating nest of dark brown chest hair curled at his throat where the robe's shawl collar didn't meet. A lock of black hair curled down onto his forehead, drawing attention to his dark eyes.

"Did you go downstairs like that?" Kate pushed herself up onto her elbows and squinted up at him.

He grinned at her, his teeth flashing against his lips. "Mrs. Webster and Odetta both say I am a fellow without parallel." He straightened his spine and puffed out his chest as he delivered this line.

Kate snickered. If only they knew how without parallel he was. Still, there was no reason to feed his ego. She tipped her chin at the tray he still held. "Is that breakfast?"

"Yes it is, my love." He set the tray on her side table and sat on the bed next to her and leaned in for a kiss. One kiss turned into several. She nuzzled his neck, breathing him in. These days Hazzard carried with him an intoxicating whiff of gunpowder. She made a low, soft sound as she moved to his mouth. Hazzard had the most delicious lips. They nibbled at her own lips, and then trailed a line of kisses across her cheek to her ear and down her neck. She slipped her hand inside his robe, enjoying the contrast between the soft furriness of his chest hair and the hardness of his muscles. He growled and pulled away from her. "Siren," he whispered in her ear. "If I'm not back at Fort Washington by mid-day they'll cashier me out of the Army."

Kate grinned and held her hand out for her cup of coffee. "More artillery lessons?"

He nodded. "I wish McClellan would make up his mind. Either Washington City's fortifications are the priority or Fort Washington's readiness."

"He's punishing you," Kate said, sipping her coffee. Odetta made coffee the New Orleans way, with chicory, which added just the right combination of sweet and sour slipperiness and a dash of cream, which she claimed made the coffee bloom. "He's jealous of your influence with Mr. Lincoln."

Kate watched Hazzard eat a beignet. How could he eat first thing in the morning? "And he's been down with the typhoid fever."

"Which he wouldn't have if he wasn't so enamored of military parades. That's where the General got sick, reviewing Porter's division. We ought to be fighting, not parading. It's stupid," Hazzard said through a mouthful of pastry. "And Mr. Lincoln agrees. I suspect the president is as infected with all the 'On to Richmond' talk as the rest of Washington."

She rolled herself out of bed and reached for her robe. "See? You have Mr. Lincoln's ear and Mr. Lincoln is less enamored of his general-in-chief than he was a few months ago. For that alone McClellan hates you."

Hazzard snorted. "For all his efficiency and modern ideas, McClellan's jealous of anyone else with power. That's half the reason General Scott had to go."

"General Scott is also just about two-hundred years old. You know I adore the old ma, but this is one war too many for him. But you're right, McClellan's insecure. People say he thinks he's grander than the president. It's why they call him the Little Napoleon behind his back." She kissed Hazzard's cheek and headed for the door. "I'm going downstairs to ask Odetta for bath water. Would you like to join me?" She shot him a look over her shoulder, eyebrow arched in a query.

Hazzard threw back his head and laughed. "Heavens, no. I'll never get out of here."

Kate closed the door to her bedroom with a smile. It was nice to find out the lady's magazines were wrong— succumbing to a Hazzard's charms didn't cause him to lose respect for her. Instead, their feelings seemed to expand and expand again. And Hazzard hadn't developed an unfortunate tendency towards possessiveness either. He came and went, as did she, and they met in the middle, as equals. They couldn't go on forever like this, but for now, it was enough.

She came down the stairs to find the kitchen air redolent with the scents of coffee and frying potatoes. The kitchen was Kate's favorite room in the house, and not just because it often smelled like heaven. The Washington contingent of the Pinkerton Detective Agency gathered around the extra large table several times a week, sometimes just for food and company, sometimes for strategy and planning meetings. This morning she found Uncle Juba at the table, and Odetta at the stove stirring potatoes, but no one else was around. Given it was mid-morning Kate was unsurprised.

Juba rattled the newspaper he was reading and then folded it halfway down and peered over it. "You see?" He rattled the newspaper again.

"President Tyler died? I did see that. I wasn't aware he was still alive."

"No, not that." Juba shook the newspaper again.

"Oh, you mean the fighting on the Cumberland River?" She smiled her sweetest smile.

"Kate." Juba's eyebrows lowered and tightened.

Odetta nudged Kate with her elbow. "Quit torturing the poor man."

Kate couldn't face her cook's censure. "Fine. You mean the news about Mrs. Greenhow?" Kate laid a kiss on Odetta's cheek. "Thanks for breakfast in bed."

Odetta smiled at Kate. It was a smiling sort of morning. "After I saw the paper it seemed you deserved a little treat. It's a good day." She inclined her head at Juba's newspaper.

Kate turned back to the table and held out her hand. "Here, let me see it."

Juba folded the newspaper so that its headline showed. "Mrs. Greenhow Moved to Old Capitol Prison!"

Late last summer Mr. Lincoln ordered the now notorious Confederate spy Rose Greenhow arrested. Lincoln and General Scott charged the Pinkertons with investigating Greenhow's spy network and supervising Fort Greenhow, as the Washington newspapers dubbed her home. Greenhow's house arrest allowed her to continue her spying activities, though she had no idea her Pinkerton guards knew what she was doing. One evening she escaped. Kate followed her, fought her and threw her in the canal. Then she hauled Rose out of the water and drug her back to her prison home. Kate couldn't remember the evening without a smile.

In December Rose sent an acid-laced letter to Mr. Seward, Lincoln's secretary of State. To compound the offense, she sent a copy of her Seward letter to a newspaper in Richmond, the Confederate capital, thus demonstrating her own ability to circumvent all efforts to contain her network. Her letter accused both Seward and the Union government of abusing women, using words like 'tyranny' and 'atrocity' to great effect.

The letter solved two problems for the Pinkertons. First, they had solid evidence that Mr. Seward had passed important military intelligence to Greenhow before Bull Run. The letters he wrote the lady spy had been those of a lonely man trying to impress an attractive widow, not the purposeful acts of a treasonous turncoat, but they presented a military intelligence problem. But Mr. Seward was not the sort to fall to public pressure or embarrassment. He'd severed all relations with Mrs. Greenhow and shifted her to his enemy list. Plus, the tone of Mrs. Greenhow's letter was so vituperative that it discredited her in the eyes of all but the most enthusiastic Confederate sympathizers. Worse, at least for the lady, Mr. Lincoln rethought his policy of house arrest for lady spies and ordered Mrs. Greenhow to prison. Kate couldn't have gotten better results if she'd written the letter herself.

Mr. Lincoln let it go on longer than he should have. The diplomatic mess with the British over two captured Confederate diplomats took most of the president's attention in November and December, as had a storm of corruption charges swirling around his secretary of war Simon Cameron. Compared to those problems the shenanigan of a nest of imprisoned lady spies must have seemed like small beans to the President.

Four days ago the diplomatic crisis resolved, ending British threats of war. And the Senate confirmed Mr. Stanton as the new Secretary of War. With the worst of his troubles resolved Mr. Lincoln's ordered Rose's removal from her home to the Old Capitol Prison. That had been two days ago. Yesterday Kate oversaw a contingent of army privates boarding up Rose's windows and removing from the house all papers and valuables. At 4 PM a windowless carriage pulled up in front of the house and Kate had the great pleasure of escorting Rose to a real prison.

The infuriating woman insisted her nine-year-old daughter Little Rose accompany her to the Old Capitol Prison. As Rose stepped into the carriage she turned to Kate and said, "I hope that in the future you will have a nobler employment than terrorizing decent and defenseless women and children."

Kate barked a laugh. "Madame you are a traitor and as defenseless as a rattlesnake. And you're the one taking your daughter to jail, not us." Resisting the impulse to shove the lady spy, Kate instead handed Rose and her daughter into the carriage and shut the door, sparing a moment of pity for the little girl. What sort of mother took her child to prison with her? Kate shrugged it off, powerless to improve Mrs. Greenhow's parenting skills. She rode home, had dinner and two glasses of wine and retired to her bedroom with her dashing artillery captain. And thought about Mrs. Greenhow not once all evening.

Kate shook her head as she read the newspaper Juba handed her. "I'd like to hang this headline on my bedroom wall and gaze upon it every day."

Juba heaved out a deep breath. "Took long enough, didn't it?"

"Too long," Kate agreed as she handed Juba's newspaper back to him. She pulled out a chair and sat down next to Juba. "The important thing is she's not a Pinkerton problem anymore." The Old Capitol building was so called because the government moved to the massive brick building after the British burned the Capitol in the War of 1812. Four years later, with the Capitol restored to glory, the Old Capitol became a school and later a boarding house. After the war began, the Army converted the building into a jail for political and military prisoners. That meant everyone in the Old Capitol Prison was the Army's problem and the Pinkerton's were at last free of Rose Greenhow.

Kate leaned back in her chair and appraised Juba. He was a small, dark-skinned man and her father's half-brother. He'd also been her mainstay after her parents died in a circus accident and for the last few years her favorite detecting partner. Juba had little to do with Fort Greenhow the past few months because it would have been unacceptable to all but the most radical liberals to have a black man guarding a white woman. And he'd been busy with some project of his own, though he'd been mighty secretive about it. "When are you going to be ready to tell me what you've been up to?"

15

Juba pulled on a wide-eyed, innocent face. "What are you going on about, Katie dear?"

Kate resisted the impulse to punch her uncle in the arm. "You know what I mean. You and Columbus are up to something."

"We are. It's just that Columbus and I agreed you had enough to worry about. And it don't concern you. Not yet."

Kate tried not to feel hurt. Behind her Odetta snorted. Kate's heart lifted a little.

Odetta came over to the table and stood between them, hands on her hips. She glared at Juba. A firm stare from Odetta could wilt men stronger than Juba. Kate was glad the cook had Juba in her sights and not herself.

Juba rubbed his hands over his head and looked up at Odetta. "You're right." He looked back at Kate. "It's not that I don't want to tell you. It's just that you've been through a lot. I wanted you to have a little break from all this spy nonsense."

Before Kate could say anything he held up his hand and continued.

"Remember when we were in Richmond and we met the Van Lew ladies."

Kate nodded. "Eliza and her daughter Elizabeth. They were wonderful, weren't they?"

"They sure were. And you know Miss Van Lew had all her slaves, really her pretend slaves, organized to spy on the Confederate government." Juba shared a meaningful look with Kate. The Van Lew women had freed the family's slaves when Mr. Van Lew died, but in Virginia an ex-slave had to leave the state. In an act of unimaginable bravery, they'd stayed with the Van Lews to fight slavery from the inside. "So me and Columbus figured we could organize colored folks here in Washington and connect them to the Van Lew's network."

"Huh." Kate tipped her chair back on its hind legs then thumped it forward. "Think you can pull it off?"

He nodded. "Yeah. We're working with people who are used to making sure white folks don't take no notice of them."

"And what kind of information would you move?" Kate saw a half a dozen uses for a black spy network, but she wanted to know what Juba thought.

"All sorts of things. Fortifications. Troop movements. Leadership changes. General attitudes. Mr. Lincoln would want to know all that. Mr. Stanton too."

"Hmmm." Kate bit her lip. "Have you considered the Irregulars?" Last summer their kitchen maid Louisa organized a band of street children into an effective surveillance unit. When one of them asked if they were regular Pinkertons Kate had joked that they were Irregular. The name stuck.

"The children? No. It's too dangerous."

Kate shook her head. "Not for moving across enemy lines or anything like that. Just for informational gathering around town. People don't see children and children see things adults don't. Plus we'd have a reason to keep paying them."

"And feeding them," Odetta said from her post at the kitchen sink.

"Right," Kate said. Odetta took pleasure in the pack of children that invaded her kitchen most days. "And Louisa's a good liaison."

"Speak of the girl and she appears," Odetta, proclaimed in her testifying-at-church voice. A second later Louisa burst through the back door.

Louisa brought with her into the kitchen a host of stable smells, from saddle soap to horse manure. A small black and white dog followed behind her and bounced into Kate's lap.

"Miss Kate," Louisa half-hollered, her light brown face crinkling with excitement. "I taught Excelsior a new trick. All by myself."

Kate dropped a kiss on Monty's head, partly to disguise the small smile growing on her face. She very much doubted a sixteen-year-old maid had taught the big white circus horse anything he didn't already know. He was smarter than most people and had been performing since before Kate was born. Still, the girl's excitement was infectious. Kate looked up at her horse-crazy maid. "What can he do now?"

"I taught him to play Tip Tac Toe." Louisa's face broke into a broad smile.

Kate tried not to laugh. "Excelsior can hold chalk?"

"No silly," Louisa said with a giggle. "We don't use a chalk and a slate. I draw in the dirt with a stick." Louisa chattered about Excelsior's training and the games they'd played together until a knock at the door interrupted them. "I'll get it," Louisa sung out and ran off toward the front of the house. Monty jumped down from Kate's lap and ran after her.

Kate stared at Juba.

"What?" he asked, hands raised palm up in surrender.

"See? She needs more to do. Something meaningful."

"Fine," he said. "But if anything happens to her or your irregulars, don't blame me." He smiled when he said it, taking the sting out of his words.

Hattie came into the kitchen then, followed by Charlotte and Timothy Webster. Charlotte nodded at Kate, who noticed her cheerful housekeeper and bookkeeper had a rather tight hold on her husband's arm. Hattie frowned at the Websters and crossed her arms over her chest.

Timothy patted his wife's hand and sat his battered carpetbag down on the kitchen floor. "Give me a kiss Katie, for I'm off to the wilds of Virginia." His blue eyes sparkled in good humor.

Kate pushed back her chair and stood tiptoe to plant a sound kiss on Timothy's weathered cheek, just above where his beard started. "You sure?"

He nodded. "I've got letters I collected in Baltimore. My job is to get them across the lines to Richmond."

Kate looked from Charlotte, who hadn't let go of her husband's arm, to the still-frowning Hattie. Hattie unfolded her arms and moved to the stove to pour herself a cup of coffee.

Timothy saw it all. "I'll be fine. Those Baltimore boys never figured out I was undercover, which means I've got as good a set of rebel credentials as anyone."

Kate agreed. The previous year Timothy and Hattie had infiltrated a web of Confederate sympathizers in Baltimore and uncovered a plot to assassinate Mr. Lincoln. Timothy's current idea was to volunteer himself as a letter courier to those same people. As the intermediary he'd have access to the information crossing the lines between Baltimore, a rebel stronghold and Richmond, the Confederate capitol.

Louisa pushed open the swinging kitchen door and, taking in the scene, slipped an arm around Charlotte's waist. Charlotte smiled down at the girl and hugged her back.

Timothy turned and kissed his wife, then pulled her, Louisa, Kate, and Hattie into a hug. "I'll be fine. I've got a thousand Rebel contacts and no one suspects me. And I'll be back in ten days."

"And if it works the way it should, I'll go back with him as his wife just like we did last year in Baltimore," Hattie said. "It makes for a great disguise."

This was the part of the plan that Kate both loved and hated. Hattie was right. Timothy's performance as a Confederate mail carrier would be a lot more convincing if his wife went south with him. And it was better if Hattie pretended to be Mrs. Webster. Charlotte had no experience pretending to be someone she was not. And the Washington branch of the Pinkertons needed Charlotte in Washington to keep their records. But Hattie would be gone for months if it worked out like they planned. Kate liked them all living in this house together and while Charlotte, Louisa and Odetta were all perfectly nice, Hattie was her best friend.

Charlotte blew out a loud breath and pushed her husband toward the door. "If you're going you best get going."

There was a flurry of goodbyes. Juba went out with Timothy. The plan was for two men to travel to Alexandria together. From there Timothy would go on alone and Juba would come home. Kate had learned not to ask what they were doing. They weren't talking about it, at least not yet.

Louisa pulled a yellowish envelope out of her apron pocket. Monty stood on his hind legs like he thought she had a treat for him. "No, silly boy. Telegram, Miz Kate." She handed Kate the envelope and then gave Monty half a cookie. Odetta pretended not to notice.

Kate grabbed a kitchen knife and slit the envelope open. She looked at the slip of paper inside and sighed. "Could you be more cryptic Allan?"

"What is it?" Juba held his hand out for the telegram.

Kate shook her head and handed him the slip of paper. "If it's what I think it is, it's bad news."

Jan. 5, 1862

If you are today without employment take next train to NY. Mr. S will meet you at depot. Black Widow possible.

EJ Allen

She handed the telegram to Charlotte, who read it and held it at arm's length as if it were a rotting carcass. "Is this that case from a few years ago? What would it be? 1858?"

Kate blew out a deep breath. "57 I think. I'd been on the job less than a year."

Charlotte sat the telegram on the table and stepped away from it. "No one catches them all, not even you. And that Black Widow was one of the worst."

"She was a monster." It seemed to Kate like she was admitting something shameful. "I should have found her."

Charlotte hugged her and let her go. "It looks like you've got another chance."

Kate wasn't so sure she wanted another chance. How many people had the Black Widow killed in the years since Kate's failure?

Hazzard stepped into the kitchen just then, still buttoning the brass buttons on his navy blue uniform jacket. He took one look at Kate's stricken face and froze. "What did I miss?"

Kate looked at Hazzard, resplendent in his officer's uniform. She didn't want to leave him. Not one bit. But the Black Widow could not be ignored.

Peg A. Lamphier

"We might have a break in an old case." She took a deep breath and blew it out. "I have to catch a black widow."

Chapter 3

1855-1856

Kalamazoo, Michigan

rom nearly the first her plan had gone terribly, horribly wrong. Farmer Gosford answered the door to her knock and invited her right in. Just as she knew he would.

She was sitting at his kitchen table while he bustled around the kitchen, stirring up the fire for tea when Lily came out with it. "Mr. Gosford, you have been courting me, have you not?"

He stopped his fussing at the stove and turned to stare at her. After a moment he spoke. "I have Miss Nettleton. I took a chance on the gold fields so I could come home with the money to buy a farm. I have that now, but I'd like a worthy wife to work it with me. And of courser I want sons." He blushed, pink to his ears. "And a daughter or two if they were as pretty as their mama. If you'll excuse me saying so."

Lily repressed a shudder at his vision. It wasn't college in Detroit and a life of independence. But what were her options? With no money, no schooling past eighth grade, nothing to call her own, not even the dress on her back, what choice did she have? She lowered her chin and looked up at him through her thick black eyelashes. Blink. Blink. Blink.

He fell to his knees before her. "Would ye marry me then Miss Nettleton? Would you consent to be my wife?"

She looked down at her hands and demurely nodded her head so she missed the piggy look of triumph that swept over his face when she said yes.

He left her alone that night, insisting he ask her father for her hand before making her his wife. He returned mid-morning with the black-clad preacher and her family. After a swift ceremony in the little white house's front parlor, Gosford and Pa shook hands and shared a drink from a whiskey bottle, bought for just that purpose. Ma said nothing. Her distant sadness made Lily angry. After the ceremony Lily watched Polly run around the farmyard chasing chickens. She caught a little black bantam rooster and brought it over to Lily for her inspection. "Can I come visit you?" Polly shifted her feet and avoided Lily's eyes when she asked.

Lily grabbed her sister's hand. Polly was fifteen years old, but not nearly so developed as Lily had been at that age and not so pretty either. She'd inherited their mother's wan complexion and mousy brown hair. Polly's cornflower blue eyes were her best feature, that and her sweet disposition. "You come visit me anytime you want. And if you have any trouble with Pa, you tell me, you hear?"

Polly nodded and blinked her watery eyes. "I'll miss you."

"I'm right down the road," Lily replied, trying to keep her voice steady and firm. Crying wouldn't help the situation. "We'll see each other all the time. And remember, tell me if

Pa bothers you." She stared hard at Polly to make sure the girl got the message.

But she didn't' see Polly all the time. Not at all. Mr. Gosford didn't like visitors, not even Pa. What he liked was Lily. Or Lily's body, more like. Her new husband took her for the first time right there on the living room floor only minutes after her family and the preacher left. He'd pushed her down on the floor and thrust his knee between her legs while he tore at the buttons on her dress.

"You're mine now and I can do whatever I want to you. You got a wife's duty now."

Lily recognized the fevered expression that flushed over his face. She'd seen it on Pa's face.

Impatient with her buttons, he tore at her dress, and scooped her breasts right out of her corset. "I thought I'd die before I got my hands on these great big tits of yours." He licked and bit them, groaning like a stuck bear as he did. Then he'd pushed himself up on his knees and unbuttoned his pants. The only good thing about it was he didn't notice she wasn't a virgin. When he finished, he collapsed on her, crushing the breath out of her. But before too long he pushed himself up, chewed on her breasts some more and was ready to go again in no time. That night seemed to have extra hours in it and when Farmer Gosford fell asleep at dawn Lily didn't even have the strength to wash herself.

He made her follow him around the farm, ostensibly to help with the chores, but really to control her every waking minute. He made her eat dinner with her dress down around her waist. "One day the kiddies will come and we'll have to be a mite more careful," he told her in between noisy, slurping bites of beef stew, "but for now I'm getting all I can." Lily

25

didn't understand his bottomless need but she learned she didn't have to understand. Only endure.

By fall Lily was pregnant. It didn't stop his lust, nor even slow him down. She became a thing, a great, gaping hole into which he emptied himself again and again. He never kissed her, not even when she told him she was going to have a baby.

One day in late February a Chinook began to blow. Warm air from the south turned the snowdrifts into piles of mush and the icicles all dripped and dropped off the eaves. The false spring drove Gosford into a frenzy of rutting. On the second day of his almost continual assault her belly ripped apart in great waves of pain. She screamed and screamed as her baby bled out of her.

The noise and mess made him angry. He stood over the bed where she laid leaking blood, his hands balled into ham sized fists. Lily didn't know if the baby had been a boy or girl. She'd not seen it. He'd taken the tiny thing, a still warm clot of flesh, outside, wrapped in the bloody sheets. She assumed he buried it. She hoped he buried it.

When he'd returned he'd stormed around the bedroom, yelling at her. "Dammit. Now I gotta start all over. How am I to make this farm what it ought to be without sons? What good are those great big tits of yours if you can't make a baby?" He made her get up and strip and remake the bed. Then he had sex with her. Somewhere in the middle of it she passed out.

She bled and bled. They didn't have enough sheets and towels to keep the mess at bay. The cold returned and the laundry wouldn't dry. Once her parents visited. He wouldn't let them in the house. He told them she had influenza. From

26

the bedroom window Lily watched them drive away, Polly looking over her shoulder at the house as they drove down the road. Lily thought she should worry about Polly, at home alone with Pa, but she had her own problems and couldn't spare any pity for her baby sister.

The next time her family visited Farmer Gosford let them in the house. Lily crept down the stairs and listened at the parlor door. Mr. Gosford and Pa were in the there. She assumed Ma and Polly were in the kitchen cleaning up. Lily hadn't been keeping up with her housework. It enraged Gosford.

"You were right," Gosford told Pa. "She's a fine lay, for all she cain't keep a baby in her. She was worth every penny of the three hunnerd dollars I paid you for her."

"I tole you," Pa said. "When you get a son off my daughter, you'll pay me the rest. Don't you forget. I got my eye on Johnson's meadow. I'm gonna run sheep on it. The gal's looking peaky though. A little break should help her catch pregnant by spring. Like a milking cow."

"Maybe. But what about my needs?" Gosford asked. The two men chuckled together. Lily thought she'd never heard a more awful sound. Unable to listen to any more she crept back upstairs.

She was huddled in bed when she heard Pa's wagon drive away. Not long after a high, thin scream pierced the quiet like a needle through the air. A thump followed and then it was quiet once more.

Lily crept downstairs, hoping against hope that her husband had somehow hurt himself. She cracked the kitchen door and peeked in. Her husband had Polly pressed to the table. He had one hand on her little sister's mouth to keep her quiet, another pressed to her abdomen, pinning her down. He

27

stood between her legs, his pants puddled about his boots, grunting into her baby sister like a boar rooting in its trough.

Something in Lily broke. She pushed open the kitchen door and grabbed her cast iron fry pan off the stove. He never knew she was there, not over the terrible sounds he was making with her sister's body. Lily swung at her husband's head, putting everything she had into her swing. The pan connected with his skull with surprisingly loud crunch. Blood sprayed over Lily's hands and nightgown. Farmer Gosford dropped to the floor like a mishandled bag of corn meal. He twitched once, twice and once more before he stilled, his expression blank and stupid.

Lily considered her husband for a moment, then lifted the iron pan and brought it down on his face once, twice, three times. Behind her Polly scrabbled off the table. Lily dropped the pan on the floor, sure the mass of red and grey mush meant she'd have no more trouble from the bastard.

Polly squealed a high hurt sound. "Pa told me to," she cried. "I didn't want to." She cowered into the corner, her face was white as the kitchen curtains and burst into wet tears.

Lily stared at her sister. It took a moment before it occurred to her that Polly thought Lily would be mad at her. She stepped over Mr. Gosford's body and around the table. "It's not your fault," she whispered. She wrapped her arms around Polly and hugged her hard. "It's not your fault baby. It's Pa's fault. And Mr. Gosford's. Not you. Never you." The sisters held each other, crooning and rocking in shared horror. Then Lily had an idea.

She hauled Polly around the table, grabbing her best knife as she did. Lily stood over what remained of Farmer Gosford, contemplating his manly appendage. She leaned over and sawed at it. "Now you," she said to Polly, handing her the knife. Polly finished the job. He didn't bleed much, which surprised and disappointed Lily.

They left most of what was left of Farmer Gosford on the kitchen floor, his severed phallus abandoned beside him. Lily saddled the horse and the two of them rode home, Polly behind Lily. When they arrived home Lily grabbed her mother's fry pan off the stove, walked upstairs and bashed her father while he slept. It took less than a minute. Ma stayed downstairs with Polly. When Lily came down the stairs, her mother had the kettle heating.

Lily drank a cup of tea, packed a bag, and went out to the horse. Once mounted she looked down at Polly and her mother. She nodded, mostly to herself. They'd be fine now that Pa had joined Farmer Gosford in hell. "Tell them, when they come, it was me. But give me a day's head start before you call the sheriff. You can say I went crazy and locked you in the barn." She paused. "Tell them I always wanted to go to Chicago."

Ma nodded and put her hand on Lily's foot. "Wait," she said. Ma walked into the house, leaving Polly and Lily to say their goodbyes. When Ma came back she had a small wooden box with her. She handed it up to Lily. "You earned it."

Lily opened the box. Inside lay a wad of bills.

"Three hundred dollars," Ma said. Then she whacked Lily's horse on the rump and sent her daughter away.

Chapter 4

January 7-8, 1862
Cincinnati, Ohio & Rochester, New York

*A*llan looked out the window over Cincinnati's busy riverside port. Though he'd had an office at General McClellan's headquarters, just out of town, he also had a private office. It wouldn't do to let the army subsume his detective agency when the need for a military intelligence organization had become so urgent. Better the generals develop their own intelligence units and he keep his Pinkertons independent. The lead grey sky suggested it was still cold out there. His friend, General McClellan thought it was time to move down to Washington.

Allan was glad to go. No city on earth could be as miserable as Chicago in January, but Cincinnati gave Chicago a run for its money. It would be nice to leave winter behind and go south.

Like Chicago, Cincinnati was an industrious city. Despite the cold, men and wagons rushed to and fro, from steamboats to warehouses, carrying all manner of things, from coal to dress goods. From Allan's fourth-floor window, all the rushing around seemed as comic as an Italian burlesque.

A knock on the door interrupted his reverie. He was more than a little surprised to find Mr. Harcourt standing in the hall.

"Sir, I told you to return in three days time." Allan heard the impatience in his voice. He took a deep breath before continuing. It was never good to let the customer know you found him irritating. "I have nothing for you yet. I should by tomorrow."

Harcourt doffed his hat and held it before his chest. "I'm sorry Mr. Pinkerton. I am beside myself with anxiety."

Allan had to admit, the man looked upset. Mr. Harcourt was a handsome man, mid-thirties, with a thick, light brown beard that matched his hair, which he wore a wee bit too long for the current fashion. His plump, red lips suggested a man who appreciated his creature comforts, as did the straining buttons of his waistcoat. Allan wasn't sure he liked the fellow much, but he often found his clients less than savory. Years of experience taught him that his feelings about clients didn't change the color of their money or the depth of their problem.

Allan waved at his client chair. "Settle yourself Mr. Harcourt. Perhaps I could offer you a drink?"

He took a seat and accepted a short glass of Scottish whiskey from Allan. They appraised each other. Harcourt's top hat had the soft shine of quality materials and his suit fit him like no off-the-rack suit ever did. Allan did not understand how gentlemen kept the silk of their hats unsullied. His hat always had fingerprints and scuffs on it.

After a sip, Harcourt sighed in pleasure and spoke. "I apologize again, sir. It's just that I am so anxious about my friend. This woman will ruin him and he is a good man."

Allan suspected there was no friend. There rarely was. Men hired detectives to spy on their wives or their mistresses, but they would not admit that they needed help so they invented friends in need. "I appreciate the gravity of the situation Mr. Harcourt. Or I appreciate that you appreciate it. But as I told you two days ago, woman cases are almost always about jealousies and social abuses and the Pinkerton Detective Agency is above such inquiries."

Harcourt took his hat off his knee and slapped it down on Allan's desk. "That is not what this case is. This woman is a thief. She steals my friend's money and his reputation."

Allan nodded. "I believe you feel threatened. But in my vast experience, women are more often the victim of these situations than men. You must assure me the woman in question is not one of those young women led astray by a man with power and position. I will not take part in an attack on a woman whose only crime is that her older lover has tired of her and wishes now to avoid the consequences of his behavior."

Harcourt pursed his lips in a pantomime of thought. "I admire your sense of honor sir, which makes me even more eager for you to take this case. The woman in question is no victim." Harcourt finished his drink and stood. He reclaimed his hat and bowed toward Allan. "Once again, I apologize for coming without an appointment. Did we say 4 o'clock, Tuesday?"

"We did." Allan stood and held his hand out over the desk. The two men shook hands before Harcourt took his leave.

Allan returned to his window. After a few moments, he saw Harcourt exit the building. He hailed a passing hansom cab, climbed in and disappeared from sight. Seconds later so too

33

did the cab. Allan wondered if he should have followed the gentleman.

If, for example, Harcourt's friend really was a millionaire, why did Harcourt not have his own carriage? Didn't rich men have other rich men for friends? And why had he come today? He said he was anxious and Allan thought he was telling the truth. But anxious about what? In Allan's experience men didn't get as worked up as Harcourt over a bit of feminine fluff. But if the man's description of the lady was accurate he had good reason for alarm, whether he knew it or not.

Allan pulled his watch from his waistcoat pocket and clicked it open. Kate would be here soon. Together they'd decide what to do. They'd have to decide. General George McClellan wanted him in Washington post haste. He needed to close the Cincinnati office and move on to the next thing.

Kate stepped off the night train from Baltimore into the swirling steam and sulfurous stink of the train engine. She stepped across the platform of the New York City depot, lean-ing a little against the weight of her carpet bag. Her gun and lockpicks weighed down her bag, but she suspected she'd need both on this mission.

"Halloo," called a male voice off to her right.

Kate turned toward the voice and tried not to laugh. Mr. Scully strode through the steam and mist toward her. He was one of Allan's most trusted operatives and he'd disapproved of her for years, a steadfast believer in 'women should be wives, not detectives.' They'd reached a rapprochement last year. They'd shared some nasty case in Baltimore with a bunch of other Pinkertons and Kate's part had been a piece of grueling

deep cover. Mr. Scully had come to see the value of lady detectives, though they'd never be best friends or anything close.

"Mr. Scully, as I live and breath. Why are we meeting here
in the middle of the night?"

He shook her hand and led her over to a bench. "I'm sorry
to be abrupt, but the train for Rochester is leaving in twenty
minutes and you must be on it."

Kate swept the skirt of her brown traveling dress under her
and took a seat on a nearby bench, shivering at the cold night
air. "Rochester?"

Mr. Scully folded up his lanky form to sit next to her. He
removed a file folder from a leather case he carried and handed the file to Kate, before pulling a pair of delicate spectacles
from his jacket pocket. He perched them on his nose and
squinted down at file folder he'd just handed over. "Mr. Pinkerton asked me to meet you and give you that file." he nodded
to Kate's packet of papers. He pulled a folded piece of paper
from his pocket. "I'm supposed to read you this before you get
on the next train." He shook out the letter and read from it.

My dear Miss Warne,

*I have only a few minutes to write this before Mr. Scully must leave to
meet you in New York. I had an unusual client request this morning. A
Mr. Harcourt, representing himself as a friend of a millionaire named
Lyons, based in Rochester, claims that a lady of dubious morality is
blackmailing Lyons. I have my doubts, but his description of the woman
alarmed me.*

*Please go to Rochester and ascertain if this Mr. Lyons is real and if
so, find out if he is rich enough to bribe. If Mr. Lyon does not exist, please
determine what the truth of Mr. Harcourt might be. You have only one
day for your investigation as I require your presence in Cincinnati at 3*

PM, day after tomorrow. Mr. Harcourt will return to my office to hear whether the Pinkertons will take his case.

Harcourt reports the woman is in her late twenties, dark-haired, violet eyed and enjoys significant physical endowments in that most womanly of regions.

You must know what this means.

Yours,

A. Pinkerton

Kate turned to Mr. Scully. "Have you seen this woman?

He looked at her, perplexed. "No. She's in Rochester. I'm here."

She jerked her chin back and forth, trying to clear her head. "Why didn't he send you to Rochester? Instead of me?"

Scully frowned. "I'm on another case. Something about one of McClellan's messengers. I can't say more. Plus it sounds like it's one of your old cases."

She stared down the platform at the locomotive coming in. After a long moment, she said, "I'm afraid so." A train's whistle shot a shrill alarm into the night.

Mr. Scully stood and jerked his chin at the train. "That's yours." He dug into his pocket again, this time extracting a first class passenger ticket. "Here."

She took the ticket, fumbling a little with cold and anxiety. Mr. Scully leaned into her and kissed her on the cheek, surprising her more than a little.

"Take care in Rochester. I'll see you in Cincinnati day after tomorrow." With that he walked away into the cold night, leaving Kate wide-eyed in astonishment. Mr. Scully had never once, in all the five years she'd known him, kissed her cheek.

It was mid-day before she reached Rochester. Kate wanted nothing more than to check into a decent hotel and sleep for a few hours. No one slept well on a train. They were loud, either cold or hot and uncomfortable, even the first class cars. But a nap was not to be. Investigate first, sleep later.

She found a newsstand and bought a slim city directory. She'd heard the Erie Canal caused a population explosion in the towns along its route, but it was a whole other thing to see it up close. Tall brick buildings crowded the streets near the depot, and people hurried everywhere and nowhere. She shouldn't feel so surprised. Mr. Douglass wouldn't publish his famous abolitionist newspaper from a wide spot in the road.

A porter at the train station directed Kate to a teashop only two blocks from the station, across from the city post office. The winter sun shone off the muddy Genesee River, illuminating her walk with a thin, but clear light. Kate ordered a pot of tea and a small plate of sandwiches to sooth her cranky stomach. The file Mr. Scully handed contained notes on the old case. She'd reviewed it on the train, but truth be told, she remembered most of the contents all too well. After her food arrived, Kate perused her new directory while she munched and sipped. There were four Lyons in the L section. One Lyon was a blacksmith and the other a hairdresser. Those seemed unlikely occupations for a millionaire. The third Lyon was listed as a lawyer and the fourth was a businessman. The last two seemed most likely. She checked the addresses against the map at the front of the directory and set out hunting Lyons.

Lawyer Lyon had his offices on Clinton Avenue, several blocks down from the tea shop and one block east of the river. The other Lyon listed his address as building called 'The Arcade' on East Main, across the river. Kate tried the lawyer first only because his office seemed closer. Her walk, fortified by her lunch, turned out to be the best part of her day. Though upstate New York could have difficult winters, this day the sun shined enough to melt the snowdrifts and set icicles dripping. Kate was still glad of her thick wool coat and velvet muff, but it was nice to be out of the train and on her feet.

After less than fifteen minutes she stopped in front of a small, street front office. The expansive plate glass window suggested the space had once been a shop of some kind, while the hand-lettered sign on the door announced Lawyer Lyon's place of business. Kate peered through the window. The office held a paper covered desk, with more papers piled on the floor in uneven towers. On the sidewall stood two straight-backed wooden chairs that made it clear this lawyer didn't hob nob with the city elites. Kate stepped away from the window, certain this was not her Lyon.

Kate headed back the way she'd come, toward the Main Street Bridge. The sun stayed warm on her cheeks as she walked down the slushy sidewalks. Fifteen minutes later she came to a block sized Greek revival building that proclaimed itself 'The Arcade.' The building had a grandness that felt right. This was exactly the right place to find a millionaire.

Kate stepped into a wide hall that widened into a vast central space. Five stories up a monumental glass ceiling flooded the hall with a brightness not found inside other buildings, even on clear summer days. She walked down the center hall, taking in the shops that lined each side. Shoppers could buy books, cigars, hats, luggage, candy and stationary in the shops. A gentleman could get his hair cut or his boots shined. Railed balconies lined the second floor. They opened to yet more shops, while the third and fourth floors had interior windows that looked out over the hall. A massive fountain tinkled in the center of the hall, while a two-story mural of what looked to be Niagara Falls decorated a wall near the far entrance. Kate stood near the fountain and turned in a slow circle to take in the marvel that was Rochester's Arcade. Prosperous looking men and well-dressed women hurried by her, everyone with a place to be.

Kate spied a building directory next to the building's small post office. She ambled over and took a look. There it was. *Mr. Abelard Lyon & Lyon Enterprises, 324.* Kate found the bathroom on her way to the staircase before making her way to the third floor. At room 324 she found a discreet sign that read *"Lyon Enterprises: Purveyors of Seeds for City and Farm."*

A small bell tickled when she opened the door. Kate perused the space. The front office had a set of comfortable chairs along one wall and a sturdy wooden desk that appeared to be gatekeeping the door behind it. No clerk occupied the desk.

Kate thought about rifling through the papers on the desk but before she could the door behind it opened. A silver-haired gentleman stepped through, smiling as he did. "May I help you Madame?"

"Ah, yes," she said, fluttering a little as she did, "I wonder if Mr. Harcourt is in today?" She figured this was a safe thing to ask because Mr. Harcourt was supposed to be in Cincinnati.

"Oh, I'm very sorry my dear lady. Mr. Harcourt is out of town on personal business just now."

Kate resisted the impulse to do a small happy dance. She was in the right place.

The silver-haired gentleman shook himself slightly and made a shallow bow. "I'm sorry. Allow me to introduce myself. Mr. Abelard Lyon at your service. Could I help you? Or did you need my assistant Mr. Harcourt?" He tipped his head as he spoke, making himself look like an inquisitive squirrel.

Kate smiled at the man. "No, no. Thank you though. I met Mr. Harcourt several weeks ago. He mentioned your seed company. I find flowers so fascinating and . . . ." Kate looked down at her feet. Men liked it when ladies got flustered. They could rush in and help.

Lyon bustled over to the desk and pulled open a drawer. "My dear, you must take one of our catalogues. You may peruse it at your leisure. If you find there's something we could help you with, please come back. It is never too early to plan for spring." He held a thin catalogue out to her. "Most of our seeds must be ordered in quantity, but I'd be happy to arrange a smaller order for a pretty thing like you. Or any of your delightful lady friends."

Kate hated it when men talked to her like that, but somehow Mr. Lyon made it seem rather nice, like a genial grandfather about to hand out butter toffees. She took his catalogue, thanked him and left

Kate walked out of the Arcade with a satisfied smile and a light heart. She hadn't thought this Mr. Lyon really existed. If Mr. Harcourt was telling the truth about his friend, maybe he was also telling the truth about the woman. The next question was a simple one. Was the woman also the Black Widow? If so, nice Mr. Lyon was in a great deal of danger. Kate shuddered. So much death. And so much failure.

Chapter 5

1856

Detroit Michigan

*L*ily lowered her eyelids and took another look. He'd boarded the train at the Toledo station. She recognized him. Well, not him. But his type. He was an opportunity. He was young, but past the first flush of youth, smooth shaven and as self-confident as a man who'd accomplished all his dreams. His slightly long, dark blond hair and waxed mustaches announced his vanity, while his dark suit and cleric's collar suggested a man of devout discretion. She suspected the latter was no more hokum. This man might be dressed as a minister, but he was not a man of God. Eighteen years with Pa and one with Farmer Gosford hadn't been a total waste—she recognized a predator when she saw one.

He took a seat near the rear of the car, facing forward. His grey eyes gobbled her up, lingering on her chest before they travelled upward.

Lily waited a few minutes and peaked at the man again. She needed to make sure he noticed her noticing him. Three hundred dollars wouldn't get her far.

The night she rode away from Polly and Ma, she'd gone to Battle Creek, the next town over from Kalamazoo. She reached Battle Creek at dawn, left the horse at a livery stable and bought a ticket on the first train out of town. That train took her to Fort Wayne. She took a room on the wrong side of town. Once checked into the hotel she fell into a boneless, dreamless sleep.

The next morning she forced herself to get moving though she would have liked to have stayed in bed for a few days. A lady who'd just killed her husband and father did not get to lounge around in bed, even if she was still recovering from a lost baby. At a small dry goods store, she bought herself a dress of plain calico, two sizes too large, an old-fashioned poke bonnet and a small leather traveling bag. She returned to her hotel room and changed her clothes. She tried making herself look fat by tying the old dress around her waist but her thin face and stick-like neck gave her away. Instead, she tipped the bonnet down over her forehead to cover her face and returned to the train depot and bought another ticket, this one for Columbus, Ohio.

By the time she arrived in Columbus, late that same day, Lily felt quite ill. She was still bleeding down there and her head spun every time she moved. It occurred to her she'd not eaten anything for two days. She found another modest hotel and checked in. The next morning, feeling somewhat revived, she had a private conversation with the innkeeper's wife. The kind lady helped her with the realities of her lady problem, providing her with a warm bath and a pile of clean rags.

Lily changed hotels again after telling the kind lady she was well enough to travel the rest of the way home. Lily stayed at the next hotel two nights in a row. On the morning of the third day she felt better , having made a deal with her body that if she slept and ate, it would quit draining her of all her blood.

She went shopping again. This time she bought a better tailored, more discrete dress and a fetching little hat to go with it. She also bought herself some pretty undergarments and a new corset. Then she took the train north to Detroit. Time to begin her new life.

About an hour into the train ride the fake minister stood and walked up the carriage aisle toward Lily, swaying with the rocking clack of the train as he did. He stopped before her and clasped his hands at his waist like he was about to burst into prayer.

"Excuse me Ma'am."

Lily pretended to notice him for the first time.

"I'm a pretty good judge of character and you look like a young lady in need of ministry." He paused like a man too delicate to say more. Then he did. "Allow me to introduce myself. I am Reverend Bland. Edwin Bland."

Lily inclined her head, then motioned to the seat opposite her. He took it, pretending he hadn't expected her to offer a seat. She tried not to laugh at him. "Miss Lily Winslow," she said, being careful to take a deep enough breath to draw attention to her bosom. For all the trouble her body caused her she might as well use her assets to her advantage.

"Allow me to say that you are the exact image of a dear friend of ours. My mother's and mine I mean." He pulled a handkerchief from his jacket pocket and pressed it to his forehead.

Lily regarded the Reverend Bland. Men like this were generally the poison fruit of excessive maternal admiration.

45

His mother probably adored him. And he couldn't settle on a story. Did she need ministering or did she look like this imaginary friend? She bet his mother had raised him to believe he was smarter than everyone else. And most men thought they were smarter than all women.

"On second glance though, I realize you the finer looking of the two. There is something of the noble in your brow that adds depth to your looks."

Lily pushed down a derisive snort. He liked her brow, did he? How stupid did he think she was? She resolved then and there to use the Reverend for her own ends. It would serve him right.

By the time the train arrived in Detroit Lily thought she had him hooked. After several hours of discussion, on matters ranging from their mutual dislike of mutton to the spiritual teachings of Franz Mesmer, they struck a bargain of a sort.

It began with Reverend Bland's confession.

"My dear Lily, I have developed a deep interest in you. I'm sure you know about affinities?"

Lily didn't but thought it best to answer in the affirmative.

"So do I," her eager swain gushed. "I feel as if good spirits were all around us, whispering the sacredness of our affinity. We were destined to meet."

Lily watched the reverend's rhapsody of faux emotion with interest.

"Don't you feel it, my dear? Can you hear the spirits?" He cocked his head as if he could hear angels on the Detroit train.

Not trusting herself to speak, she nodded and batted her eyelashes.

He reached for her hands and held them in his own. "Then we must meet in Detroit. You will take a room at the Michigan Exchange Hotel and wait for me. I must visit my mother, but I will come to you soon after."

She fluttered her eyelashes and brought his hands up to her chest. "Is it a very expensive hotel?" She put a little tremolo into her voice and lifted his hands so his knuckles brushed the front of her dress.

He looked into her eyes. "Oh, my dear. How thoughtless of me. I have money. I shall pay for your rooms. Only to assist a helpless woman. As any man of God would do. You understand."

She understood all too well.

She held him off for almost three weeks while her body recuperated from losing the baby. Reverend Bland visited her in the evenings. They talked some and kissed more. Lily found that she enjoyed the kissing. Neither Pa nor Farmer Gosford was ever much for kissing and she found she enjoyed it. It didn't hurt that he signed for her hotel and restaurant bill.

During one of their evenings together Lily learned several interesting things about her suitor. His mother had inherited an old, established fortune. And he her only child. She was a pious sort, of the Methodist persuasion and when her son drank himself out of Harvard her approbation had been severe. After mommy threatened him with disinheritance, young Edwin appeared to embrace moral rectitude and began studying with a local minister. Four months ago, in a liturgical ceremony that delighted his mother, he made his vows and embraced the clerical collar. And yet he had neither religious convictions nor moral compunctions. He did have a narcis-

47

sist's self-regard. He needed to be in his mother's good graces long enough to inherit her considerable fortune, after which he would abandon his clerical collar for a life of luxury he knew himself already entitled.

As she'd suspected, Edwin's mother had raised him to expect feminine admiration and his youthful successes had convinced him he was irresistible to women. Lily had to admit that she found his cat-like self-assurance more than a little attractive. Also, unlike her father and husband, he always smelled good, his citrusy men's hair tonic a welcome change from manure and body odor.

In return for room and board, she told him about herself, of her family farm and the never-ending, soul-crushing work. She intimated that her father was violent, but she didn't tell him she'd been married, nor that she'd lost a baby. And she never once considered telling the Reverend Bland that she was a double murderer.

Lily immensely enjoyed her time at the Michigan Exchange Hotel. Pink Polly wallpaper adorned the walls and the bed wore a covering of leaf green, satin. It was like sleeping in an English garden. The view out the window contained not one farm, or even a stray chicken, but instead looked out over the bluffs of the Detroit River and the lovely city of Windsor just beyond. Most nights a porter brought meals to her room though Saturday nights she and Edwin took dinner at the hotel restaurant. She spent her days reading and daydreaming about the future. Lying in bed she tried not to think about her lost baby, nor Ma and Polly. At least now she could be sure Pa would never hurt Polly. Part of her wanted to return to the Gosford Farm in search of her baby's tiny body, but she didn't dare. Instead, she vowed to never forget the poor little mite. Like her, it had deserved better.

Over time Edwin's kisses became insistent. On their third week anniversary, as they snuggled on the room's pink velvet settee, he came out with it. "I must have you, my dear. You intoxicate me."

She pushed him away from her, stood and walked to the window. She reminded herself to be brave and then turned to face him. "Edwin, you promised to introduce me to your mother." She used her iciest voice.

"I know darling. And I will. But she's not well right now. We must wait." He stood and joined her at the window, wrapping his arms around her waist.

"Then I will go home."

"We both know you will not," he said, matching her coldness.

Before Lily could regain control of the moment, a knock came at the door. It was room service. The waiter pushed a small, linen covered cart into the room and left. Lily returned to her senses. And to the sofa. Edwin joined her there, kissing her between bites of chicken. She let him caress the tops of her breasts, thanking all that was holy that she'd had the foresight to wear her lowest cut dress.

After dinner he buried his face in her cleavage and then raised his head. "Lily, you have ruined me. I am a good Christian man but you have me in your power. God forgive my cursed weakness." His face returned once more to her bosom.

Lily tried not to laugh. He really did think she was stupid. But if he said he was in her power, wouldn't he have to act like it? Pressing her advantage she asked, "Well?"

"Well, what?" he cried in exasperation, pawing at the buttons on her dress.

She pushed his hand away. "Well?"

He cupped his hand to her breast. "I am rich Lily. Or will be. You must be patient. One day I will give you everything."

"But that won't give me respectability, my dear." She removed his hand from the front of her dress. "If I yield my virtue to you, I will lose the one thing that should mean the most to you. My respectability."

"Not if we love each other. I can do a great deal for you in the meantime. I could buy you a small house. Hire a housekeeper. No one would have to know where the money came from. You could be accepted into society."

Lily bit her lip, pretending to consider his offer.

He misunderstood her hesitation and made his first blunder. In a tight, mean voice he said, "You must either accept me or go back to your parent's dirty farm. You have no choice."

She heaved him off her, pushing him onto the floor, and stood above him. "Take care, Edwin. Never insult my home or me again. I may be a simple country girl, but you are a seducer. Insult me again and I will kill you." Lily drew back her foot to kick him, then remembered herself. She looked down at him in shock. Had she lost this opportunity with her temper?

He gazed up at her from the floor, his eyes afire with passion. He wrapped his arms around her knees and begged her forgiveness. After that he was putty in her hands. Or so it seemed at the time.

The Reverend Edwin Bland took Lily to a small grey house on the west side of town. Trellis's covered the front porch, the vines just beginning to fuzz out green, a pretty contrast to the glossy black shutters on either side of the front window. Once inside Lily's excitement mounted. This was more like it. The parlor was small but, elegantly appointed in soft grey fabrics and well-cushioned chairs. Bland tugged on a bell pull in the corner of the room and moments later a stout, older lady appeared.

"This is Mother Cawley," he said with an airy wave of his hand. "And this, my dear Mother Cawley is your new charge, Miss Winslow, a young lady late of Terre Haute, come to Detroit to expand her education."

Mrs. Cawley approached Lily and kissed her on the cheek, welcoming her to her new home.

And thus Lily learned of her new identity. And though he didn't know it, he was right when he told Mrs. Bland she was in Detroit to improve herself. She learned an awful lot the next few months. For example, it didn't take a genius to figure out she wasn't the first woman Edwin kept in the little gray house. Lily determined to be the last in Bland's line of mistresses, or at least the first one to become his wife. What he did after they married was up to him. To that end, she pretended to believe him when he made weak excuses for why he didn't give the house to her as he'd promised. She also pretended to believe his even weaker excuses for why she had not yet met his mother.

Instead, she made sure that Reverend Bland had ample use of her body. Their first night together he'd been so eager to bed her he'd failed to notice that she required no deflowering. She performed as a shy virgin at first, before transforming

51

into an eager lover. Lily also discovered that if she plied the reverend with enough wine or brandy, he would fail to perform, but would not remember his failure in the morning. He believed her stories of his prowess, confirming as they did, his belief in his own perfection.

Mrs. Cawley and Lily got along tolerably well. The housekeeper knew which shops had the finest dresses, hats, and jewelry, and better yet, which had charge accounts. The lady appeared all jolliness and good cheer but she was, above all, Bland's creature. Mrs. Cawley fawned over him every time he appeared in the little house and did his bidding in all things. Lily often caught the two of them whispering together, though she pretended to notice none of it. Her position in this house was too comfortable to jeopardize with honesty. Instead, Lily rose late, luxuriated in soft clothes, warm baths, good food and a comfortable place to live. And then, one glorious fall day Lily's fondest dream came true. A doctor came, examined her, and informed her that she was with child.

Lily exalted in the news. She would have another baby, one to replace the child she had lost. Bland would have to marry her now. Lily dressed in her prettiest nightgown, careful to leave the top strings untied to better show off her swelling bosom, and took to her bed. She knew Bland liked to come to the house from Sunday services and find her in bed, awaiting his arrival. And so he did. The nightgown found its way to the floor, like every Sunday. Afterwards Lily shared her news.

He rolled toward her, careful to keep one of his hands on her breast. "Why, that is wonderful my dear. We must speed up our plans now." He kissed her on the mouth so hard their teeth clicked together.

"Oh, darling," she whispered in his ear. "We'll be such a happy family." One thing led to another. He professed his undying adoration for her. She tried ever so hard to believe him.

When he was getting ready to leave Lily pressed herself against him. "Couldn't I come with you? I could meet your mother."

He pressed a kiss to her forehead. "Not yet, darling. Let me prepare the way. But soon you shall be Mrs. Bland."

A week passed before he returned to the little house. Outside the leaves had fallen, pushed by the cold wind off the lake. An ice rain fell, hitting the windows with sharp pings that made it seem as if she were under attack. She sat knitting and worrying. He'd never been away this long and he'd never missed a Sunday afternoon in her boudoir. Then she heard it. The door unlocked and thrown open. Reverend Bland's voice called out, "Mother Cawley!"

Lily sat frozen in her seat. Her future would be determined here, today. She listened to her lover and his housekeeper murmur in the hallway. When he entered the parlor, he flung his coat upon a chair and fussed with his cravat before he even looked at her.

Lily's heart stuttered.

"Darling, I have filthy news for you. The Church elders require that I go west. It seems there is business of vital importance on the frontier and they can trust only me to take care of matters to their satisfaction." He thumped his thigh with his fist. "Curse my effectiveness. If I were a lesser man they would send someone else."

Lily sat still as could be, knitting needles frozen mid-stitch. Outside the sleet continued to ping against the window.

53

He pretended not to notice. "But don't worry darling. Not one bit. This cursed inconvenience presents us with an opportunity. I shall go west and prepare a place for you. I must sell this house though, to raise the funds for our new house. When I return, I will marry you. Hopefully by Christmas. Once married we can return to the frontier until such time as I complete my work there. When we return to Detroit Mother will be none the wiser about the discrepancies between our marriage and the age of the child."

He beamed at her, all charm and witless self-love.

Careful to keep her tone light she asked, "How long shall you be gone?"

He waved his hand in the air as if her question was not important. "Oh, a few weeks. No more than four. While I'm gone my little bird can wait for me at the hotel."

"So I'm to leave this house?" She wanted to be sure she fully understood his plan. His real plan.

He nodded. "But only until I come for you." He knelt before her and curled a hand around her waist. "Would you like to retire to our downy nest now?"

She nodded, unable to trust her voice. Lily set her knitting aside and stood.

He rose with her. "Give me a moment. I have matters to discuss with Mother Cawley. For our future together." He kissed Lily chastely on the cheek and then gently pushed her toward the bedroom.

Lily scampered into the bedroom and yanked off her dress. Buttons popped and flung themselves onto the floor. Grateful she'd been wearing house slippers and not her high button boots, she threw a ruffled velvet wrapper over her corset and

54

undergarments before opening her bedroom door. She peeked out into the hall. They were still in the kitchen. Lily crept down the hall and pressed her ear to the crack between the frame and the door.

"So just like before," Mrs. Cawley said. "Clear out and wait."

"Yes. When the hotel complains about the bill, she'll come here. After that, she'll have no recourse but to leave town."

Mrs. Cawley said something, but the wind howled and covered the words. It occurred to Lily that it didn't matter what they said next. She tiptoed back to her room.

The Reverend arrived in her room only moments later. "Why darling, you're not undressed." He did not look at her as he removed his clothes.

She moved into his line of sight and batted her eyelashes at him. "I thought you'd like to unwrap me yourself. Like a present."

He leered and pounced.

Outside it began to snow in earnest.

Afterward, once she was sure he was asleep, she rose from the bed and opened her top drawer. She'd prepared for this day. Lily removed a small tin bottle of liquid from its nest of silk stockings, wetted a handkerchief with the contents and laid it on the pillow just in front of his face. She watched his body stutter and jerk in reaction to the chloroform. Time stopped until he stilled. She left the room, naked as a baby bird, and walked down to Mrs. Cawley's room. She caught up a candlestick as she went, but didn't need it. The housekeeper was already asleep. Lily made sure she stayed that way.

Once assured the two of them were well and truly drugged she dressed and packed. Several weeks ago she'd purchased a wheeled traveling trunk with some of her dress money. Into it,

55

she loaded her two best dresses, her velvet wrapper and an extra pair of boots. She left the trunk, half filled and open. She took her small collection of jewelry from its box and dumped it all into her old handbag, then fished the Reverend's wallet out of his jacket and opened it. The wallet was stuffed with bills. Lily's heart broke a little at the sight. If she had any doubt about the Reverend Bland, his wallet, thick with traveling cash, dispelled it. In the kitchen Lily found Mrs. Cawley's household money in an otherwise empty coffee can. It joined her paltry jewels and the Reverend's wallet in her small bag. Then she stripped the house of every valuable she could fit into the trunk's remaining space, from the silver tea service to a small, horsey painting by an esteemed lady artist.

Before Lily left the white cottage she dripped more chloroform onto the Reverend and Mrs. Cawley's handkerchiefs. Then, wheeling her trunk behind her, she made off into the night, her head bent against the storm.

Chapter 6

*K*ate stepped off the train in Cincinnati bleary with exhaustion, rumpled and chilled to her bones. The January weather looked every bit as grey and bleak as she felt. To compound her general dissatisfaction, Cincinnati didn't have a central depot, but seven small depots, one for each railroad company that operated in the city. Kate didn't care much about grand depots, except that they had heat, teashops, and indoor bathrooms. Her stomach rumbled at the thought of hot tea and buttered biscuits.

After availing herself to the depot's icy cold accommodations for ladies, Kate found a hackney cab and directed her driver to take her to Gibson House Hotel. Kate figured that if Allan Pinkerton could afford to send her to three cities in three days he could also afford to pay for someplace swanky. Plus, the Gibson House had a connection to her old case.

The cab took her into Cincinnati's heart, near the post office, mayor's office and river. Outside the cab's window, a light snow fell, though there wasn't yet enough of the white stuff to cover the grimy city streets. Gibson House stood in all its grandeur on Walnut Street, one block off the main street. She asked her cabman, a genial light-skinned black man bundled into an oversized great coat, to wait for her while she checked in.

Kate stepped into the Gibson House's lobby, sinking into the thick carpets and church-like quiet. She conducted her business with a middle-aged, whip-thin fellow with prodigiously large muttonchops. He seemed more than a little uncomfortable with the fact that Kate had no trunks or luggage larger than her carpetbag. Kate pocketed her room key, cast a longing eye at the hotel's restaurant and returned to the cab.

This time she directed her driver to Allan's office building, which lay a dozen or more blocks to the west, down by the city riverfront. She once again asked her amenable driver to wait for her and then stood on the sidewalk, looking up at the building through falling snowflakes. How like Allan, who's Scottish rigor encouraged austerity, to have his office on the building's top floor. Kate hiked up the stairs, holding her heavy blue wool skirt up in one hand. She took a little rest on the third-floor landing, cursed Allan under her breath and assaulted the last flight of stairs.

Huffing and puffing, she threw open Allan's door. "Dammit, Allan. Would it kill you to have a ground floor office?"

Allan looked up from the papers he had in his hand and pushed his reading glasses down his nose. "That's $5 more a month and I won't be here long enough for the location to matter." Then he smiled.

Kate dropped her coat on a nearby chair with a theatrical sigh.

He strode around his desk and pulled her into a tight hug. "General McClellan requires me to move my headquarters to Washington. I'll be gone from here within the month."

"It's about time," Kate said. She didn't share Allan's enthusiasm for General McClellan. What good is an army if it never leaves camp?

Allan only nodded and gestured to a chair. "I don't want him or anyone else in the Army to know about the F Street house, so you'll continue to be in charge there. I'll have offices in the War Department."

Unexpected relief washed over her. When Allan first put her in charge of the Pinkerton's secret Washington headquarters she'd been more than a little resistant to the idea. Since then command had grown on her.

He waited until she sat and then joined her. "Anyway, you're just in time. Mr. Harcourt should be here any minute." He pushed a tin of cookies at her and flipped out his pocket watch. "We've got about fifteen minutes. What did you find in Rochester?"

Kate told her story, ending with her assessment that Mr. Lyon did indeed appear to be worth bribing and agreeable enough to be taken in by a nefarious adventuress type.

Kate watched Allan appraise her over his glasses. After a long moment he crooked an eyebrow at her.

"I guess we'll see," she said with a sigh. "I found the Black Widow's trail from this city back to Detroit and Kalamazoo, but after that, I lost her. She just disappeared."

A peremptory knock at the door interrupted them. It was Allan's turn to sigh. "That will be the anxious Mr. Harcourt. Before I let him in, are we in agreement?"

"That we should take his case? Yes. We want another crack at the Black Widow."

"Not *we* dear. You." He stood and strode to the door. Over his shoulder, he said, "This was always your case and so it shall remain."

The fellow who stepped into Allan's office stopped to unwrap a wooly scarf from his neck. "Sorry, sorry," he muttered. "A filthy afternoon out there. Simply filthy."

As Allan took Mr. Harcourt's coat, Kate examined the man. Though he couldn't have been much over thirty years old he looked like a man who had once been handsome but had wrecked himself through dissipation. Broken blood vessels contaminated his cheeks and nose though his mouth was as plump and pink as a velvet boudoir pillow. As he looked at Kate, his tongue whipped out of his mouth and slid around his lips. Kate tried not to shudder. He reminded her of a snake she'd seen behind glass at Mr. Barnum's museum, lazy and predatory at the same time. Then he smiled at her and a jovial businessman replaced the reptilian predator.

Allan made introductions and they all settled into chairs. Harcourt brushed his light brown hair back from his forehead and leaned forward. "Mr. Pinkerton, I am honored that you have agreed to meet with me once again. I hope you can help me with this unpleasant business of mine." He settled back into his chair, amiable dignity personified.

Kate leaned forward. "Mr. Harcourt, I wonder if you could relate the details of your case once more. I understand you've explained it to Mr. Pinkerton, and he explained it to me, but I'd like to hear it from your point of view."

Harcourt looked at Allan, his eyes wide in shock.

Kate suspected he thought she was here to serve tea or take notes.

Allan crossed his legs and spoke. "Mr. Harcourt the lady before you is one of my best operatives and her sex recommends her to this case. She has my complete confidence. And let me remind you, the Pinkerton Detective Agency only rarely takes domestic cases. I don't like them. Not one bit. Miss Warne is your only hope."

Kate saw temper flare in his eyes. He blinked and the friendly man reappeared.

"I work for a gentleman called Mr. Lyon. I also presume to call him my friend. He is a good and kind man, but he is also a rich man, worth over three million dollars. Last spring Mrs. Lyon died, leaving Mr. Lyon bereft. At this point, I made a dreadful mistake. I suggested to my friend that he attempt to contact his wife through the veil."

Kate found herself interested and skeptical in equal measure. "You sent him to a spiritualist?"

He blushed. "I did. I'm not sure that I believe in spiritualism, but I thought that even a charlatan might help Mr. Lyon with his wife's passing. I'd heard glowing reports about Mrs. Winslow from others of my acquaintance and the woman did not have to be the real thing. She had only to alleviate Mr. Lyon's melancholia and I cared not how."

"Did it work? Did she help him with his grief?"

"That depends upon one's perspective I suppose. He thinks he is in love." Harcourt frowned. "Let me explain. This spiritualist had him return for many sessions. She learned his habits and preferences and rapidly became quite familiar with my friend. I will admit, she is an attractive woman and poor Mr. Lyon was married to the same women for decades. I'm

61

not sure any man could have withstood the full force of this woman's attention."

Kate's stomach rumbled. Apparently, a few paltry cookies were no substitute for lunch. Seeking to move along the interview she asked, "And the problem Mr. Harcourt? Why do you seek help with the Pinkertons and not Mr. Lyon?"

Harcourt shifted in his chair. "I introduced them, you see. Mr. Lyon is the kindest of men and he cannot see how she abuses him. But I see it. My self-recrimination is not enough to save my friend and employer, but then I heard the famous Mr. Pinkerton had an office in Cincinnati and so here I am."

"But will Mr. Lyon welcome an investigation?" Kate asked.

Harcourt nodded. "Mr. Lyon has given me leave to come to you. You may speak to him yourself. The truth of the matter is that he is not too far-gone to succumb to Mrs. Winslow's blandishments regarding the marital state. She refuses to accept defeat, harrying him night and day, alternating declarations of affection with threats. The latest threat is that she will sue him for breach of promise. Which is why Mr. Lyon allowed me to take this step."

Allan interrupted. "How much does she want?"

Harcourt jerked his handkerchief from his pocket and wiped his mouth. "Marriage or one hundred thousand dollars."

The answer seemed obvious to Kate. "If your client is worth millions, why not pay her off?"

"She's doesn't really want the $100,000, which Mr. Lyon was willing to give her. Against my wishes I might add. Pay off a blackmailer once, you'll pay again and again."

62

"Exactly my sentiment," Allan said. "Blackmailers are the lowest form of criminal. They extort not only money from their victims, but safety and sanity."

"If Mrs. Winslow doesn't want the money, why would she threaten to sue?" Kate suspected she knew the answer, but it was always best to hear it from the client.

Harcourt leaned forward in his chair again. "She want's to become the next Mrs. Lyon and thus have access to all his money. The suit would bring about Mr. Lyon's social ruin and she knows it. If Rochester society were to find out he consorted with a lady spiritualist, not just visited one mind you, but allowed one into his domestic circle, why he'd be socially ruined. The Lyons would never be welcome in society again. This fact bothers Mr. Lyon not one whit being a man of sufficient age to prefer his home to society, but his daughters and their families would face ruin as well and that concerns him a great deal. No, the harridan doesn't intend to go to court. She believes the threat of a lawsuit alone will bring Mr. Lyon to the altar. She is a seductress of the highest order and poor Mr. Lyon is at her mercy."

Kate fought the urge to shoot to her feet and smack Harcourt's face. She hated it when men blamed women for giving them exactly what they desired. Like spoiled children, men wanted sexual passion and then despised any woman who offered it. They wanted a younger woman to make them feel strong and vital, then despised the woman who would do so.

Still, it wouldn't help to hit the man, however personally satisfying a short bout of violence might be. "Could you describe this woman in greater detail?"

"Of course. She has milk white skin, smooth and set off by black eyelashes and brows. Her hair is so long and thick it makes a bundle at the back of her head at least twice the size of most lady's." He paused, fidgeted with the cookie plate and continued. "Her eyes are a remarkable dark blue, so blue that in some light they appear nearly purple. She is lightly built, like you Miss Warne, but for." He stammered to a stop.

Kate shook her head. *Men.* "Mr. Harcourt, please consider me a detective first and a lady second. It would be immensely helpful if you could continue your description."

He looked at Kate, then shifted his gaze to Allan. "Mrs. Winslow must have her corsets special made for her." He cupped his hands before his chest as if he couldn't help himself. His hands froze, then dropped to his lap.

Kate almost laughed in relief. She wasn't on a wild goose chase after all. "You mean to say that Mr. Lyon's paramour has larger bosoms than most ladies?"

Harcourt nodded in quick little jerks.

Kate's heart jumped a little. She had another chance. "Mr. Harcourt, we will take your case."

After signing a contract and leaving a small purse with numerous bills in it for expenses Harcourt left the office.

Allan wanted to talk strategy after Mr. Harcourt left, but Kate wouldn't hear of it. "I'm done for the day. The cabman is waiting for me. I'm going back to my hotel, where I will eat an enormous dinner. Then I will crawl into my bed and sleep for 12 hours.

Allan took out his pocket watch, looked at it and then looked at Kate.

She tried not to laugh. "I know. It's 4 o'clock. I don't care. I'm hungry and I'm exhausted. I haven't slept more than four hours at a stretch since I left Washington. The Black Widow will keep for one more day."

Allan kissed Kate on the cheek. "I'm sorry my dear. This case makes me anxious. Plus I can hear the clock ticking on my time in Cincinnati."

Kate stood in the doorway and thought. "If this is the Black Widow, I may not catch her in the next two weeks. She's given me the slip before so I'm going to have to be extra careful not to let her do it again."

She paused and thought. "OK. Here's what we do. When do you need to leave?"

"Like I said, McClellan wants me in Washington by the first of next month." Allan walked back to his desk and picked up a calendar. "I'll have to leave by the 23rd or 24th."

Kate nodded. "I'll send you a telegram in a week, updating you on my progress. If I need help I'll let you know."

"And I'll tell Mr. Harcourt that you're in charge of his case from now on. "

Kate stifled a yawn. "Fine. We can work out the details tomorrow."

Allan walked Kate down the hall. "Just tell me this. Is it her?"

Kate shook her head, biting her lower lip as she did. "It feels like it is, but it may be wishful thinking. The description sounds like her and this business about bribing a rich man into marriage sounds like our Black Widow."

Kate paused at the top of the stairs. Allan was right behind her. She was so tired she just stared at him.

He turned and smiled at her confusion. "I'll make sure you get to your cab before you fall asleep on your feet, collapse into a snow drift and freeze to death. My wife would never forgive me. And I agree. It sounds like our gal. Your gal."

Kate didn't know whether to feel exhilaration or horror at his words.

Chapter 7

lexander Gibson watched his new wife over the dinner table. She held her hand up to the light cast by the gas light chandelier, admiring the heavy gold ring upon her third finger, a ring he'd put there during their Christmas day wedding ceremony. She smiled over the table at him, her eyelashes fluttering. Alexander contemplated the delights waiting for him after dinner. They married almost three months ago and yet he found his wife as alluring as when he'd first laid eyes on her. His two sons were less than happy with his second wife, objecting to their hasty marriage, but he didn't care. He wanted dear Lillian the moment saw her. That he waited four weeks to make her his bride was a testament to his patience. After a lifetime of hard work, building a small boarding house into the finest hotel in Cincinnati, meeting his guests and family's needs before his own, he deserved this one happiness. The second Mrs. Gibson was his just reward for a lifetime of hard work and moral rectitude.

Even pregnant with their first child, she fired his imagination and his passion. The dear girl did not bar him from her bedroom when she found herself with child as his first wife had done. Instead, she continued to practice marital delights, even though her swelling belly created certain challenges. She did other things, things he'd never done before. She knew her bosoms thrilled him and would pull her nightgown off her shoulders when they were in bed, though she kept her belly covered, no doubt shy about its burgeoning shape.

He was not so distracted by his love life that he forgot the plain facts of reality. A woman as young and beautiful as Lillian surely found his wealth more attractive than his person. But what of it? Shouldn't a man be rewarded for amassing a fortune? She seemed fond of him and at this stage in his life that was more than enough. She'd given him his youth back, a youth he'd never really had because he'd been busy making something of himself. Her pregnancy, with its proof of his potent manhood, made him feel like a stallion in his prime instead of the old man he saw in the mirror.

As if she could read his thoughts, she smiled at him again, pinning him with her astounding lavender eyes. "I'm so lucky to have found you, my darling. Perhaps we should cut dinner short so I can show you just how lucky I am." She pulled a lawn handkerchief from her sleeve and dabbed at her cleavage.

Alexander Gibson, who in his other life had been a dour, restrained hotelier, groaned with anticipation. He threw his napkin on the table and swept his wife into his arms to carry her to their bedroom. He staggered only a little.

Lily thought maybe her luck had changed. She left Detroit with a trunk of clothes, some pilfered silver and a bag of money and jewelry, but once again on the run. She took a train to Toledo. From there she went to Columbus and then Cincinnati. Each time she changed trains she changed her clothes, on the off chance Edwin had set the authorities on her.

She was nearly sure he would not. He wouldn't want his mother to find out what he was up to—and while Reverend Bland was a slippery, lying snake, his rich mother was real. She'd seen the house and heard people gossip. Still, while the rational part of her mind told her she was safe and had enough to keep herself until the baby came. She would lie awake at night worrying about the past like a dog with a rotten bone.

She'd stepped off the train in Cincinnati determined to never rely on a man again. She'd never met a man who didn't take what he wanted. Oh, she supposed they existed, but she'd never met one. And with a baby on the way she had to quit being stupid. It was time to reinvent herself.

At the train depot, she asked a porter for the city's finest hotel. He directed her to Gibson House. At first, she'd been dubious. Though it was a large and attractive building, it was on the far edge of town. In her short experience, the best hotels were in the city center, or with port cities, near the water. Cincinnati, for example, lay on the busy Ohio River and its downtown, with its fashionable shops and restaurants, lie near the river port.

Later Lily would thank the heavens she hadn't told the hansom cab driver to turn around when he first brought her to Gibson House. The sumptuous lobby and comfortable rooms convinced her to stay for a few days. She would find a pawnshop and turn her stolen silver and jewelry into cash. Then she would buy a little house, establish her identity as a respectable widow woman and raise her baby. She would need a husband eventually, when the money ran out. But not right away. But her plan had flown out the window when she'd seen Mr. Alexander Gibson.

On the second morning of her stay at Gibson House, she'd woken to a pitching stomach and bleak mood. She dry retched into her washbowl and rinsed out her mouth with cold tea. A peek outside proved the day as grey and gloomy as her mood, so she laced up her best corset and slipped on a rather daring purple velvet dress that turned her dark blue eyes an almost matching shade of amethyst. She needed to buy a plain black dress or two for her new life as a young widow, but there was no reason to rush into it. Cheered by her reflection, which showed her body still as lithe as ever and her breasts swollen with the as yet otherwise undetectable pregnancy, she made her way to the hotel lobby. She had a fun day of shopping planned.

She approached the concierge stand, hoping for directions to a good dress shop and help with a cab. On her way across the lobby, she saw an older man, dressed in a tailored black suit, speaking to the desk clerks. At first, she took him for a guest, but the concierge hailed him as Mr. Gibson.

A Mr. Gibson. In the lobby of the Gibson House. She knew she shouldn't but she couldn't help herself. Lily paused in the middle of the lobby, waiting for Mr. Gibson to notice her.

After a long moment, Mr. Gibson turned from the front desk and ran his eyes over the lobby. His eyes saw Lily, moved on, and then returned to her. He stared at her, his hands hanging forgotten by his side. She smiled in an absent-minded way. She watched him consider his options and decide. He was a tall man, but old enough to be well past his prime. The width of his shoulders and thickness of his torso suggested a body once powerful but now settled into comfortable old age.

He stepped up to her and performed a small bow. "Madame. I am Mr. Alexander Gibson, proprietor of this establishment. You seem at a loss. I wonder if I might help you." His grey and black beard waggled at her as he spoke, his voice a rich Scottish burr.

Lily found his grey eminence reassuring after the Reverend Bland's slick youthfulness. She fluttered her eyelashes at the old fellow, knowing how men felt about her eyes, and laid her gloved hand upon his arm. In that way, though she hadn't set out to do so, Lily caught herself a rich man.

Determined not to make the same mistake again, Lily kept her pose of respectability until Mr. Gibson brought her before a minister. They married on Christmas day, four short weeks after they met. By then Lily had teased the old gentleman into a froth of physical desire that made poor Mr. Gibson blind to the holes in her story and the size of her waistline.

Her new husband was so obsessed with her he'd have believed the sky was green if she said so. Her plan was simple. Keep him in her thrall so he didn't notice her too rapidly expanding waistline and pass the baby off as his. He certainly didn't seem to have any significant knowledge of the female body and its workings. He and his first wife must have had only the most furtive, under-the-covers, type of marital relations, a fact that made him eager to cooperate with his own seduction.

They lived in a suite of rooms on the top of his five-story hotel. Once again Lily found herself surrounded by luxury and pampered by servants. Alexander never lost his temper and never, as far as she could tell, ever lied to her. As winter turned to spring, he continued to treat her with respect and courtesy. If she didn't love him, Lily found herself growing fond of her second husband.

One April day, about four months after becoming Mrs. Gibson, Lily went looking for a morally flexible midwife. One of the few benefits of corsets and belled skirts was that only Alexander knew how large she'd become and she took care never to expose her abdomen to him. And as his adult children refused to receive Lily there were no uncomfortable questions about dates from that quarter. Her last refuge was the fact that her second husband ran his hotel like a private fiefdom. No employee was likely to risk his or her job to tell the boss his wife had cuckolded him. All Lily needed now was a midwife to attest that the baby had come early.

She found the woman she needed in a German neighborhood north of downtown, across the Miami Canal. Called Over-the-Rhine by locals, the neighborhood teemed with German-born workers and their families. Mrs. Schmidt kept a clinic for poor women just north of Liberty Street, in a neighborhood redolent with the yeasty smell of brewing beer. Lily and Mrs. Schmidt came to an agreement based on their shared belief that men had no business asking reproductive questions of their wives. Lily's ready supply of cash didn't hurt either.

"Ja, Ja, das ist gut," Mrs. Schmidt said over the head of a small child she was examining. "I vill be dare, and den after you pay me de rest." She looked up from the child and scrutinized Lily. "And you best quit de eating zo much. Zo da baby is not zo big."

Lily took her advice, figuring that whatever discomfort and hunger she had the next few months would be nothing to the freedom she'd have once Alexander accepted the baby as his. She returned to the hotel confident her future would turn out fine. Just fine.

The feeling did not last.

She went into labor early, even by her own calculations. It was hard to be sure. Her water broke at dinner, seconds before a massive contraction hit her, the wave of pain so sharp she screamed. Her husband, thinking the baby was coming three months too soon, came unhinged with anxiety. Once that first contraction passed Alexander helped her to bed, fluttering about her and wringing his hands all the while. Another contraction tore through her. She managed not to scream that time. Her husband screamed for her, a high pitched, old man scream that made Lily want to slap him. When it passed she gave him Mrs. Schmidt's card and told him to have one of the porters fetch her.

He looked aghast at the name and the address on the card. "My darling, you need a real doctor, not some ignorant, immigrant woman."

She'd expected this objection. "I don't want a doctor dear. He'd be a man, wouldn't he? It would be awful. Only my husband should see me like this." She tried to blush, but another contraction ripped through her. Yet another scream tore unbidden from her mouth.

He rushed from the room, returning minutes later with their maid. "Stay with my wife. I'm off to get the doctor." Lily opened her mouth to protest but Mr. Gibson left the room so quickly she didn't have time. And so her neat little plan fell apart.

Alexander returned with a man Lily had never seen, a tall, greyhound nosed doctor who'd been treating hotel guests for years.

"The child is out," the doctor announced just before dawn, his voice flat like a dead thing. Lily, nearly incoherent from exhaustion and blood loss, missed the look that passed over the doctor's face as he examined the child. Before Lily was aware enough to ask for the baby, the doctor had it whisked out of the bedroom, along with Mr. Gibson. The maid came in and tended to Lily but no one brought her the baby, not then and not later. A maid helped her into a clean nightgown and took away the pile of bloody towels and sheets. Exhausted, Lily fell asleep. At one point she awoke to find a bowl of soup and a pot of tea by her bed. She ate her lunch and waited. And waited. No one came.

Sometime late the next afternoon the doctor returned to examine her. He refused to look her in the eye and answered none of her questions. The maid came with dinner that night and breakfast again the next morning, but she wouldn't speak to Lily either. Lily cried until she ran dry, then cried again. Her plan had unraveled. She shifted from asking, "Where is my baby?" to "Is my baby alive?" She got no answers.

The third evening after the baby's birth Alexander entered the room. He carried a sheaf of papers with him. He laid one set of papers before her, keeping his eyes on the carpet beneath his feet.

"Sign these." His flat dry face was like a slap to Lily's cheek. "They are adoption papers."

Lily ignored the scream that grew in her throat. "Alexander, what are you doing?"

His eyes were like chips of Arctic frost. "Just sign them, whore."

She ignored the papers and grabbed at his hand. "Give me my baby and I'll go. Please. You'll never see me again, I swear."

He yanked his had away from her. "Don't tough me. Your whelp is mine in the eyes of the law, if in no other way. I'll not have a whore's child carry my name or inherit my fortune."

Lily clutched at his arm and cried, "No, no, please, no. I'll do anything. Please."

He shook her off like she had some kind of dread disease. "You'll do anything? That's the problem. You are a fallen woman. Don't make it worse for yourself."

"I'll go away. I'll change my name. You'll never see us again. I promise. Just give me my baby." Lily tried to keep the panic from her voice.

"Your promise means nothing, harlot. I mean to rid myself of you and your little bastard." He tucked his chin and glowered at her from his lowered brows. All traces of the man who'd made enthusiastic love to her had disappeared. "I want my baby," Lily wailed. She couldn't lose another child. If it happened again she'd go mad.

"It's already gone. And good riddance. Dr. Pope took care of it."

Alexander set the second set of papers atop the first. "These are the divorce papers. I have already signed them. Sign the adoption papers and these, admitting you are an adulterer, and I will pay you to absent yourself from my life. One thousand dollars now, another thousand when the marriage is over. I'll go to Indiana. It will take less than three months to get a divorce." He removed an envelope from his jacket pocket and laid it on the side table, next to her empty dinner plate. "A cashier's check. For services rendered. Suitable payment for you are a whore." He stood and left the room. He didn't look back.

Lily considered her choices through the night. Why did she have no good choices? She never did. She inspired lust in men, but not love. Never love. Did she ask so much? All she wanted was a chance to raise her baby in safety. In return, she would have given him anything, done anything, been anyone. Not even twenty years old and four men had used her and thrown her away. And two babies gone. Just gone. Tears were not enough. She cried them anyway.

The next day Alexander returned to her room. She pleaded with him, but he remained unmoved. She tried seduction though she was in no shape for it.

"Whore," he hissed. He pushed her away and stomped from the room.

They left her alone all the next day. No one came, not even the maid. Someone sat a tray of food outside her door about midday, knocked and left by the time she struggled out of bed and opened the door. She ate the roast chicken and bread with her hands, tearing at the meat like a ravenous and guilty dog.

That night she rose from her bed and dressed. She packed a bag and left it near the door. She stopped for a moment, looking down at the envelope with the check, still lying on her bedside table. Then she shrugged and added it to her bag. She hated to do it. It was admitting he was right. She was a whore. But a girl had to be practical. You couldn't eat pride.

Once packed, she retrieved her little bottle of chloroform from a box in her closet. She opened the bedroom door and peeked out. There was no one guarding the room. It was the story of her life. One of the stories. Men underestimated her.

Lily crept down the hall to Alexander's bedroom and pushed open the door. Moonlight illuminated the room. He slept, as he always did, on his back, elevated by a ramp of pillows, his hands folded on his chest. The chloroform bottle squeaked a little when she opened it, but her second husband slept on. She held the cloth over his nose until he stopped moving. It took a while. Then she re-wet it from the bottle and held it to his face again. After several long minutes, she checked his pulse. When she was sure he was dead she left his room, closing the door behind her without a sound. Empty of thought and child, she left the hotel.

Out on the dark street a cool, damp spring breeze tugged at Lily's bonnet. The scent of coal smoke and river water rode the air, like a dark perversion of spring. Lily tied her bonnet under her chin with a hard tug and squared her shoulders against the coming dawn. She wasn't sure where she'd go or what she'd do, she knew one thing for sure. She'd never trust a man again. Or let one use her. She was done with that life.

Chapter 8

*K*ate walked down the Gibson House's grand stairway in much better humor than when she'd gone up the afternoon before. A revivifying ten hours of sleep and a breakfast as large as the previous day's supper and she was ready to face the day, no matter how cold and grey. She'd braced herself for a return trip to Allan's office, wearing her warmest brown wool dress and matching coat, only to find him waiting for her in the hotel lobby.

He stood at the sight of her and examined her like a piece of evidence. "I see you have your traveling dress on again. And your cheeks are blooming."

"I am a woman reborn," she quipped, kissing him on the cheek. "More so now that I don't have to hike up all those stairs to your office."

"And so you will give my wife a positive report of my conduct?"

"Just this once," Kate said with mock sternness. She sat her traveling bag on the floor next to a small settee and took a seat. "Shall we conspire?"

Allan's laughter rolled through the lobby of the Gibson House. Wiping tears from his eyes, he looked around at the crystal chandeliers and velvet-covered furniture. "I would have thought you'd begin your investigation here."

"Where it all began, you mean? Did you notice?" She gestured at the front desk. "He's the same clerk as five years ago."

"And yet you packed your bag."

Kate reached down and patted her bag. "The clerk isn't going anywhere. We have to determine if this woman in Rochester is really the Black Widow. And we took on a case for Mr. Harcourt to rid his Mr. Lyon of an adventuress which we must do, regardless of the woman's ultimate identity."

Allan took a cigar from his pocket and rolled it in his fingers. "True, true. So you'll go back to Rochester?"

Kate nodded. "I'll approach it like any case of this type. I'll tail the suspect, investigate her activities, and infiltrate her circle, that sort of thing. The simple solution to Mr. Lyon's problem is to catch Mrs. Winslow in improprieties of her own."

"Would you like me to have your effects sent from Washington?" He put a match to his cigar and made a selection of unseemly sounds to get the thing lit.

"Good idea. I've got my gun, dagger and picks with me, but I need a few additional supplies." Kate told him what she wanted. He laughed at that too.

Kate stared out the frost etched train window at the swirling snow. It's dressing took the dreary, grey colors of winter and turned them into a suit of shining white. Few things in life offered such a brilliant makeover. Kate's parents had spent so many of her childhood winters traveling the southern circuit with one circus or another that snow seemed like a thrilling novelty, even after five years in a New York girl's school and another five years working from Chicago.

She touched her forefinger to the window, melting a tiny oval in the ice crystals. She had a good seat on the train, close to the small coal stove that sat in the middle of the aisle. It was odd to be running around the Northeast again, alone, chasing the sort of case like the old days. She'd grown used to living in a household full of people, all of them cooperating to uncover Confederate spies. Lately, they'd been dismantling Rose Greenhow's Washington spy network. Uncle Juba, Hattie, Odetta, Louisa, Samuel, Timothy and Charlotte Webster had all helped. Collectively they made up the Washington branch of the Pinkerton Agency. She missed them already.

And Hazzard. Always Hazzard. Her lips curved into an unconscious smile as she thought of him. If she were a fast woman, she'd say he was her lover. Kate chuckled. She enjoyed the pleasures of the marital bed without the benefit of marriage. And heavens, did she enjoy it. Maybe she was a fast woman. Kate smiled to herself. No maybe about it. She was a fast woman of the worst sort.

She'd married and divorced before she became a Pinkerton operative. That experience had not left her with positive thoughts about marriage, nor with the desire to repeat the experience. She'd kept Hazzard at arm's length for over a year. Now she found immense, unfathomable pleasure with her romantic and patient Captain. But what else had she found besides pleasure? Love? It would seem so. She shook her head. No, it would not seem so. It was so.

Kate wasn't sure what scared her more, that Hazzard would turn out no better than her ex-husband, or that he'd be killed in the war. She'd loved her husband too, or thought she loved him, which amounted to the same thing. And he'd lied to her and abused her in all the ways a husband could abuse his wife, and then he'd betrayed her and left her with nothing. Well, that wasn't fair. His father gave her $5000 to divorce his son, so it hadn't been a total loss. It hadn't taken her long to figure out the money was more reliable and more likely to give her pleasure than the husband.

Her logical mind knew Hazzard was incapable of brutality. He'd declared his feelings long before she'd been sure she wanted him in her life and then he'd waited for her, never pressing his suit. What sort of man did that? Maybe that was the problem. He was too good to be true. Why would a man that handsome wait around?

She knew what respectable ladies would say. But they'd be wrong. He hadn't seduced her and refused to marry her. She was the one who didn't want to marry, not Hazzard. They had a war to survive. And wasn't that a problem? She was a spy for Mr. Lincoln's government and had already taken two bullets. Hazzard was a captain in the Fourth Artillery and, despite Lincoln's and the Pinkerton's efforts to keep Hazzard in the spy business, he'd have to go to war. Hell, he wanted to go. He'd missed the battle at Bull Run. His regiment's orders had been to hold Fort Washington, the city's defensive fortification on the Potomac, but that didn't mean the regiment wouldn't be ordered into battle.

The things a woman could learn in wartime astounded Kate. She learned that lieutenants and captains died in battle at much higher rates than did colonels and generals. Field artillery soldiers died at even higher rates than fixed fortification artillerymen. What would happen if he got his wish and his company marched to Virginia?

And what then? How would she survive losing Hazzard? The dangers of wartime love chilled her heart. Love was like cannons in war. It committed great havoc on its targets and occasionally exploding as the result of operator error.

Kate jerked her head as if to shake off her thoughts. The train car rocked back and forth, the coal fire popped and smoked, and a man down near the rear door snored like he was in his own bed. She having all these dire thoughts about herself and Hazzard so she wouldn't have to remember the Black Widow? *No. Lily Nettleton. There.* She'd said it, if only in her head. Bad, bad Lily Nettleton.

It started on one of those icky, sticky summer days that Chicago seemed to specialize in. She'd been working for the agency for less than a year when Allan gave her the Nettleton case. Only they'd called it the Gibson case then. Mr. Conall Gibson came to them with a story of family murder. He explained how his father, a well-off hotel owner, had suffered after the death of his wife of thirty years. Yet only months later the father met and married a young and attractive woman. Six months after that the second Mrs. Gibson killed her husband while he lay sleeping and absconded into the night with a suitcase full of money and family jewelry. The Cincinnati police had little luck tracing the murderous wife, so the younger Mr. Gibson thought to enlist the Pinkertons in the hopes of bringing the young woman to justice for his father's cold-blooded murder.

Allan sent Kate to Cincinnati on the premise that it was just such cases for which he'd hired a woman. She spoke to all the hotel employees, finding a clerk who remembered that the second Mrs. Gibson's bags had tags from Columbus and Toledo. A glance at a railroad map suggested that while Toledo was an unlikely stop for a woman traveling to Cincinnati from Columbus. A traveller would first have to travel northwest, then at Toledo turn back southeast. Unless Columbus was a red herring, used by the woman to disguise that she came from points north of both Toledo and Cincinnati. Which was just the sort of behavior people fleeing the law engaged in. This made sense to Kate. A normal woman did not get up in the middle of the night and murder her husband.

She interviewed the hotel's head clerk. He remembered he'd once heard Mrs. Gibson discussing Detroit's finer points with another lady. The conversation had centered on the city's best modistes and milliners. Kate thought a lady who knew a city well enough to discuss its dressmakers might return to that city in times of trouble. And Detroit lay just north of Toledo. So that's where Kate took her investigation, hoping that by tracing the murderous lady's past she might find her present.

She started with dress and hat shops but found that ladies that ran those establishments took their customer's privacy more seriously than lawyers and priests. Next, she turned to hotels. Given the reported quality of Mrs. Gibson's trunks and clothes, she started at the finer hotels. She started at the National Hotel before moving on to the Steamboat Hotel. Having no luck at either of those she tried her luck at the Michigan Exchange Hotel. That's where she struck gold.

Three dollars encouraged the desk clerk's recollection of Mrs. Gibson. He said she was easy to remember because she'd been checked in with a man who'd done the same thing with other women.

"A wily one, that fellow," the clerk said with an admiring tone. " He weren't no minister, no matter how white his collar. Had him an oily way of turning ladies into admirers if you take my meaning. "

Kate knew the type. The world was full of men only too eager to take advantage of the vulnerable. They preyed on women, children and old people and usually got away with it because the police had bigger fish to fry. Two more dollars bought the address to a house that the hotel had, on three different occasions, transferred a young woman's luggage.

The address proved to be a modest house on the west side of town. Pinkish white Roses climbed up a trellis in front of the house, providing a pretty contrast to the light grey paint. A grandmotherly looking woman answered Kate's knock, invited her in and served her lemonade. The woman introduced herself as Mrs. Cawley, the housekeeper.

"Oh, my goodness, I do remember Lily," the lady said when Kate described the Black Widow to her.

"The young master was quite taken with Miss Lily. He very much wanted to marry her and if you'd seen the girl you would not blame him. But his mother wouldn't allow it. She had her eye on some rich young society girl for her precious only son."

"The desk clerk I spoke to had quite a different story about your young man. He said your minister made a habit of seduction."

"Well, yes, I am sad to say that the young master was a hellion in his youth, with the drinking and gambling and fast women. All the vices of fashionable young men you understand, but one day he awoke from a night of sin and repented. He began attending church and soon after enrolled in the Methodist seminary here in town. Why he's out west right now ministering to the heathen Red Men."

Mrs. Cawley explained that her minister met Miss Lily on the train and fell in love with her. He brought her to this cottage, where he'd brought women before, intending only to care for her until he convinced his mother she would make a suitable bride.

"But I guess it took too long," the lady said, her mouth tight with disapproval. "One night Lily, who I'd taken care of like my own, drugged the young master and me. Drugged us. Can you imagine? And then she stole the silver and my housekeeping money and fled into the night like a common sneak thief. I've always thought the master and I was lucky she didn't murder the two of us in our beds. Everyone knows how easy it is to kill someone with chloroform."

Considering Lily murdered her second husband with chloroform, Kate thought Mrs. Cawley was right. Kate questioned Mrs. Cawley at length about Miss Lily Winslow, learning about the young woman's food and clothing preferences. She also learned where she'd come from.

"Tuscaloosa, if I remember aright," Mrs. Cawley said after some thought. "No, that's not it. Tuscaloosa's not in Michigan is it?"

After the two women agreed that Tuscaloosa was most surely not in Michigan. Mrs. Cawley clapped her hand to her forehead. "I'm such a ninny. Kalamazoo. That's what she said. She came from a farm outside Kalamazoo."

The tiny town with the odd name was a long train ride west of Detroit. She could hardly go from farm to farm asking about missing daughters. Instead, she found the town's newspaper office and asked to look through their back issues. The newspaperman, a portly, red-faced man with a shining bald dome of a head seemed happy to help, so Kate took a chance and asked him about girls named Lily.

He scratched his head, smearing ink on himself in the process and said, "Well, there's a couple. How old? What's she look like?"

So Kate described her quarry. Halfway through her description, his face lit up. "Why, you're looking for Lily Nettleton. Good luck. The sheriff never found her and he put considerable effort into it."

The newspaperman told a chilling tale of a young woman who, in one night, killed both her husband and her father before disappearing. "She locked her mother and sister in a storage shed. I suppose they were lucky to survive. The next day the mother escaped, discovered her husband's mutilated body and sent for the law. Sheriff Miller found Lily's husband later that day, also murdered and mutilated. Bit of a scandal there. They say she cut both men to bits."

The newspaperman paused and shook his head. "She was a pretty thing. Far too pretty for Kalamazoo. And only eighteen years old when it happened. But she never seemed happy. She had a friend who said Lily talked about being a schoolteacher in Detroit. Hard to believe a girl like that would kill two men. But the Sheriff said it was her."

The Sheriff told the same story, adding that Lily had also stolen a horse. He'd tracked her as far as nearby Battle Creek, but he'd lost her trail after that. He thought she'd taken a train, but he didn't have the resources to trace her, so he'd had to live with the unsolved case. They agreed that the young lady's specialty was absconding into the night, leaving violence and mystery in her wake.

Kate didn't have any more luck in Battle Creek than the sheriff had. She returned to Cincinnati and scoured the city's ticket offices, hotels, and boarding houses. The hotels and boarding houses seemed like a waste of time, but Kate checked them anyway. A woman who'd just killed her husbands and father was likely to get out of the area as quickly as she could, but then again, triple murderers weren't notoriously logical people.

After checking the hotels boarding houses Kate asked around in tea and dress shops. She even checked the libraries. No one remembered seeing anyone matching Lily's description. During the weeks she searched Kate thought a lot about the sort of woman who would murder three men. A woman like that wouldn't stop. And each murder would be easier than the one before.

After two weeks of fruitless searching Kate had to admit the murderess wasn't in Cincinnati. She never found even one trace of Mrs. Gibson, Miss Winslow or Miss Nettleton or any other lady matching her distinctive description. Kate returned to Chicago, her case open and unsolved.

That failure haunted her like a great black mark against her soul. She felt sure the Black Widow was out there wreak-ing havoc on people's lives. And now, five years later, she had another crack at her. Maybe.

Chapter 9

January 11-12, 1862
Rochester, New York

Kate stood in the middle of her hotel room and twirled around, taking it all in. She had stayed nowhere this nice since last year in Baltimore and then she'd been pretending to be a senator's mistress, which had taken some of the fun out of the accommodations. There were few things more delightful than a good hotel. She noted the hotel stationery on the desk by the window. She'd write a letter to Hazzard later. And another to Juba, who would share with everyone at home.

When she arrived back in Rochester, Kate had asked a hackney cab driver to take her to the city's best hotel. He took her into the heart of the city, driving past snowdrifts already grey with mud and manure. She'd watched out the window as the cab turned onto Main Street. They crossed the river that ran through town and a block later stopped. Her driver, a red-cheeked, older man with a lilting Irish accent, hopped down from his perch and handed her bag over to a hotel bellman. Kate took one look at the hotel and tipped the cabbie enough to make him laugh out loud.

It was a five-story brick and stone building that appeared to take up most of the block. Shops, including a bakery from which emanated the heavenly smells of warm bread, lined the front walk. A sign at the main entrance announced the establishment as Osborn House.

"Timothy O'Malley, at your service Ma'am." He swept his hat off and bowed at her, bouncing on the balls of his feet as he did. A cold gust of wind blew his orangey grey curls around his head.

Kate tightened her scarf about her neck, looked at the cabbie for a moment and decided. "Mr. O'Malley, I am a stranger to your city it would be helpful to me to have someone who knew their way around town. I wonder if you would like to return here tomorrow and drive me around town? I could pay you for the whole day."

O'Malley beamed at her, revealing a gap-toothed smile that made him look like a puckish boy. "Nothing would give me greater pleasure Ma'am. What time would you like me?"

"Nine should be fine." Kate intended to have another full night's sleep after yet another long day on a train. She nodded at his cab, a large, four-wheeled conveyance where the customers sat inside and the driver up top. "I wonder if you have another conveyance, something smaller, so we could talk to each other."

"Hmmm." He grabbed his coat lapels and looked thoughtful. "I know just the thing. You don't worry Miss. I'll take care of it or Timothy O'Malley ain't my name."

"Then I will see you on the morrow." She tipped her own wool felt hat at her new friend and allowed the bellman to whisk her inside.

At the reception desk Kate informed the clerk that her trunks would arrive in a day or two. This news both reassured him that she was not a lady of low repute and had the advantage of being true. By now Allan should have cabled Charlotte in Washington with a list of items to send on to Rochester. Kate asked the clerk to have someone check the New York Railway luggage offices tomorrow. She also asked him to send up a selection of the city's newspapers.

On her way to her room on the third floor, she stopped to examine the menu posted outside the second-floor dining room. Partridges. Oysters. Champagne. Kate's stomach rumbled at the words. Even better, the dining room offered room service. She would dine like a queen, while wearing her robe. What could be better? Her mind strayed to Hazzard. Well, it would still be a good dinner, even without him.

Her room proved superior to even the dinner menu. A thick, rose-colored Brussels carpet covered the floor. Ivory wallpaper sprigged with tiny pink roses made the room light and cheery as did the ivory velvet drapes. A small, gas chandelier battled the failing winter light. Kate sat her bag on the bed and walked over to the window to peer out. A radiator sat under the window. Steam heat was almost as exciting as room service.

One of the room's two doors opened into a small closet. She held her breath and opened the other. There, gleaming like the crown jewels she found a private water closet with a flushing toilet and a small sink. If she could get Hazzard to move here she'd never leave, especially with a bakery on the first floor and a dining room with room service on the second.

She'd just finished unpacking her bag when a knock at her door signaled her newspapers' arrival. The hotel maid who delivered them looked no older than fifteen and Irish enough to be Mr. O'Malley's kin. Bridget, for so she said was her name, agreed to bring Kate some dinner and a pot of tea within the half hour. She even helped Kate unbutton her boots, using a buttonhook she kept in her apron pocket for just such occasions.

A half-hour later Kate had all the comforts of home, but for her favorite blue velvet wrapper, left behind so she could travel light. She had more comforts than home. How did the F Street house not have radiators and plumbing? She made a note to herself to find out what it would cost to update her house. She also had a tray with a plate of partridges and glazed carrots and a pot of tea that smelled like apricots. Bridget made Kate sit in the room's pink velvet chair and pulled the little side table in front of her. Upon it she put the tray of comestibles and the pile of folded newspapers. Kate thought about asking Bridget to run away with her.

Kate examined the newspapers while she ate her dinner. The clerk had sent up the *Rochester Democrat*, the *Evening Express* and the *Evening Herald*, the *Monroe Democrat*, the *Rochester Courier* and a thin thing called *Northern Freeman*. All of them, even the *Freeman*, had advertisements for reform meetings, including those for helping the indigent poor, the insane, and the orphaned. There were announcements for temperance, anti-slavery and women's rights societies. Kate knew you could tell a lot about a town from its newspapers and clearly Rochester was a do-gooder kind of place.

Best of all, Rochester had spiritualists. Every paper, from the conservative *Monroe Democrat* to the reform focused *Express*, had advertisements for spiritualists. Some specialized in spirit rapping, some in automatic writing, others in ectoplasmic manifestations. Trumpet mediums claimed to hear the spirits, trance mediums said they could feel the dead and ectoplasmic mediums could make the dead dimensional. There was even a man offering to debunk any spiritualist, both in public talks and private consultations.

In the *Evening Herald*, she found what she was looking for. Mrs. Winslow advertised subscription séances several evenings a week. Kate took down the address and times in a small notebook and crawled into bed. She lay in the cozy hotel room, upon a soft feather bed, wind and sleet rattling at the windows outside and thought about her plan of attack. She needed to better understand spiritualism in general and Mrs. Winslow in the specific. Only then could she figure out if the lady in question was also the Black Widow.

The next morning dawned clear and cold, the sky a brilliant azure dotted by fluffy white clouds that chased each other across the sky, like sheep herded across a field. Kate donned her brown wool traveling dress once more and looking forward to her trunk's arrival and with it a fresh dress or two. She availed herself to the second-floor dining room, where she ate a breakfast of corn cakes dolloped with a chunky peach jam that sang songs of summer in her mouth. At five minutes after nine Kate stepped out into the brisk morning and tried not to laugh. Sweet Mr. O'Malley was waiting for her in a small, two-wheeled dogcart harnessed to a shaggy grey pony not much taller than a mastiff. The pony wore a bright purple knitted blanket under its harness and a matching purple ribbon braided into its forelock.

"Mr. O'Malley, you are a sight to see." Kate walked to the pony's head, noticing the diminutive equine was a lady pony.

"Good morning' to ya, Miss." He'd doffed his hat, allowing his curls to wave about in the gusts of morning air.

"Warne, Miss Kate Warne." The pony allowed Kate to kiss her velvety pink nose.

"Well, Miss Warne, I know it don't look like much, but me wife fixed up the cart so we'll be snug as bugs in a rug and Buttercup, here, why she's a tough old girl and she'll take you anywhere you want to go today."

Kate glanced up at him, back to the pony, then back to her driver.

He grinned. "My granddaughter wanted to dress up Miss Buttercup after I told her what a fine lady you are." He had the good sense to look chagrinned.

Kate tried with little success to keep a straight face as she stepped into the cart. The floor was lined with flannel wrapped hot bricks. She pushed her boots against the radiant warmth, grateful to the efficient Mrs. O'Malley. Mr. O'Malley pulled a thick, woolen blanket over both of their laps, making a cozy tent over their lower bodies.

He nudged her with his pea coat bolstered shoulder. "The Missus says I'm to bring you to the house for tea in two hours. She'll re-heat the bricks while we fortify ourselves. If that's all right with you, Miss."

Kate beamed. "It sounds like a capital plan Mr. O'Malley."

He clucked Buttercup into a trot. "Where to Miss Warne?"

Kate pulled her little notebook out of her coat pocket, opened it and held it out to O'Malley. "Can you take me here?"

"Orange Street? Sure. It's on the other side of the river, by the canal."

Kate spent the ride admiring the scenery. Rochester sat in a valley, surrounded by tree-covered rolling hills. O'Malley pointed out the observatory high above the city on Mount Hope, taking great delight in his city's scientific bent.

Macadam street surfaces made their progress smooth even though the carriage and wagon filled streets saved Buttercup from anything more strenuous than a walk. Rochester businesses lined the downtown streets, their signs as bright and cheery as a new hatbox. He spoke with great pride of how Rochester had grown in the last few decades.

"Used to be a no account town, back when I was a lad. But the Erie Canal came to town and with it came all kinds of industry. We're the City of Flour on account of all the mills, but also the City of Flowers on account of all the seed companies. Doesn't that beat the band? Now there are jobs aplenty and rich men everywhere, building big houses and hotels. And they all take cabs, from here to there and everywhere. The wife and me are in the clover. Oh, I know. I'll drive you by the Opera House after this. You never seen anything like it."

After they passed a second park, no more than a wide square blanketed in snow this time of year, O'Malley turned on Orange Street. Midway through the first block he pulled Buttercup to a stop and motioned toward the house on his left. It was a brick house, two stories high, with a wide front porch held up by round white columns.

From the street, Kate could see a large front door and windows curtained in some dark material. "Hold on while I see if anyone's home," she said as she climbed out of the cart.

Someone had shoveled the house's front steps, though a thin coat of ice remained. Kate picked her way to the front door. A sign over the door read Barlow's Boarding House. A sheet of paper was affixed to the door's small window.

Mrs. Winslow
Spirit Guide and Medium
Public Welcome Thursday, Friday & Saturday, 7 PM
Private Séances By Appointment Only
Inquire Second Floor, Left.

Kate peered in through the window. What she saw appeared more apartment house than a home. She glanced over her shoulder at O'Malley, who tipped his whip in her direction. Kate felt for her pocket revolver, finding its cool metal weight reassuring. She pushed open the door. The foyer's warm air wafted over Kate. Somewhere a clock ticked in the quiet. She walked up the wooden stairs, almost wincing when a loud creak came from the risers. Upstairs, more dark woodwork outlined the doors and walls. The first door on the left had a small card pinned to it that read: Mrs. Edwina Winslow, Medium.

Kate's heart galloped, though she wasn't sure why. She'd never seen Lily Nettleton so there was no danger of being recognized. Either the woman that lived here was the Black Widow or not, but either way the lady had no reason to think Kate anything but a run-of-the-mill customer. Kate knocked on the door. The sound echoed in the quiet hall. Nothing happened. She knocked again. Behind her, a door opened. Kate's shoulders jumped at the noise.

She forced herself to relax as an English accented voice said, "Mrs. Winslow's out. She takes a carriage to do errands and such in this weather."

Kate turned to see the speaker, hoping she didn't look as frightened as she felt.

A red-faced man of medium build and neat mutton chop whiskers stood at the door opposite. He wore an under-stated dark waistcoat, white shirt and matching trousers. "Would you be inquiring after the lady's services?" This time his voice was quieter. Kate considered the possibility that he'd scared her on purpose, and then dismissed it. Why would he?

"Well, yes," she replied, putting considerable flutter and stammer into her words. "A friend recommended Mrs. Winslow. I hear she is the best in the city. I rather hoped . . .." Kate stammered to a stop.

"It's all right dearie. Mrs. Winslow helps all kinds."

Kate stepped closer to the man. "May I ask, are you a believer?"

His smile transformed into a self satisfied expression that made him look as if he'd stolen the crown jewels and gotten away with it. Kate decided he'd scared her on purpose.

"I am. Mr. William Bristol at your service." He nodded his head at Kate. "I am proud to say that upon occasion Mrs. M uses me as her assistant. I know many of the city's spiritualists and I can assure you the lady of whom you inquire is no charlatan."

Kate fluttered her eyelashes at Mr. Bristol. "That is good to hear sir. So I should come back another time?"

"Come back Saturday night, 6 o'clock. She has two empty chairs that night. Two dollars for one evening or you can buy a subscription for six dollars a month. That allows you to come as often as you please." He nodded at her again, stepped back and closed his door.

Kate returned to Mr. O'Malley and Buttercup with the beginning of a plan. "Mr. O'Malley, I wonder if you could point out the livery stable nearest this house."

She pulled her notebook from her pocket again and showed him the second address. "And here as well?" He doffed his hat at her, jostling her with his elbow as he did. "I can my dear, but it's way on the other side of town, with my house halfway in between. I have my orders from the wife. How does a nice cuppa sound?"

Kate thought tea sounded like a good idea indeed.

The O'Malley household turned out to be as whimsical and entertaining as Buttercup. Mrs. O'Malley provided currant scones and a huge pot of tea, while two granddaughters provided entertainment. The oldest, who announced she was six years old, hopped about the room and sang songs. The little one stared at Kate with her thumb in her mouth until Mrs. O'Malley picked the child up and dropped her in Kate's lap.

Kate hid her astonishment at finding a fragrant bit of damp humanity in her arms, in part because both the elder O'Malley's seemed to think it normal and because the little girl felt sort of nice. Kate fed the little girl crumbs of scone and sips of sweet tea while Mr. O'Malley hauled bricks in from the cart. Mrs. O'Malley popped them in the oven and stirred up a pot of what looked like rough oatmeal. She poured it into a wooden bucket and held it out to the singer of songs. "Mary my dear, take this out to Buttercup. Get your coat first."

Kate thought of Odetta's penchant for feeding street children. Odetta and Mrs. O'Malley were cut from the same cloth.

A half-hour later she and Mr. O'Malley were on their way again. He drove her around the east side of town and past the second address though they did not stop to make inquiries. Along the way, he pointed out the building that had once housed Mr. Douglass's abolitionist newspaper, *The North Star.* "He were a brave fellow, that Mr. Douglass," O'Malley breathed, staring at the building as if he remembered something long gone.

Kate couldn't hide her astonishment.

O'Malley saw her face and laughed. "Were ye thinking all the Irish hated the Negroes?"

Chagrined, Kate admitted that's exactly what she thought.

"Oh, I 'suppose a lot of us do, but me and the wife, we admire the way Mr. Douglass and the free blacks in this city stood up to the rich folk who'd not have them here. Being Irish we know a thing or two about not being wanted." O'Malley looked at his hands and frowned. "I think Mr. Douglass and the radicals are right. No man is free if some are slaves. Surely no poor man."

Kate felt more than a little ashamed. "I'm sorry Mr. O'Malley. I should have known better."

He patted her knee and they drove on in silence.

As they drove to their next destination the sky turned an ominous slate color. A damp breeze that smelled of snow worked itself into wind, encouraging Kate to cut her reconnaissance mission short. Mr. O'Malley dropped her at the Osborn house just as the first flakes of snow swirled in the air. She kissed him on the cheek, hopped from the cart, bestowed

101

upon Buttercup a similar kiss and went inside, but not before Mr. O'Malley extracted from her a promise to send for him should she need help.

As Kate walked past the hotel bellman she sighed. So many plans to make. In every investigation there came a moment when it woke up and began to speak. The Black Widow case was doing that now.

Chapter 10

January 13, 1862
Rochester, NY

Her large traveling trunk arrived, delivered to her room by one of the hotel's dark-skinned porters. Kate flung open the lid to find a letter from Hazzard. Kate all but tore the envelope open.

Dearest Kate,

Hattie has packed the contents of this trunk, with some help from Juba, with an eye to the beastly upstate New York weather. Brrrr. If only I were there to keep you warm.

No one here knows what you are doing. If safe, please send an explanatory letter to Mrs. Webster, who will share the information. I have every faith in your ability to slay monsters by yourself, but if you require my help I shall come at once.

Yours Always,

G. W. Hazzard

P.S. Samuel should be one day behind this trunk, with the big guy and the little guy in tow.

Kate resisted the impulse to squeal in girlish delight. It was a very Hazzard-ish love letter, both practical and charming. And she was getting company. She used to relish working alone, but not so much anymore. The past year had given her a family and she missed them. She missed breakfast with people who loved her and working with people she trusted. She wondered if Uncle Juba could afford to lose Samuel's help with his spy network, even if only temporarily.

After hanging up her clothes, Kate dressed in one of her men's suits, being sure to pull on a set of woolen undergarments first. Once dressed she shrugged into a heavy black great coat, pulled a dark grey slouch hat low over her ears and tied a black scarf around her neck. She tucked her Colt revolver into one pocket and her dagger into the other, adding to that pocket a pair of padded gloves. A bead of sweat trickled down her lower back as she did so. She peeked into the hallway to make sure no one saw a man leaving Miss Warne's room before high tailing it out of there.

Out on the street, she pulled the scarf up over the lower part of her face and strode west on Main Street. The snowstorm had passed in the night, leaving the skies a brilliant, arctic blue. After twenty minutes of brisk walking, she found herself in front of a livery stable. The livery stable, in fact, that Mr. O'Malley said was closest to Mrs. Winslow's apartment. The building sported a wooden false front painted with the words "Livery, Feed & Sale Stable." Even in the cold, the comfortable bouquet of manure and hay wafted from the building. Kate stepped inside and looked around. A scrawny stable boy directed Kate to the office at the back of the stable. Kate knocked on the open door and, taking care to keep her voice low, said, "Excuse me, sir."

A middle-aged man with a dark Quaker beard looked up at her. "What can I do for you?" He rose and offered his hand over his desk.

Kate, still wearing her gloves to disguise her small hands, stepped forward and shook the man's hand. "My sister is coming for a visit and she's bringing her horse. I live in a boarding house so I've no place to put him." The man sat and motioned for Kate to do likewise.

"Well, look no further than my stables, sir. We can take care of the beast. If you care to look around, you'll see I run a clean stable with healthy stock."

Kate offered a dry smile. "I noticed on my way in and commend you. I also wonder if you have carriages for hire. My sister cannot ride in this weather."

"I do have a carriage I hire out."

"One a lady might be comfortable in?"

The man pushed himself to his feet again. "Let's go see it. It's going out within the hour."

Kate followed the stable man and pretended to inspect the carriage. She thanked him for his time, promised to return with the horse on the morrow and left.

Next, she walked over to Mrs. Winslow's and took up a post across the street, behind a large, unhitched wagon. She waited. The sun felt warm on her cheeks, but she kept her scarf pulled up. Last summer she'd sustained a male performance for weeks with only a bushy mustache, men's clothes and an entitled attitude. But she'd been around men. Women were harder to fool. It had been a woman who'd seen through her disguise last summer. And if Mrs. Winslow was who she thought she was, she was likely to be more aware of her surroundings than the average woman.

Kate waited and watched in the weak warmth of the winter sun, her mind drifting into a comfortable blank space. The solid thunk of a closing door jerked her out of her reverie. A woman walked down the stairs across the street. Kate peered over the edge of the wagon. The lady wore a heavy blue coat and a midnight blue velvet bonnet, but Kate could make out dark hair and brows. And because of the coat's meticulous tailoring, she could also tell the lady was both petite and curvy. This had to be Mr. Lyon's lady love, Mrs. Winslow.

Kate followed her. The lady walked straight to the livery stable. Minutes later the stable's wide doors swung open and the carriage rolled out. Kate followed it. Though she was on foot, the streets were so crowded with freight wagons, passenger carriages, hacks and the occasional omnibus that the carriage was easy to keep in sight.

They traveled down Main Street until it turned east. The traffic stayed heavy even after they turned north. Not too many blocks later the carriage came to a stop in front of a two-story wooden building. A sign affixed above the door read 'Schmidt's Beer Garden and Tavern.' The driver hopped down from his seat and opened the carriage door. The lady in blue stepped out. She waited for the driver to open the tavern door before stepping inside.

The driver climbed back into his seat and clucked the horses forward about fifty feet before he stopped, pulled a heavy rug over his lap and lit a cigar. Kate watched the interaction with interest. These two were familiar with each other.

Kate checked the traffic, crossed the road and stepped into the tavern. The scent of sausages, bread, and beer made her stomach rumble. A fire crackled in a huge stone fireplace at the far end of a large dining room, while a bar lined the back wall. The blue-coated lady sat at a small table near the fire.

She removed her gloves and bonnet, revealing a mass of dark hair. Kate took a table near the bar and watched the woman.

The lady folded her bonnet ribbons inside the hat so they wouldn't wrinkle, then smoothed out her gloves, folded them and tucked them into her coat pocket. Then she unbuttoned her coat and slipped it off her shoulders, revealing a cobalt blue dress that revealed somewhat more décolletage than was strictly decent for a day dress. She laid the coat on a chair and resumed her seat. A barmaid approached her and was waved off. The barmaid sauntered over to Kate. Instead Kate ordered a small beer and a half loaf of dark rye bread. It came with a miniature tub of thick, pale yellow butter. Kate did her best not to gobble the bread with unseemly haste though she took advantage of the fact that no one expected men to be delicate about their food.

As Kate finished her bread, the tavern door opened to admit an exquisite man. It was clear by the way he paused in the doorway he found in himself much to admire. He was none too tall and slender as a nymph. His wide blue eyes and delicate facial structure only enhanced his fairy-like qualities. The young gentleman looked around the room, twitching his waxed mustaches like a rabbit testing the breeze. He swept a shining silk top hat off his head, exposing dark blond hair just long enough to pull into a short tail. He was as pretty as a debutante.

Then his face brightened, his smiling lips exposing fine white teeth. With his free hand, he tugged at the sleeves of his tailored dark blue frock coat. When he did he exposed a canary yellow waistcoat into which he'd tucked a waterfall tied cravat of the type rarely seen outside ballrooms. He stepped across the room like he knew all eyes were on him. Something that looked like a diamond stickpin glinted in the white cloth of his neckwear.

As he passed Kate, she found herself confronted with lavender pantaloons, tucked into butter yellow boots. So astounded was she that she nearly failed to notice who he was meeting until he took a seat at Mrs. Winslow's table. The two clasped hands in a lingering, almost caressing manner, before Mrs. Winslow removed several coins from her reticule and slid them across the table.

He scooped up the money and made his way to the bar, his precise, mincing steps allowing Kate and the other patrons a full view of his glorious self. The barkeep poured two brandies, took the bill and pushed coins at the young man. Neither man said a word. Kate guessed this exchange was not their first.

Kate nursed her beer and watched the man return to the blue lady. He leaned toward his companion, while she sat back in her chair, making it clear which of them had the upper hand in the relationship. Kate silently cursed the patrons that kept her from sitting closer. She wanted to, no needed to, listen to all conversations between ladies of dubious character and elfin men in lavender britches.

After about fifteen minutes the lady pushed her empty glass away and stood. Her companion followed suit and lent her his elbow.

As they walked toward Kate, Mrs. Winslow said, "My dear Le Comte, I couldn't agree more."

Kate waited until the two left the tavern, then followed. It was snowing again. Mrs. Winslow spoke to her carriage driver before her companion handed her into the carriage and climbed in behind her. The driver slapped the reins and the carriage took off, rolling north up the now empty street. Kate watched as it rolled away, its wheels clattering against the macadam. Traffic had thinned out and the carriage moved too fast for a person on foot to follow. She stood there, shoulders hunched against the cold until Mrs. Winslow's conveyance was nothing but a memory. Kate shook off a shiver and headed back into the tavern.

She approached the empty bar, leaned her elbows against the counter and waited. The innkeeper was one of those fat men that were, despite their size, light on their feet. He twirled out the kitchen door, two plates of sausages in each hand and delivered them to a table of working men.

The barkeep stepped behind the bar and eyed Kate. "Anodder beer, den?" He had a mug in hand and was pouring before the words were out of his mouth.

"Yes. Thank you. Could I buy you one?"

He smiled, his facial wrinkles suggesting he'd had a good deal of practice with the expression. "Ah, ya. I dank you." He poured himself a mug of his amber brew and touched glasses with Kate. "Here's luck."

Kate glanced around the tavern's great room. "This is a nice place you have."

"Dank you. You never come here?"

Kate shook her head. "I'm in town from New York City and had time this morning. I took a stroll and ended up here."

"Ya, I get a good many customers dot vay. Peoples strolling to der Bort."

"The Bort?" The bartender's accented English finally defeated her.

"Ya. Der Bort Charlotte. Eferbody goes to der Bort. For da entertainments, ya know."

Kate's brain struggled to interpret words. Port Charlotte. She'd seen it on the directory map, just north of Rochester where the Genesee River emptied into Lake Ontario. "The Port has visitors even in winter?"

"Oh, ja," he said, beaming and nodding. "Like dat lady and gentlemen who just left here. Dem two meet 'ere all de time and dey go to der Bort. Lotsa hotels up der. Ones dat don't care 'bout virtue."

"Really?" Kate leaned her elbow on the bar and sipped her beer.

"Vell, I would never rent rooms to two such as dem. I don't get mine living dat way. If I did, I might as vell be a politician." The German snorted at his own joke. "And dat gentleman is too much a dandy." He nodded at Kate. "I mean, you be small too, but you at least dress like a real man. And you drink good German beer."

Kate stifled a smile at the thought of her manliness and bought her new friend a cigar from a box he kept behind the bar. For the hour the big German puffed on his cigar, poured beer, wiped counters, picked up plates, and gossiped with Kate between his duties.

The blue lady and her lover met at the tavern two or three times a week, a pattern they'd established the previous summer. During one of their early visits, they'd asked to rent a room, but he'd refused them, saying he was full up. He'd directed them to Port Charlotte, after which they made it a habit to use his tavern as a meeting place. They would return four or five hours later, or so the German assumed because Le

Compte sometimes came into the tavern for dinner and more brandy.

Having ingested one too many barley based beverages, Kate asked for a private room. Three hours later, refreshed by a nap and a cold basin of water, Kate took up a post outside the tavern in a narrow side alley. Dark came early in January, which meant she didn't have to put much energy into concealing herself.

She waited in the dark, shivering against the cold, wishing for one or two of Mrs. O'Malley's heated bricks. Carriages passed on the road, but none of them slowed. As the dark deepened, traffic died down to nothing. Time dragged. Kate shivered. Time dragged some more. The familiar rumble of carriage wheels woke her up. She peeked around the corner to see the carriage door opened. Le Compte stepped out. He stumbled and caught himself on the carriage wheel.

"Good night my darling," came a high, girlish voice from the carriage's interior. Giggles followed as Le Compte reached into the carriage with one of his arms. "I'll see you on Saturday. I'll try to be early so we have more time."

Le Compte bowed, wobbling as he did. "I shall count the moments Ma Cherie." He stepped back and the carriage rolled away.

Kate watched as the little Frenchman turned toward the tavern, then shook his head. Instead, he walked away, up the street in the same direction as the carriage.

Kate followed him, careful to keep about a half a block back. She suspected in his inebriated condition she could have followed right on his heel, but better safe than caught. After several blocks, he turned onto Main Street. Kate sighed in relief. She knew where she was now. After too many blocks to

111

count they crossed the river, it's damp cold aroma rising to meet them as they did. Kate recognized the Arcade standing on the corner of Main and State. Her quarry turned onto State Street, walked past the Arcade and up one more block, before turning and disappearing.

Kate scampered up the street and found a stairway embedded in a tall brick building. She bounded up the stairs two at a time and grabbed the door at the top. Offering up a silent plea, she turned the knob. The door opened. She entered as the Le Compte disappeared down a hallway and up yet another set of stairs. Kate followed, running on tip toe to keep her heels from clacking on the floor boards. A single gas light at the top provided a thin yellow light for her pursuit.

By the time she'd made it to the top of the stairs, the Frenchman had disappeared. Again. She tiptoed down the hall, examining the doorways. Several doors had cards tacked to them. With the gas light at her back, she couldn't make out the words. Kate stood in the hallway undecided. Good sense dictated she return in the morning when the light would be better. Caution and curiosity fought a little battle in Kate's mind. Caution lost. It usually did.

Kate pulled a tin of lucifers from her interior jacket pocket, thanking the powers-that-be for men's jacket pockets. She struck one and held it up to the card at the first door. An accountant. Shielding the little flame with one hand she stepped over to the next door. A lawyer. Neither seemed likely. Men with professions did not wear lavender trousers.

Her match guttered out. Kate paused and listened. Nothing. She lit another and checked the next door. And there it was.

112

Claude Le Compte
Healing and Trance Medium
Clairvoyant and Mineral Locator
Appointments upon Request

In the spirit of the moment, Kate whispered, "Voila." She turned to go, already thinking about the hot water tap and steam radiator in her hotel room.

Chapter 11

January 14, 1862
Rochester, New York

Kate stood on the depot platform and looked down the track. She checked her watch again. The train was late. It was probably a weather delay. The day was as cold as a brass corset and snow had fallen through the night. She paced and thought about yesterday. If the lady she followed yesterday was Mrs. Winslow, then she'd solved Mr. Harcourt's case. She couldn't sue Mr. Lyon for breach of marriage contract if she was indulging in secret assignations with French fellows. But so far all Kate's evidence was circumstantial, meaning she had more investigating to do. After the train arrived. If it ever arrived.

The shriek of a steam whistle broke Kate's thoughts. She looked down the track. There it was. She beamed, unable to help herself. The train slowed with a screech of brakes, billows of white steam coming from every crevice of the locomotive. Kate walked to the end of the platform and waited, tapping her foot against the frost-covered floor boards.

The train was a small one, with only two passenger cars and two freight cars. She watched the cars slow and stop, before the doors open. People stepped out. None of them were

Samuel. Craning her neck, she looked down the track. No, there wasn't another train.

She turned to go inside, intent on querying the station master, when a man's voice above the engine's racket.

"Miz Kate!"

Kate whirled. Samuel was leaning out the first freight car's door. She waved. "Samuel!" A small black dog leaped out of the freight car, ran up the tracks, bounded up the stairs and flung himself into her arms. Kate squeezed Monty in her arms. "Oh, you are a good dog aren't you? Are you the best dog? Are you?"

He squirmed in her arms, applying lavish swaths of warm dog spit to her neck and chin as he did. She kissed his nose one final time and set him down. He ran back down the steps and back into the freight car. She followed him, taking care on the icy steps.

"I got him in here but he's cold and cranky." Samuel's dark-skinned face broke into a wide, gap-toothed smile as she approached. "He'll come out for you and a walk will warm him right up."

The freight car, redolent with the bouquet of horse, hay and oats, was dark inside. "Celli," she called in a soft voice. A shrill neigh answered her.

Samuel held out his hand and pulled her up into the car. Her pure white Kentucky stallion had once been the most famous circus horse in the country and he acted like he still was. Excelsior stamped his front feet at her and issued a high pitched neigh.

Kate turned and looked at Samuel. "Did you ride in here with him?" Samuel had him blanketed and his legs wrapped, but the train car was icy cold.

"Yes Ma'am."

"You must be near froze to death."

",, Miz Warne. I got the big boy to lie down last night. Me and him and the little fellow snuggled up close and kept as snug as could be."

Kate doubted Samuel's words but didn't say so. A man had his pride. "Would they not let you in second class?" Up north most railroad companies let negroes ride in the second class car.

"Oh, I 'spect they would, but all them white folk make me nervous. I just as soon ride with the horse."

Kate gave Samuel a close look. She'd first met him in the yard of a slave market awaiting sale. A succession of bordello madams had owned him, but beyond that, she didn't know much about his life.

He smiled at her. "I was fine Miz Warne. No need to worry yourself."

A wave of cold shame rode through Kate. She'd wanted her horse and her dog and hadn't thought about the man who'd deliver them. At least not enough.

They got Excelsior unloaded and walked him over to the same stable she'd visited yesterday, only this time Kate was dressed as a woman. She presented herself as the sister with the horse, reminding the stable owner he'd met her brother the day before. When the man remarked on the siblings' uncanny resemblance Samuel barked out a laugh so loud he startled Monty.

Once they'd rubbed down Excelsior and fed him a bucket of hot mash, Samuel, Monty, and Kate left the stable. Kate kissed her horse on the nose several times before she did, an act Excelsior withstood with dignified patience.

Outside Samuel paused and turned to her. "Where to next?"

He was asking where he should go. Even Rochester hotels were not tolerant enough to allow negro guests.

"Mrs. O'Malley is expecting you," Kate answered with a broad smile. She linked her arm in his, not caring of what people thought and took Samuel to the O'Malley's. Monty followed along, peeing on every other lamp post as they went.

That evening Kate left Monty in the hotel room and presented herself at Madame Winslow's rooms for the lady's Friday night séance. She'd dressed in her best traveling dress, a navy blue polonaise with red braided trim and wound her hair into a tight, low bun. Before she knocked on Mrs. Winslow's door she adopted her most forlorn expression.

Mr. Bristol opened the door, this time wearing a hunter green frock coat. "I'm pleased you returned my dear. You look in need of spiritual assistance." He stepped back from the door and waved her in. "Mrs. Winslow is preparing herself, but the others have gathered in the parlor. If you'll join them, I'll see if she's ready."

He led Kate down a short hall, turning into a mid-sized room. Maroon velvet drapes with soft gold tiebacks matched a maroon and black patterned wallpaper. A large, carved wardrobe like cabinet stood between the two draped windows, while a round table sat in the middle of the room. A soft gold damask cloth covered the table, its hem nearly touching the floor. Eight dark wooden chairs gathered around the table, though none of them were pushed in far enough to interrupt the smooth fall of the tablecloth. Another, smaller table held an unusual assortment of items on it, including a harmonica and tambourine and a small drum. Two fair-haired women who looked enough alike to be mother and daughter stood by the table, doing their best to ignore a pair of older gentlemen across the room.

Kate headed for the ladies. Before she could introduce herself Madame Winslow entered the room, pausing at the parlor doorway like a diva taking the stage. Her dark hair shone in the gaslight. Kate breathed a sigh of relief. It was the same woman Kate had followed to the German's tavern. The lady held her curtsy for a moment, allowing the gentlemen a glimpse of her substantial décolletage. Kate fought the urge to roll her eyes and snort. Instead, she joined the others in polite clapping. Mr. Bristol took up a position in front of the large cabinet.

Mrs. Winslow broke her pose and made her way through the room, speaking to first the ladies and then the gentlemen. Kate was the only newcomer in the room.

After a few minutes, Mrs. Winslow made her way to Kate. "My dear, how nice to meet you," she said, holding out her hands to clasp Kate's hands. "Are you here for a particular purpose? Is there a loved one you'd like to contact? Or are you a spiritual seeker?"

Kate found herself so transfixed by Mrs. Winslow's eyes she almost failed to answer. For years people had talked about the Black Widow's purple eyes, but she never believed such a color existed outside of people's imaginations. If this was Lily

119

Nettleton, the descriptions had not been hyperbole. Kate mentally shook herself and said, "Both I think. Mr. Barley has been gone for over a year and I miss him so. If you could contact him or assure me he's safe and happy, that would be a great benefit to my uneasy mind."

"Are you unsure about the afterlife Mrs. Barley? Do you struggle with standard Christian belief?"

The conviction in Mrs. Winslow's voice surprised Kate. She'd expected something less genuine from a woman who must be a charlatan. "I, I don't know," she stammered. "I only know I miss my husband."

Mrs. Winslow pressed Kate's hands again. "You must have loved him very much. I should be able to contact him, my dear. If not tonight, then soon." The lady stepped past Kate and announced, "I feel the spirits pressing close. Shall we begin?" She gestured to Mr. Bristol, who'd not moved from his station in front of the cabinet.

He opened the cabinet door like he was revealing ancient Egyptian secrets. A straight-backed chair sat inside the cabinet. Mrs. Winslow stepped up to the cabinet and held out her hand. He took it and helped her step up, into the cabinet. She turned sideways and sat in the chair. Then she smiled at the séance attendees and said, "Would you all please take your seats and join hands. We shall see if the spirits are with us tonight. Mr. Bristol, since we are short a gentleman, would you take a place in the circle once you've put out the lights?"

Kate couldn't help but admire the lady's quiet charisma.

Bristol closed the cabinet door and snapped the door lock with a loud click.

From behind the door, Mrs. Winslow called, "And the slate Bristol?"

He plucked a thick, hinged, book-sized contraption off the table and opened it, revealing a double slate, both sides blank. He placed a piece of chalk inside, closed the thing and put it on the table. Everyone found a seat at the table, arranging themselves to they alternated men and women. Kate sat between the two older men, each of whom offered her a distant smile as they placed their hands on the table. Kate joined hands with her companions while keeping an eye on the cabinet and Mr. Bristol. He shut off the gas to the lights. The room went black. Unable to help herself, Kate gripped her gentlemen's' hands a tiny bit harder. A chair scraped against the polished wood floor, presumably Mr. Bristol taking his place at the table between mother and daughter.

Again, Mrs. Winslow's voice came from the cabinet. "I will now attempt to call the spirits. I will need your help. Concentrate on the person you are here to contact. Keep quiet and keep contact with each other's hands. Once we have a clear signal that the spirits are amongst us we shall proceed."

And then nothing happened. Kate heard breathing, then a quiet sniff. Someone shuffled their feet. The gentleman on the left had moist hands while her other hand stayed dry and cool. The air moved against her cheek. Then came a soft single note from the harmonica. The note transformed into a tuneless group of chords.

Kate strained to see, but the room's darkness admitted no peeking. The tambourine rattled, then stopped. Another high note sounded from the harmonica. The drum rat a tat tatted. Then nothing. Quiet reigned for several long moments, then

Mrs. Winslow's voice sounded through the cabinet door. "They are here and will stay."

By the end of the evening, Mrs. Winslow claimed to have spoken to a dead son, a dead wife and a dead husband. She did not contact Kate's imaginary dead husband, in either of the séance's two stages.

Kate spent the evening holding back snorts of derision. Life among circus folk taught her there were more fools in the world than there were foolers, but the world was full of both types. Mrs. Winslow's act was not much different from the gypsy fortuneteller act Hattie taught Kate more than a decade ago. People wanted to believe in the unseen so all you had to do was give them a half-credible performance. And it wasn't fraud, not to Kate's way of thinking. People wanted reassurance about their future, their lost loved ones, their choices. The person who did that provided a service worth paying for. It was blasphemy to say so out loud, but Kate didn't think there was much difference between spirit calling and church. Fortunetellers, mediums, ministers and priests were all engaged in the business of pretending to know of the unknowable.

No, it wasn't Mrs. Winslow's fakery that bothered Kate. It was her customer's fatuous acceptance of cheap emotions that made her want to smack each of them upside the head. Johnny was happy in a soft, fluffy heaven, Lizzy's husband missed her and adored her, that sort of thing. No one was ever angry about being dead or irritated that their family bothered them from beyond the grave.

After about an hour in the cabinet, Mrs. Winslow announced she was ready to rejoin them at the table. Bristol unlocked the cabinet and let the lady out. She took her seat and opened the spirit tablets, which is what she called the hinged slates. Lo-and-behold, there was a message written upon them, incoherent scribbles Mrs. Winslow declared a love note to one of the men from a long-dead wife. Not only did he believe the message, but everyone at the table seemed impressed and astounded that Mrs. Winslow's mediumship was so strong that she could summon spirit writing. No one questioned the fact that the room was pitch black when the writing appeared on the slates, nor did anyone question the medium's interpretation of meaningless scribbles.

After they examined the tablet, they all held hands and summoned other spirits, finding one who communicated only by rapping sounds. Mrs. Winslow asked the spirit questions and the spirit answered yes or no with one or two raps. No one seemed to notice the rapping sound seemed to come from Mr. Bristol's region.

At the end of the evening, Mr. Bristol appeared with the two gentleman's overcoats and the lady's wraps and ushered them out into the hall. Making a show of being too exhausted to stand, Mrs. Winslow held out a hand to Kate. "Would you stay for a moment, my dear?"

My dear? Kate stifled a laugh and settled back into her chair at the table.

"I am so very sorry," she said, her voice throbbing with emotion. "I failed to contact your husband. Perhaps next time."

Kate nodded, but before she could speak the lady spoke again.

"I sensed a disturbance in the room this evening. I think it was you. You are not a believer are you?"

Kate took a deep breath. "I don't know. I *want* to be."

"What do you understand of spiritualism, my dear?"

There was that 'my dear' again. Who did this woman think she was fooling? "Very little I'm afraid."

"Are you religious?"

"I am, but I haven't been to church since my husband died." In fact, Kate had only rarely attended church. Life on the road with a circus hadn't been conducive to regular Sunday attendance and most townspeople didn't like it if the circus folk mixed with them. Now, when she needed God, she just talked to him. Or her. Kate wasn't sure.

"Spiritualism is a religion. Spiritualists believe in God. Or rather, we believe in an Infinite Intelligence."

She said the last two words so Kate could hear the capitalization. "We believe the Infinite Intelligence wants us to improve ourselves, both before and after death. We believe humans have an immortal soul, a soul that never dies, never dissipates, but simply changes form."

"Is that who you contact? A person's soul?"

Mrs. Winslow nodded. "Without a body the soul becomes spirit, but the spirit yearns to communicate with the living. Mediums are open to spirit communication. We help both the spirit and the loved ones left behind because death is not the end. It is a new state of being."

Kate watched Mrs. Winslow as she spoke. She delivered her con with an almost perfect sincerity. Kate might have believed her if she hadn't known how the lady performed her tricks. And that's what they were. Tricks.

Chapter 12

Mrs. O'Malley pulled open the door, exposing Kate to a rush of warm, cinnamon-scented air. "Hurry dear. Don't let the cold in."

Kate stepped into a bustling kitchen, Monty hard on her heels. Pots burbled on the stove, writing slates covered the table and Samuel lay on the floor covered with O'Malley grandchildren. Monty jumped on the pile and slathered Samuel with kisses.

He pushed the little dog off and tipped his head up from the floor and grinned at Kate. "Miz Kate, you jess in time for a little 'arithmetic lesson.'"

She smiled back at him while the children bounced on him, the older girl astride his chest and the smaller one across his legs. "One plus two?"

"Equals chaos," Mrs. O'Malley sang out. She pushed aside the slates and slid a teapot onto the table. "You two go wash up and come get your tea. And no petting the doggie after you've washed your hands or I'll give all the cookies away."

The children scrambled off Samuel like he was on fire and ran out of the kitchen, hollering about cookies as they went.

Samuel rolled over and pushed himself to his knees. "I'm jess about too old for roughhousing with chilluns. Jess about." He stood and helped straighten up the table. "We really was doing some learning but little 'uns cain't sit still too long."

Kate looked over at Mrs. O'Malley. "Seems like you got yourself a nanny. Can you spare him this afternoon or is he full time?"

The ladies shared a knowing chuckle. "Mr. Samuel has been a help this morning. Mr. O'Malley is out with the cab and the baby's parents work every day but Sunday. At the seed packing factory."

Samuel pulled a slate over in front of him. "Mrs. Webster been teaching Odetta and me and Louisa some reading and some sums. I kin read the Bible now. Slow as all get out, but I kin do it. I never taught no one though."

"Not till now," Mrs. O'Malley said as she slid a plate of cookies onto the table. When she thought no one was looking she tossed one to Monty, who gobbled it down with nary a chew. "You're good at it."

Samuel ducked his head but Kate could see the pleasure he felt at Mrs. O'Malley's words in the set of his shoulders.

Kate took a cookie. "So, can you spare him this afternoon?"

Samuel shifted in his seat. "You're not thinking of keeping me here long are you Miz Kate? In Rochester?" Kate shook her head. "I'm sorry. I haven't been clear. I know you and Juba have business in Washington, but I need some help. For a day or two. And I hated to send you straight back on the train. I don't know about you, but I don't like riding the train two days in a row." Before he could speak she added,

"And when you do go back, you're riding in the second class car. You need to learn to do that just like you're learning to read." "

The little ones bounded into the room. Mrs. O'Malley looked at them, then at Kate and Samuel. "You two go into the parlor where it's quiet. I'll feed the babies their snack."

Kate grabbed her mug of tea and two cookies and followed Samuel into the tiny house's front room. Monty stayed in the kitchen, clearly aware that small children meant food for an attentive dog.

"I don't need much. I need to know when Mrs. Winslow takes out the hired carriage. So I can follow her." Kate bit into a cookie and nearly moaned in pleasure.

Samuel walked to the window. "She uses the same livery stable we put the big boy in?"

Kate nodded, her mouth too full of cookie to risk words.

"So I hang around, fuss over the horse? Ask questions?" Kate swallowed so she could talk without spitting cookie crumbs. "Yes. The thing is, I thought about watching her place, but it's cold and there's nowhere to hide where the watcher won't freeze. Last time I followed her there was a big wagon across the street and it wasn't so cold. But that was just luck. A man inside the stable would do the trick."

"And they won't pay me no attention."

Kate shook her head. "No, they won't. As far as they know, you're a spoiled rich woman's servant. Mrs. Winslow drove out the day before yesterday. I think she'll go out again today or tomorrow. I need to know ahead of time so Excelsior and I can follow her."

Kate described the carriage and driver to Samuel, and then she described Mrs. Winslow.

127

"Whew boy. She sounds like a number."

Kate agreed. "She takes advantages of the male weakness for female beauty."

Samuel shrugged. "Some men's weakness. And stupidity be more like it. Nuthin' more foolish than a fellow in a lather 'bout a woman." Samuel patted Kate on the shoulder and headed back to the kitchen.

As Kate followed him a disturbing thought rolled into her head. She made her living much the same way this Mrs. Winslow did, using men who underestimated her because of her sex. And like the Black Widow, she'd killed people. Two people. Both times it had been self-defense, but dead was dead.

From the O'Malley's Kate went to see a man she'd meant to visit since her first day in Rochester. It would have been nice to ride Excelsior, but Samuel needed the horse at the stable so he'd have a reason to be there. Considering the cold she left Monty with the O'Malley children. She heard his claws scrabbling at the door as she walked away, but hardened her heart and left him behind. The little guy's heart was bigger than his good sense.

It was just about mid-day when she reached Dr. Hubbard's house on the east side of town. The sun came out again as she walked and though it wasn't warm enough to melt the snow and ice, it felt pleasant against her face. She arrived at a small, square house and knocked on the door. While she waited she examined the shabby sign next to the door. The peeling paint revealed Dr. Hubbard specialized in 'Nervous Complaints' and 'Advice on Spiritualism.' The good doctor's newspaper advertisements claimed he specialized in the latter.

After a few moments, the door flew open and hit the wall behind it with a bang. A small brown and white spaniel bounced in the doorway, barking as if its life depended upon it. Good thing she'd left Monty with the O'Malley's. A dog fight probably wouldn't incline the doctor to help her.

"Sorry about the wait," a heavy set, red-cheeked man said, his voice cheerful against his companion's ebullient yapping. He looked down at his dog and squinted in a parody of sternness. "Mister Brown, you cease that racket at once." The dog stopped barking and stepped forward to sniff at Kate's skirts.

She had no doubt the dog could smell Monty on her.

The doctor welcomed Kate into a short, narrow hallway and closed the door behind her. Before she could speak he'd looked her up and down.

"Now let's see. You don't look neurasthenic or otherwise delicate. No, quite the opposite." He rubbed his hands together. "You're not here for doctoring are you?"

Kate smiled. Between him and Mr. Brown, she'd yet to get a word in. "Mrs. Barley," she said, holding out her gloved hand.

He took her hand in his and pumped it up and down. "Dr. Hubbard. But you know that."

"Well, yes. I saw your advertisement in a local newspaper. I require some advice on Spiritualism."

"Oh, good, good. I can tell you whatever you want to know." He paused and blushed. "For five dollars."

Kate agreed to his terms and handed over a stack of coins.

He slid them into his pocket and gestured her into a room off to the left of the hall. It was a small front parlor, crowded

129

with comfortable chairs, small tables and a chaise lounge that stuck out into the middle of the room.

Once seated Dr. Hubbard leaned forward, hands on his knees and squinted at Kate. "Someone you love got themselves embroiled with the damned Spiritualists?"

"Something like that."

"A pox on the lot of them. They're all trouble, from the tricksters selling the claptrap to the believers that buy it. And the believers are stubborn. They don't want to know its all fakery."

"I'm finding that out, which is why I'm here. Do you mind if I ask for your qualifications?"

"Oh, no, not at all." Dr. Hubbard leaned back in his chair and folded his hands atop his substantial belly. "I graduated from medical school two years after my dear brother. We set up a practice together and had a couple of good years until a spiritualist trapped him. She drained him of every penny he had and then some. He became obsessed with contacting the spirits, looking for proof of the soul and the afterlife. He missed the damn point if you ask me and I suppose you did. We're not supposed to know. Life is a mystery. Even the corporeal body has secrets."

"What happened?"

Dr. Hubbard took a deep breath. "My brother and his spiritualist friends decided they needed someone on the other side. Someone to come back and explain it to the rest of them."

"No." Kate didn't have to fake her horror.

"Yes. My brother killed himself. His damned fool friends waited for days, then weeks, but of course he never made contact.. A good man's life was wasted by puerile religious mania. That's why I do what I do. I attend trance lectures, séances, anything I can, and I find the weaknesses and expose the charlatans. And they're all charlatans."

"I have some thoughts of my own on that subject. I went to my first séance last night, with a Mrs. Winslow. Some of it seemed explainable, some not." Kate thought it was all explainable, but she wanted to hear what Hubbard would say.

"It's all humbug." The doctor's voice rose into a near shout. He sat forward and took a deep breath. "It's all lies, lies and more lies. Though your Mrs. Winslow is one of the craftier ones. Tell me about your séance. What did she do?"

Kate described her previous evening, from the cabinet and the musical instruments to the trance speaking, spirit writing, and rapping.

Dr. Hubbard rubbed his hands together. "Some of that is child's play to explain. The musical instruments and the spirit writing both happened in absolute darkness because the medium needs someone to sneak around the room playing instruments and switching the tablet. You'll never see a spiritualist do that trick with the lights on. They'll give you some hokum about how the spirits need dark, but I've caught 'em at it. If you go back listen for footsteps or the rustle of clothes. The cabinet is a newish fad. Since people like me came along the Spiritualists are always trying to prove they're on the up and up. So they'll lock themselves in a cabinet. Sometimes they have someone handcuff them or tie them up before a minion locks them in."

"Mrs. Winslow wasn't restrained in any way," Kate said. "But her assistant locked the cabinet and the lock made a loud sound so it doesn't seem likely she unlocked it and snuck out. We'd have heard it unlock."

"You're focusing on the door. If I examined Mrs. Winslow's cabinet I would find a hinged side or back panel. That's how they work. Was the cabinet against a wall or curtains?"

Kate nodded, trying to keep the smile off her face. "Both. Curtains on one side, a wall at the back." He knew the tricks like he was circus-born.

"So there you have it. She climbs out the side of the cabinet, plays some musical instruments, switches the tablet and slips back inside. I bet she spoke from inside the cabinet when she was first put in, and later when she was ready to come out, but not otherwise."

He waited for Kate's confirmation before continuing.

"The trance sessions are the easiest to fake. Like all spiritualists, she's adept at getting information out of people, then parroting it back to them. She may also use her assistant to investigate customers so she can appear to know more than she should. Tell me, what did you tell her about yourself and your reasons for being there?"

"Just that I'd lost my husband and missed him."

"And she didn't contact him?"

"She said maybe next time."

"She wants you to keep paying her. And she needs more information so she'll stall you until she or the assistant gets it. Was there someone else there? I mean besides her customers?"

"Yes. A man. He lives across the hall."

Hubbard nodded and rubbed his chin. "He's new since I investigated her. She's improved her act."

"And the rest? How did she fake it all?" Kate knew the answer but wanted to hear what Hubbard had to say.

"The spirit rapping is also easy to fake. The table clothes always go to the floor so the customers can't see what's happening under the table. Right?"

Kate nodded.

"I've seen it done a variety of ways, but the easiest is to have something hard on the floor where the medium sits, something like a marble tile. The medium either has something on the bottom of their shoe or something on their sock. They'll slip off a shoe once they've taken their seat."

"Her assistant was wearing carpet slippers."

"Then you know who did the rapping. And it makes sense. Everyone is looking at her, right?"

"Oh, absolutely. She's mesmerizing." Kate smiled at her little play on words.

Dr. Hubbard threw back his head and laughed. "When I investigated her, I was so taken with her I almost forgot what she is. She made quite a splash when she first arrived here and she remains one of the city's preeminent spiritualists. Which is saying something. There are more spiritualists in Rochester than thorns in a blackberry patch. I hear she's got a rich fellow in her clutches."

"Oh?" Kate's investigative antennae quivered.

"Yep. A Mr. Lyon. He made his fortune in the seed business. More money than King Midas, or so I hear. I also hear your gal's got him buffaloed. I'd bet he's not her first rich man either."

"Why do you say that?"

He leaned back, opened a cigar box and extracted one. "Do you mind?"

133

She didn't. Anyone who spent any appreciable time with Allan Pinkerton built up a tolerance for cigar smoke.

Once he'd clipped and lit his stogie Hubbard continued. "She's what I call a bouncer. I've made a study of the spiritualists, not just in Rochester, but elsewhere too. It's a simple matter of taking the newspapers from all the major cities and keeping track of the advertisements. Some of the mediums stay in the same city, but others, like Mrs. Winslow, bounce from city to city. Most of the bouncers are running from the law, so they change their names when they change towns. At least some of them do."

Hubbard puffed on his cigar. "The Mrs. Winslows of the world are sharks looking for rich fish and they move from place to place looking for bigger and bigger prey. Men like Mr. Lyon for example. And when they can they extort money from people in return for keeping quiet about whatever secret they've unearthed or manufactured. People pay for silence so the bouncers crimes never come to light." He put his cigar down and stood up. "Hold on, let me get my book."

When Dr. Hubbard returned, he held in his hands a large account book. "I keep track of them all in this ledger." He pulled a small table over between the two of them, sat his book on it and flipped it open. "W. Ah, here she is. Winslow. I'd forgotten. Last year she was in Terre Haute. And Syracuse too. And Chicago the year before that. About six months each place." He looked up at Kate, his cigar forgotten. "I wouldn't want that woman's claws in anyone I know. I'd bet ten thousand dollars she's ruined more men and broken more families than I can count."

Kate thought Mrs. Winslow's history sounded an awful lot like the Black Widow's history, always moving, always looking for new victims.

She left the tidy little house thinking the pile of silver dollars she'd given Dr. Hubbard was the best five dollars she'd ever spent.

Chapter 13

January 16, 1862
Rochester and Port Charlotte, New York

"It's the curious young gentleman." The German tavern keeper waved at Kate from behind the bar. The tavern was chock full today. Kate supposed the German and Irish clientele attended church Sunday morning and the tavern Sunday afternoon. It seemed like a reasonable way to split the day.

Kate pushed a fifty-cent piece across the bar at him. "One of your excellent brews, sir. And one for yourself."

"Ach, I dank you, but I don't got da time to talk wit you today." He waved his arm around the tavern's great room. "I'm busier den a one-legged man in an ass-kicking contest."

Kate laughed and assured the man she'd be fine without him. He bustled off to the kitchen, emerging a few moments later laden with plates of bratwurst and dark bread. She'd eaten lunch at the hotel only two hours ago, but her stomach rumbled a little at the sight of the plates.

In fact, she'd been in the hotel dining room finishing a bowl of pea soup when a porter appeared at her table in the dining room. He'd bowed and said, "Your stable man is outside Ma'am, with your horse."

She found Samuel and Excelsior waiting outside, each puffing ribbons of steam into the frosty air. Excelsior nickered at the sight of Kate. She put her face up to her horse's, enjoying the warm, horsey smell that came from him.

Samuel waited, aware that everyone came second when Kate was with her horse. Monty danced around her feet until she noticed him. She patted her chest and he leaped up into her arms. She nuzzled his short soft fur and looked at Samuel.

"They rolled their best for-hire carriage out and polished it 'bout half hour ago. I asked around. Seems a fine looking woman is taking it out this afternoon, 'bout two. So me and the boys," Samuel gestured at Excelsior and Monty, "we hurried on up here to pass the word."

"Excellent." Kate bit her lower lip. "I don't dare go upstairs, change into men's clothes and come down and ride away. How about this? Could you ride him up to Schmidt's Beer Garden and wait for me there? I'll change and walk down to meet you." Samuel agreed and Kate gave him directions to Mr. Schmidt's place.

True to her word, she arrived at the beer garden before 1 o'clock, Monty trotting alongside her. Better to be early. At first, she didn't see Samuel and Excelsior, until it occurred to her to check behind the tavern for a stable. She found them back there, huddled against the cold.

"Here, money for the trip home." She thrust a handful of banknotes into Samuel's pocket.

"You sure Miss Kate? I could stay."

"I could use you, but I suspect you've got more important things to do right now than hang around Rochester keeping me and the animals company." She resisted the impulse to hug him. Still, it had been nice to not be alone, even if only for a little while. She took a moment to feel sad at the sight of Samuel walking away, then Excelsior nickered. Right. She wasn't really alone. Not as long as she had her horse and her dog. She left Excelsior in the stableman's care and headed for the front tavern door.

Inside Kate nursed her beer and kept a close eye on the door. Monty took up a station under her chair curled into a tight ball and snoozed. After a quarter of an hour's wait a slim figure bundled into a scarlet cape came through the door. With a whirl, the cape came off to reveal a pair of glorious red and black plaid trousers. Monty growled at the cape's movement, his hackles at full attention. Kate agreed with him. She watched Le Compte from the corner of her eye. He took the same table he'd sat at the first time she'd seen him, removed his gloves and waited.

Kate waited too. Not long after Mrs. Winslow entered the tavern, only a little less gorgeous than her companion. She had on an embroidered, sapphire blue coat so beautiful it was almost a work of art. It had belled sleeves with a gold border of vines and leaves around the cuff and up the sleeve. The same border, also in a satin gold thread, circled the hem and ran up the front of the coat. The collar and cuffs were lined with a silky blond fur. More fur peeked around the neckline, suggesting the coat was fur lined. Kate didn't care much for ladies fashions, preferring daggers and handguns, but Mrs. Winslow's coat was awfully nice.

Mrs. Winslow took a seat at the table and once again slid money across the table to the French man. He fetched a pair of brandies.

Peg A. Lamphier

The lady took a sip and frowned. In a carrying voice, she said, "You tell that damned Dutchman to get better brandy or I'll never pay him another dime." She pushed her glass aside and stood to go. Le Compte hustled out behind her, like a small tender boat in the wake of a grand passenger ship.

Kate swallowed the last of her beer and sauntered out the tavern's back door to the stables. Five minutes later she had Excelsior saddled and on the road north, behind the pair's hired carriage. Monty rode snuggled inside her coat to keep them both warm. Charlotte lay only five miles up the road but the bitter cold air promised a long, uncomfortable ride.

The carriage approached what looked to Kate like the only hotel of any significance in the town, a two-and-a-half story brick affair just off the waterfront and in view of a beautiful stone lighthouse. Kate waited outside to give Mrs. Winslow and her Frenchman time to check in before entering the small hotel. She tapped a bell on the desk and an elderly clerk appeared. When Kate asked for a room the old man nearly capered in delight. When he spun his book in her direction, she saw why. Aside from a Mr. And Mrs. Jones of Rochester in room 2 and a Mr. Swingly of Syracuse in room 11, the hotel was empty.

"Quiet this time of the year isn't it?" Kate signed as Mr. Barley and returned the man's pen.

"Well, it's winter, don't you see? Ever been here in the summer?"

Kate shook her head and reminded herself to keep her voice pitched low. "I'm afraid not."

140

"Well, it's a whole other town in July. People come from Rochester to escape the heat. And there's all the lakefront amusements."

"Since you're not too busy I wonder if I might request a lower floor room. She peered down the hall. Room number one was on the right. Its windows would look out the front of the building. "Something facing the back, so it's quiet?"

He put her in room 4 and offered to stable her horse. He also offered to take Monty to the stable, but an extra dollar convinced him Monty should stay with his master.

Once the clerk left the lobby to take care of Excelsior, Kate tried one of her favorite detecting tricks. She marched up to Room 2 and rattled the knob and then scratched her key around the lock. In her loudest, deepest voice, she said, "Why doesn't this damned key work?" She rattled the doorknob one more time, then pressed her ear against the door. From the other side Kate heard a thump and harsh whispering. Some of it was not at all polite.

A female voice hissed "under the bed," then came a thump and someone half yelled, "Sacré bleu!"

For fun, Kate pitched her voice low and half-yelled, "Get out of my damn room." She followed up by thumping her fist on the door a half dozen times.

The high pitched female voice screeched, "Go away!"

Kate stifled a giggle. Instead she half yelled, "Say, why are you in my room?"

"Who's there?" The lady seemed genuinely perplexed.

"The man who hired the room!" Kate banged some more.

The locked clicked before the door opened a crack to reveal Mrs. Winslow's pretty eyes and dark hair. "You've made a mistake. My husband and I have this room."

141

"No. I do," Kate barked.

"You fool, show me your key."

Kate held it out.

"This is the key for room 4. Now go away." Mrs. Winslow's words dripped with venom. She was not having as much fun as Kate.

Monty objected to the lady's tone and barked at her. That proved to be Mrs. Winslow's last straw.

"Sir, take that awful creature and remove yourself from my door." The door closed with a hard thump.

Kate retired to room 4 and collapsed on the bed to indulge in a quiet fit of giggling. Monty jumped up and licked her face. "Oh, Monty," she said and hugged his squirming little body. "Detecting is soooo much more fun than teaching school."

As she unpacked Kate discovered Room 4 had a door that adjoined Room 2. She considered jiggling that doorknob too but took pity on poor Mrs. Winslow and her lover. The door had a dark glass transom above the frame. Kate dragged the room's only chair over to the door and climbed aboard to try the transom knob. Locked. She didn't bother to retrieve her lock picks from her overnight bag. Instead, she plucked a hairpin from her bun and had the lock popped open in a trice. She tipped the transom open a scant half inch. Words wafted through the crack like ghosts on a breeze.

"We shouldn't come here anymore," the female voice said in a doleful tone.

"Oh, my precious angel. Why ever not?" asked the French man.

"I fear we're being watched."

"Never. How would anyone know?"

"I don't know, but Mr. Lyon's acting odd. I fear I'm losing him."

"Surely not. You've nearly broken him. He's as weak and defenseless as a baby."

A pause.

"That is so," said Mrs. Winslow. "I'll take his fortune. I swear it. At least one of these men who uses their money to buy women will learn what it really buys."

"And we'll leave this cursed country, with its war and endless indignities."

"Paris." Mrs. Winslow giggled like a girl at a tea party. "You'll show me everything won't you my dear Comte?"

"Everything darling. The beautiful, the sublime, the heavenly city. I will lay it before you like a silken carpet."

Lips smacked and slurped, followed by the whisper of clothes falling upon the floor.

"Wait." More scrabbling sounds ensued. "Take this money and get us a bottle of wine. And bring me the change this time."

Kate heard the sound of a door opening and closing. After a bit she heard it again. After that there was the sort of noises that made her ears burn with embarrassment. Kate fought the urge to poke out her ears with sharp sticks.

She left the room, retrieved Excelsior, tucked Monty back in her coat and they returned to Rochester. It was time for a new plan.

Chapter 14

January 17, 1862
Rochester New York

A hot bath, three-course dinner and a full night's sleep convinced Kate it was time for her to lay her cards on the table, one suspect at a time. She would begin with the divine Le Compte.

Kate and Monty presented themselves at Jerome Le Compte's rooms at nine that morning. She knocked on his door and waited only a moment before it whisked open. The little Frenchman stood before her, once again dressed in his lilac trousers, accented with a deep purple waistcoat, and a black velvet smoking jacket. He'd waxed his mustaches to immaculate points. Kate though he bore a startling resemblance to a fox that had assaulted and consumed an unsuspecting chicken.

"May I help you, Madame?" His voice was soft and his intonation oh, so French.

"I hope we can help each other Le Compte." She might have sounded a teensy bit menacing.

He gripped the door hard enough to turn his fingers white. "Do we know each other?"

"We've never been introduced, but I know you. Or I know something of you."

Le Compte stared at Kate, his eyes pinched with worry. He sighed. "I suppose you should come in."

He ignored Monty but offered Kate a seat at a table set up for séances. "I live modestly. This suffices for my sitting room."

Kate assured him she was comfortable and began. "Monsieur, I should tell you I have been investigating Mrs. Winslow at the behest of one of her clients. Yesterday I followed you to Port Charlotte." Monty stared up at Kate, seemingly fascinated with her story.

"Who are you?" Le Compte looked Kate up and down, baffled by her claims.

"My name's unimportant. I assume you're familiar with the Pinkerton Detective Agency?"

He nodded. "Everyone is. Even a stranger such as myself."

"All you need to know is that I am a Pinkerton operative and I was hired to investigate Mrs. Winslow's suit against our client."

His shoulders slumped. "What do you want?"

"A written confession of your affair with Mrs. Winslow and your agreement to testify in court, should Mrs. Winslow's suit for breach of promise go forward."

His eyes took on a crafty gleam. "What suit? I know of no suit."

Kate snorted. "Come now Le Compte. I know that you know. You and Mrs. Winslow discussed it yesterday." She'd heard a good more than that, but good manners prevented Kate from mentioning the rest.

Now his eyes widened. "You were there?"

Kate nodded. In her deep voice, she said, "I think this is my room."

Le Compte gasped. "Sacré bleu."

Kate could hardly disagree. "Your paramour can expect no claim to Mr. Lyon's honor and fortune if she's dallying with you in hotel rooms."

"But it would ruin me," he said, looking up at Kate. "I would lose her and the future she offers me. I would also ruin my career as a spiritualist in this city. And hers."

Kate didn't fail to notice that his concerns for his lady love came last. "That isn't my problem. My job is to protect my client and your Mrs. Winslow threatens him with ruin for no better reason than greed."

He slumped even further in his chair. Then he straightened, his face brighter than she'd seen it since he'd opened his door. "I can furnish you with the names of other men. You could use them in court and leave me out of it."

Kate shook her head. "You think this man if he even exists, will volunteer to come to Rochester and offer himself up to degradation in a court of law?"

"If not he, why should I?" Le Compte cried.

Kate pushed down a wave of pity and pulled her notebook out of her bag. She shoved it towards him. "Write it all down. How your affair began, where you went, what you did. I will confront Mrs. Winslow with your written testimony and if she has any sense, she'll withdraw her suit. That will at least keep you out of court and allow you to keep your spiritualism practice."

He slammed his hand flat on the table. "I won't. I love her."

147

Kate rose to go. "Monsieur, I'll leave you the notebook. Once you have some time to consider your options you'll find you have only one—to cooperate with me."

Le Compte stood, pushing back his chair so violently it crashed to the floor. He rushed to the door and threw himself against it. He reached behind his back. The lock shot home with a loud click.

Kate froze. Monty emerged from under the table to stand at her feet. She tipped her head sideways at the French man. "Really? What do you hope to accomplish?"

He thrust his hand into the smoking jacket's pocket and withdrew a small pistol. Kate recognized it as a Philadelphia Derringer. She used to have one. She'd replaced it with a Colt revolver, a gun that held more bullets and shot with more accuracy over distance. Unfortunately, she was less than eight feet from Le Compte. She was sure even a man with a pointy mustache could hit her with a derringer at that distance.

Kate considered her options. Her dagger was only good in close fighting, at least until she became a great deal more proficient in the art of dagger throwing. And she wasn't going to get it out of her bodice faster than this man could pull a trigger. Same with her revolver. And if she pulled her gun someone would get shot and it might be her. She'd been shot. Twice. She didn't care to repeat the experience.

She did the one thing Le Compte did not expect. She lowered her head and launched herself at him. Her skull rammed into his torso, shoving him back against the door with a loud thump.

"Woof," or something like it came out of his mouth.

148

In a whirl of dark and light fur Monty seized Le Comte's ankle. A high-pitched scream emanated from the Frenchman as the little dog clamped down.

Kate wrapped her arms around his torso and threw him to the floor. It wasn't a maneuver that would have worked with a larger man, but he wasn't much bigger than she and she had the element of surprise. They fell to the floor and rolled around. She could still hear Monty's squealing growls and Le Compte's desperate whimpers. She grabbed his gun and pried it out of his hand. It was surprisingly easy. Of course the dog trying to kill him gave Kate a nice advantage.

She pushed herself off Le Compte and scrambled to her feet, his derringer in her hand. Her Colt hadn't even left her pocket. She scooped Monty up, pulling him off Le Compte's lower leg. Monty rumbled with low growls.

She nudged Le Compte with her foot. "Get up."

"My God woman," he moaned, clutching his ankle. "Have you no sense of decency?"

Kate mused on the question for a second. "Nope." What she had was his gun. And a small, furry creature ready for round two. Both were way better than decency.

Le Compte staggered to his feet, clutching his midsection and hopping on his good leg. She hooked a chair by the rung with her foot and kicked it toward him, using her gun hand to motion to it.

"I'll be back tomorrow morning and you better have it all written out."

"And what do I get?" He looked at her from under his brows, his face pale with shock.

"You get to live." She tried not to smile, but failed.

Peg A. Lamphier

"My life is worth nothing if I have no way to make a living. I need money. To start over."

Kate sat Monty on the chair she'd been sitting in and appraised Le Compte. His mustache looked bent. "So you're for sale?"

He shrugged a Gallic shrug. "Aren't we all?"

"All right. I won't pay you to concoct lies. I want you to write the truth. I will get you some money to start over once you give me your written testimony."

"And I should trust you?"

Kate heaved a sigh. "For goodness sake, you idiot. You drew the gun, not me. And I still haven't shot you though I was within my rights to do so. So I'm the only one of the two of us that has shown any kind of restraint or honor. From his chair Monty growled. She glanced at her dog. "The only one of the three of us," Kate amended.

"I want a thousand dollars," he said with a note of finality.

Kate tried again not to smile. Le Compte really was fun. "I hardly think you know anything worth that much money. Two hundred dollars."

"Now?"

"No." Kate resisted the urge to smack the little man upside the head. "Who walks around with that kind of money?"

He leaped up and ran to the window. He pushed it up and turned back to Kate.

Monty vaulted off the chair at Le Compte's sudden movement. When Kate didn't move, the little dog stood his ground, his hackles up in a manner that suggested he'd like another taste of French ankle.

Le Compte glared at the two of them and put his hand on the window. "I know a great deal about Mrs. Winslow. I even know her real name. Pay me or I'll jump out this window." He pushed the window sash up and waved his velvet clad arm through the opening.

Kate could only stare at him. This was by and far the weirdest negotiation she'd ever undertaken. "Keep this up I'll kill you myself. I'll be back tomorrow with $200. That's all you get. And you better have it all written down for me or you won't get anything."

She turned to go. Still holding his gun, she put her hand on the doorknob and looked over her shoulder at Le Compte.

He was holding the window sash looking like he was wondering how it had all gone so wrong.

"You have 24 hours." She shut the door behind her. Kate made it all the way to the sidewalk before she burst out laughing.

Kate picked up sandwiches and a pair of withered apples at a shop by the livery stable so she and Monty could have lunch with Excelsior. Excelsior was lying on his side in his stall dozing. He woke just enough to crunch down an apple before going back to sleep. This didn't surprise Kate one bit. Excelsior spent his entire life as a circus horse and star attraction. Even at nearly twenty years old, she was afraid if she retired him he'd die of a broken heart within a month. So she kept him just busy enough, but she never took him out more than two days in a row.

The stable manager didn't seem to think there was anything odd about a lady eating lunch with her horse, so she took up her favorite position, leaning back in the straw, with her head on Excelsior's rump. She tore up one sandwich and gave it to Monty, who gobbled it before she finished her first bite. Then, in the way of dogs everywhere, he watched her every bite to be sure she didn't drop any.

While Kate ate, she considered her next move. Part of her wanted to wait until she had Le Compte's written testimony before she saw the client, but another part of her recognized she was stalling. Though she'd met Mr. Lyon only briefly he'd seemed like a decent old chap, though she hadn't liked Harcourt one bit. He was too oily by far and helping him set off alarm bells in her head.

Kate swallowed her last bite of sandwich and pushed herself to her feet. She didn't want to leave here. Even with the sun out, it was still below freezing and the stable was snug and cozy. It would be easier if her coat wasn't so ugly. Damn Mrs. Winslow anyway.

An hour later Kate and Monty were strolling down Main Street toward the Arcade. She found a telegram office and sent Allan an update. She also sent Charlotte a telegram warning her of Allan's imminent arrival in Washington, knowing Allan wouldn't do it. He'd just show up at the F Street house and expect Charlotte and Odetta to have a room and a meal ready. Then he'd wonder why everyone was so surprised to see him.

A nice lady at a hat shop directed Kate to an equally nice lady that ran a dressmaking shop. That lady had several ready-made coats for sale, some as lovely as Mrs. Winslow's. She shrugged on the emerald green wool coat and admired its fur-lined cuffs, collar, and hem. It even had embroidery like Mrs. Winslow's though less ornate, which was more to Kate's taste, anyway. The lady then transformed their shopping into the best shopping trip ever by showing Kate a rack of cunning little dog coats. Though the coat that fit Monty did not have embroidery it did have a tiny scrap of fur at the collar. Kate bought it and the green coat.

Fortified by fashion, Kate and Monty entered the Arcade and made their way to Mr. Lyon's second-floor offices, where Kate would learn that coat shopping got a lady detective into trouble.

Chapter 15

January 17, 1862
Rochester New York

Kate looked down at Monty, who was waiting for her to open the door to Lyon Enterprises. "Keep your teeth to yourself, mister." Monty tipped his head at her, as if to say he was making no promises. She pushed open the door anyway.

She found Mr. Harcourt sitting at the front desk, the same one that had been empty the first time she visited. He closed the account book he had in front of him and stood to greet her. He also leered at her. Or maybe he didn't, but Kate's instinctive distaste for the man interpreted his smile as predatory and repulsive.

"Miss Warne, I'm so glad you're here. We've had some excitement today. Follow me." He walked down the hall to an open door.

Kate followed him into a grand office lined with dark wood paneling and filled with dark leather upholstered furniture. Mr. Lyon sat behind an enormous desk looking like the captain of a small ship. He seemed more stooped and grey than the first time they'd met, though his desk hadn't dwarfed him then. He pushed himself to his feet. "We've met before, haven't we?"

Kate tried not to blush. "Yes, sir we have. Last week. I'm afraid I misled you."

"Ah, the young lady with a burning interest in flowers. I gave you a catalog."

"You did." Kate inclined her head at Mr. Lyon. "My name is Kate Warne and I'm a Pinkerton operative. As you may know by now, your assistant has engaged the Pinkertons to investigate on your behalf. I'm afraid we did not believe his story about 'a friend in need.' Men so often invent friends when they are themselves in trouble." Kate shot Harcourt an apologetic glance. "Last week I made sure you were real."

Mr. Lyon chuckled. "Oh, I assure you, I am exceedingly real. As is my dilemma." He came around the desk, offering his bony hand to Kate. He leaned over to inspect Monty. Kate could almost hear his bones creaking in his lean frame.

Monty offered him his paw, causing Lyon to chuckle in delight. "How do you do small sir? I don't think I've ever met a dog wearing a coat." He straightened and motioned Kate to a chair, waited while she composed her skirts and sat himself. Monty picked a piece of carpet between them and settled in. Lyon laid a piece of notepaper on the small table between their two chairs. Mr. Harcourt closed the door and joined them.

Lyon picked up the note again. "Miss Warne, I have an interesting note here from a Mr. Jerome Le Compte."

"From Le Compte?" Kate tried and failed to keep the surprise out of her voice.

The old man nodded, but failed to meet Kate's eyes.

Harcourt spoke up. "It arrived by messenger only thirty minutes ago. Mr. Le Compte offers Mr. Lyon an exchange, information for money."

Kate cursed herself for trusting the French rat. He must have sprung into action the moment she left him. And she'd given him the time to do it while she ate lunch and shopped. "Let me guess. He wants a thousand dollars."

"How did you know?" Lyon stared at Kate, his eyebrows high, eyes wide.

"I visited Mr. Le Compte this morning." Kate paused, knowing she was about to upset Mr. Lyon. "I have bad news. He is Mrs. Winslow's paramour. He knows I have proof of their relationship. He also knows Mrs. Winslow cannot win a suit against you if she was dallying with him. These facts make him desperate." Kate smiled at her understatement. Like threatening to jump out of the window desperate. "The two of them hope to move to Paris, funded by the money they extort from you."

Lyon clutched the note in his fist, his face white with shock. "My dear Mrs. Winslow? With another man? Are you sure?"

Kate shook her head. "I'm sorry Mr. Lyon. She's not who you think she is. She's using you for your money."

Mr. Lyon hid his face in his hands His shoulders shook and mumbled into his hands, "What would my dear Minerva think of me now I wonder?"

Kate looked over at Mr. Harcourt.

Harcourt gestured at Mr. Lyon. "Minerva was his wife. They were married for forty-two years." He stood and offered his boss a large white handkerchief. "They loved each other very much and her death left him alone and lonely. These emotions made him susceptible to Mrs. Winslow's charms."

157

Monty sat up, walked over and put his paw on Mr. Lyon's knee. Lyon patted Monty's foot, but continued to weep.

"Mr. Lyon does not want the public embarrassment of a lawsuit." Harcourt pointed at the piece of paper crumpled in Mr. Lyon's fist, "The notoriety would ruin his family's social standing."

Mr. Lyon turned back from the window, his cheeks damp. He looked fifteen years older than he had the day she'd first met him.

Kate felt anger stir in her heart for the first time in this case. She'd felt anxiety about her old case, amused at Le Compte and dismissive of spiritualists, but she hadn't been angry. Not until now. Kate balled her hands into fists and spoke. "Mr. Lyon, if you intend to pay Le Compte I can't stop you, but I urge you not to. The two of them will do this to someone else. They'll leave a trail of ruined lives in their wake. I can take care of him for you."

He looked at her with watery blue eyes. "I want to know the truth. You understand? I need to know just how big a fool I've been. When my wife died I felt as if I would die too. And then Mr. Harcourt sent me to Mrs. Winslow and she offered me hope and understanding. Her tender glances, her graceful movements, her sympathy for my departed wife all moved me. She connected me to dear Minerva, who told me to love again. And so I gave up despair and came to love Mrs. Winslow. Was I wrong to do so?" He groped for the handkerchief and wiped at his face.

Kate's throat closed up, full of pity. Mrs. Winslow, or whoever she was, must have seen his pain and taken advantage of him. It was a quiet act of absolute wickedness.

158

Kate spent a half hour explaining how Mrs. Winslow pulled off her spiritualist act, from the cabinet with the hidden door to the common mechanisms for faking spirit rapping. She shared Dr. Hubbard's thoughts on the fakery of spiritualism and his insights into Mrs. Winslow's past as a 'bouncer.'

Mr. Lyon grew more shocked with each revelation, though Kate was at a loss to see why. Had he really believed Mrs. Winslow capable of communicating with his dead wife? As she watched him she decided he had been as much a true believer as any religious fanatic. By the time Kate got to the 'bouncer' part of her discussion, the poor man's handkerchief was soggy with tearful regret.

She left Lyon's office with two hundred dollars in her pocket and murder in her heart.

Kate threw open Le Compte's door hard enough for it to slam against the wall and bounce back. She caught it with the heel of her hand and shoved it again. Le Compte scrambled out of his chair, stumbling backward to put the table between her and himself.

"You worm!" Her voice bounced off the walls. "You absolute worm."

Monty echoed her sentiment with a deep growl.

"I need the money," he squealed. He'd backed up all the way to the closed window. "Don't hurt me. And keep that dog away from me."

Kate snorted. "I won't touch you, you fool. But I will destroy you if you continue your present course."

He collapsed into a chair, weeping into his hands. "We have no women like you in France. I am undone."

Kate suspected there were women like her everywhere, including France. Still, she had to fight the urge to feel sorry for him. Misery oozed out of him like sweat. His love for Mrs. Winslow was as real as Mr. Lyon's. Maybe more so.

Kate pushed away her pity and grabbed her notebook, which still lay on the table. She sat at the table, motioning at him to join her. Monty sat beside her, keeping his eyes on Le Compte.

He hesitated, but a stern look from Kate brought him to his chair. "You will tell me about your affair with Mrs. Winslow and I will write it down. Now. And then you will sign it and I will give you your money. For your trouble." She watched his unhappiness war with his self-interest. "Let's begin with how you met her."

He sighed and scrubbed at his face with his hands, being carful not to muss his mustaches. "You must understand, she is my friend. Whatever I do here today, she is my friend. She has great faith and she's taught me much about the spirits. I owe her my life and my living." He glared at Kate.

She waved her hand at him to go on.

"I came to America with nothing. Nothing. I tried to find work. I was alone, hungry and tres desespere." He paused, biting his lower lip. "How you say? Desperate. I decided to leave this country and go to Canada. I was in Port Charlotte, waiting for the ferry when I saw her. She was with Lyon. I watched them. She is a magnificent woman." He paused, smiling faintly as if remembering that long ago day. "I could not look away. I thought she was his wife, but I did not care. I loved her from that moment. And from her glances in my direction, I could tell she felt the same way. So I did not go to

Canada but followed her instead. I learned she was his mistress and a powerful clairvoyant. She taught me to find my own gift. Whatever I am is because of her."

"And then she became your mistress?"

"That and more," he said. His eyes shined with a kind of fervor one saw in religious fanatics or rabid dogs. "She teaches me. She gives me confidence and hope. She offers me a future. And because I love her unconditionally I don't care that she goes to Canada."

"Canada?" Kate tried to hide her confusion at this turn in the conversation.

"I once asked her why she made the trip. She laughed and show me a stack of money. For this, she said. But one day, with much wine and clairvoyance, she told me. Because I am her love as much as she is mine, you see?"

Kate realized her pencil stood slack in her fingers. She hadn't written a word. "What did she tell you?"

"Do you have my money?" His mustache points quivered like whiskers on a nervous rabbit.

Kate patted her coat pocket. "Mr. Lyon authorized me to give you $200. But that's all you'll get. I have made sure of that."

He slumped deeper in his chair and scrubbed his face again. "She goes to Toronto. There she meets Mr. Devereaux. He is a man of power and wealth, but not so powerful as my dear Mrs. Winslow. He gives her money."

Kate doubted it was that simple. "How long has she known him?"

Le Compte shook his head. "I don't know. More than one year, less than two."

"And she still visits Mr. Devereaux?"

"Once a month. She goes on Tuesday and returns on Wednesday." He blushed and fixed his eyes on the floor.

Kate saw his mustaches twitch. "When does she go again?"

He looked up at her, a blush full on his pale cheeks. "Tomorrow," he whispered. "God forgive me, tomorrow."

When she'd gotten all the details out of him she needed Kate put a pile of bills on the table and left. Monty followed her, but not until after he peed on Le Compte's coat rack.

As she closed the door, the French man began to cry again. Looking over her shoulder she saw the pile of cash gripped in the weeping Frenchman's hand. Kate sighed. She'd had too, too many masculine tears for one day.

Chapter 16

January 18- 19, 1862
Toronto, Canada

*H*er hands gripped the rail, numb with cold. Kate watched the horizon in an effort to ignore the way the deck heaved with Lake Ontario's waves. A frigid breeze blew across the water, slapping her in the face, plucking at her veil and once confined hair. Even her new coat couldn't keep the bone-deep chill at bay, nor her wool dress. Pants would have been warmer, but Mrs. Winslow had seen Kate's male personae, or so Kate assumed. Women's clothes were safer, but not warmer. Not for the first time she wished she had Monty buttoned in her coat. The little fellow made a first-rate heater, but she'd taken pity on him and left him with the O'Malleys for the day.

She'd tried sitting inside when she first came aboard. The steamship's interior rooms were warm and Mrs. Winslow was easy to keep an eye on from across the room. The lady spiritualist had boarded the ferry, taken a seat in the First Class Parlor and taken out a slim volume of what looked like poetry. Kate had worn a heavy black veil so Mrs. Winslow wouldn't recognize her. What would lady detectives do when veils fell out of fashion?

Kate bought a copy of the *Rochester Union* and took a seat across the room from Mrs. Winslow. She tried reading the headline article about Mr. Lincoln's General War Order No. One. Frustrated with General McClellan's foot dragging, the president ordered both the eastern and western armies to advance in February. Kate suspected that Mr. Lincoln's new Secretary of War had something to do with this change in strategy, but her roiling stomach made thought difficult. She put down the newspaper and took some deep breaths. The room's heat, combined with the constant rocking of the ship and her tight corset made keeping her breakfast in place a struggle. She gave up the fight and made a dash for the necessary room. After she forcibly ejected her breakfast a nice steward took Kate by the elbow and led her outside. He assured her that fresh air would help and it had, but not enough to make going back inside seem like a good idea. Mrs. Winslow wasn't going anywhere until they docked.

Instead, Kate spent her time on deck reviewing the case. She was sure of a few things. First, Mrs. Winslow's case against Mr. Lyon had no merit. Second, in spite of what she told Le Compte she needed more proof. Kate had little trouble imagining Le Compte in court. His ridiculous appearance, combined with his obvious reluctance to harm Mrs. Winslow made him a bad witness.

This led her to her third conclusion: she needed more evidence. That reality led to this ferry trip to Canada. Kate packed her small carpet bag and waited at Ontario Ferry Company's small port side building. Mrs. Winslow arrived with her own small bag and bought a ticket just before they boarded.

By the time the ferry docked in Toronto Kate's hands and feet were like blocks of ice and it felt like there was a pack of weasels wrestling in her stomach. She cursed Mrs. Winslow for preferring the ferry to the train.

They docked in a thick fog that turned the daylight into a murky gloom. Kate followed Mrs. Winslow up the dock to a hansom cab stand. There the lady directed her cabbie to the Queen's Hotel. Kate hired her own cab and followed. The ride from the port to the hotel was short, but revealed little of the city. The winter fog rendered the gas lights an eerie yellow-grey color that did little to illuminate the streets.

The hotel might be another grand building but in the gloom it was hard to tell. Still, Mrs. Winslow didn't seem like a woman who traveled on the cheap. Kate breathed a sigh of relief. She'd stayed in enough rat-infested boarding houses to last a lifetime.

The lobby blazed with gleaming gas chandeliers, ivory wallpaper, and soft gold carpets. Kate stood behind a large potted palm while Mrs. Winslow checked in. Once the lady had gone upstairs Kate hustled up to the desk and told the clerk that the Mrs. Winslow was her friend, whom she was trying to surprise. He gave her the next room over from hers.

Once again Kate climbed the stairs and found her room, thinking she was spending far too much time in hotels. She missed her own bed, her own house, her own people. She stripped off her lovely new coat and threw herself on the bed, indulging in a brief bout of self-pity. It turned boring pretty quickly so she decided to ring for tea. Mint maybe. It would settle her tummy. Also, she needed to figure out how to spy on her neighbor. She rolled over and looked around the room. It had neither an adjoining door nor a handy transom.

165

Kate had just removed a painting from the wall when a knock sounded at the door. She hopped down from the chair she'd been standing on and opened the door. A plump young maid carrying a silver tray with a tea service on it stood in the hall. There was an envelope on the tray. Kate reached for it. "Is this for me?"

The maid shook her head. "No Ma'am. I'm to post it for the lady next door."

"Oh, you leave that to me. She's a friend of mine and I have my own letters to post. I'll bring them all down to the desk when I'm ready." Kate tucked the envelope into her skirt pocket with perfect confidence and extracted a quarter, which she gave to the girl.

The pink-cheeked maid bobbed a half curtsy, set the tea tray down on Kate's room table and whisked herself from the room.

The moment the door closed Kate pulled the envelope from her pocket and examined it. Elegant with swoops and swirls, the letter was addressed to John Devereaux, 46 Yonge Street. Written across the bottom of the envelope in large block letters was the word "PERSONAL." Kate took the letter over to her pot of tea and held the sealing wax over the steaming spout. She counted to ten before plucking her dagger from her coat pocket. She eased the knife tip under the wax and tipped up the seal. After that, the letter was hers.

Queen's Hotel, Toronto

3 PM, January 29

Devereaux— I find myself in some difficulty. I need at least five hundred dollars. A thousand would be better. You said you have finished helping me, but if you do not call on me by this time tomorrow I will make you wish you had. Reflect carefully on the worth of your reputation, both as a businessman and as a husband and father. Once you have done so proceed as you deem best.

Yours,

Mrs. W.

Kate resisted the impulse to burn the nasty thing. Was there anything more repulsive than a blackmailer? And why were there so many men in the world willing, even eager, to step into a blackmailer's snare?

As she resealed the wax on the letter she heard a door close in the hall. Kate cracked open her door and peeked out to see Mrs. Winslow sweep down the hall as majestically as a ship leaving port. Kate grinned. It was time to go shopping.

She returned from the hardware store with a hand drill, two bits and a cheap fountain pen. First, she disassembled the fountain pen by unscrewing both its nib end and removing its end screw. She dribbled the ink into a wastebasket and swabbed out the steel tube with a slim roll of paper. Once dry, she tucked the tube behind her ear for safekeeping.

Once again Kate mounted her chair and used her dagger to cut a small flap of wallpaper where the painting had so hung. She sponged the flap with a dampened towel and when it was sufficiently wet, picked at it with her dagger. When the wallpaper didn't come loose she sponged it a few minutes more and tried again. On her second try, the wallpaper peeled off the wall with ease, leaving a 3 inch square of plaster wall exposed.

Kate grinned as she screwed the smallest drill bit into the drill, pressed it against the wall and turned the drill handle. Plaster dust fell to the carpet. She always started with a small bit. It kept the breakage on the other side of the wall minimal.

167

She cranked the drill handle until she felt the bit break through the other side of the wall. Kate put her eye to the hole and saw a pinpoint of light at the other end. Good. She'd been a little worried that she might drill into the back of a painting hung in Mrs. Winslow's room. Kate's room had nothing hanging on the wall to the right, so she was betting Mrs. Winslow's room didn't either. But it was a guess. A good guess it turned out.

Wiggling the drill, she pulled the bit back out of its hole. Next, she unscrewed the small bit and replaced it with a larger one. She drilled the hole again, enlarging it from a mere pinpoint to something about 3/8 of an inch wide. It looked as large as a drain pipe to Kate, but it would be invisible anyone not looking for it. Her experience as a detective and a circus girl taught her that most people were unobservant. They saw but did not see. Or they saw what they expected to see. With a wall, they didn't expect to see a hole, so they didn't see a hole. Wallpaper helped too because busy patterns confused the eye. And she'd drilled the hole high on the wall, making it even harder to see. People rarely looked above their sight line. For some reason, they didn't like looking up.

She leaned back and appraised her work. Thanks to the chair it was well above eye level. She pressed her ear against the wall. Nothing. Kate hopped off her chair and eyed the high boy dresser. Its top was about shoulder height. She checked its drawers. Empty.

Ten minutes later, puffing and sweating, Kate had the dresser lined up with her listening post. She placed two pillows on top and used the chair to climb aboard. Her skirts proved an obstacle, but not an insurmountable one after she collapsed her hoops and squirmed around a little bit. Her drill hole sat just in front of her. She plucked the pen tube from her hair and wiggled it into the hole. She tipped back her head and examined her work. Perfect. Time to wait.

There'd been footsteps in the hall all morning, but no noise from the room next door. Kate waited atop the room's dresser last night until just after ten when she climbed down and into bed. She'd reasoned that Mr. Devereaux wouldn't come by in the middle of the night, not if he had a wife expecting him home. Still, Kate wouldn't have bet on it but for the fact that she was having difficulty staying awake as evening lengthened. She had coffee with her dinner, ordered from the maid and delivered to her room, but the beverage made little impression on her level of alertness.

She awoke at dawn and returned to her listening post atop the dresser. She fell right back to sleep. At half-past eight a maid knocked at her door with her breakfast, startling Kate awake. She hopped off the dresser, cracked the door open just enough to take the tray and give the maid another coin.

An hour later, caught up on her sleep and tummy full of toast, sausage, and coffee, Kate heard a knock, not on her door, but from somewhere near. It was not the polite double knock the maid used, but a thundering triple pound that sounded like someone in a temper. Kate pressed her ear against her makeshift listening device and heard the clear sound of first a woman's voice, then a man's.

"It's about time."

"I came as soon as I could."

The male voice sounded reedy and thin.

"Well? Do you have money?"

Mrs. Winslow's voice did not at all sound reedy or thin. She sounded like a woman in control of the situation.

"I don't see why I should keep paying you. You've had enough off me."

"You have no choice. Fork it over and quit whining."

"I've paid a thousand times over for my mistakes. This is the last time."

Kate heard a thud, like a package thrown on a table. Then a long pause.

"This is only three hundred dollars."

"It's all I have. I told you, you've bled me dry. My sons don't understand why the business is failing. But it's not. It's just you and your ceaseless demands."

"You should have considered that when you were sating your lust. I guess this will have to do, but short me again and I'll write a letter to your wife."

"Then do it and be done with it."

Kate heard a door open and then slam shut. She leaped off the dresser and caught up her coat, but when she made it into the hall the man was already gone. She hustled for the stairs. There. A hunched man leaning on a walking stick limped across the hotel lobby. Kate followed him at a distance, the frigid Canadian air turning her face into a block of ice.

He wore a good quality coat and hat and moved like a man on his last legs, crabbing along all bent over. He leaned over his walking stick like it was the only thing keeping him upright. He walked down Front Street to Yonge, where he turned left. A block later he entered a large brick building. Kate followed him inside. While he laboriously climbed the stairs Kate examined the building directory. *Devereaux & Sons,*

202. The business could be anything, and Kate wasn't sure it mattered. She stood in the lobby, thinking hard. After a moment she decided it couldn't hurt to try. She mounted the steps and prepared to meet the elder Devereaux.

At first, Mr. Devereaux did not want to talk to Kate, let alone cooperate in her scheme. She didn't blame him. If she were him she wouldn't trust women either. She explained what she'd discovered about his interactions with Mrs. Winslow. His resistance, along with his posture, collapsed like a cake taken from the oven too soon. He admitted that he'd paid Mrs. Winslow almost three thousand dollars over the past two years, always in increments of $300 to $500. He refused to talk about their relationship before the bribery, nor would he tell Kate what Mrs. Winslow had on him. Kate didn't need him to tell her, not given the circumstances and persons involved.

Mr. Devereaux wrote out an affidavit detailing the bribery scheme, including the dates and amounts of the payments he'd made to Mrs. Winslow. He also wrote a brief description of their one-time relationship, which he only described as a 'friendship' and the significant mental duress her claims caused him. His pathetic eagerness to be out from under his blackmailer's grasp enraged Kate. No one, not even an adulterer, should be terrorized like that.

Kate left Devereaux and Sons with a two-page document that would sink any hopes the lady might have of winning a lawsuit against Mr. Lyon. She also left with a deep appreciation of the psychological damage a blackmailer could wreak on the innocent and unsuspecting. She'd put an end to Mrs. Winslow's schemes whether she turned out to be the Black

Peg A. Lamphier

Widow or not. The lady's reign of misery would end one way or another.

Chapter 17

January 19-20, 1862
Rochester, New York

Mrs. Winslow was gone by the time Kate returned from her encounter with Mr. Devereaux. Kate wanted to follow the lady, who'd most surely gone to the Ontario Ferry Company's dock for the trip back to the States. One look around her hotel room convinced Kate to reconsider. She splashed cold water on her face, dampening her murderous impulses and made a mental to-do list.

She left her hotel once more, found an English chop house and ate a hearty lunch of steak pie and tea. The beer looked tempting given the morning she'd had, but remembering the fit of her lady clothes she abstained. After lunch, Kate stopped at the same hardware store she'd used the day before and bought a small pot of glue, which she carried back to the hotel. Once in her room she climbed aboard the dresser once more and re-glued the loose flap of wallpaper, having first removed the pen tube. Then she rehung the painting, a rather dreary picture of a ship tossing about on foamy waves, and pushed the much-abused dresser back where she'd found it. Once she'd returned the room to its original gloomy glory she washed up and packed up her bag and tools. She left a dollar on the pillow for the maid, and left the Queen's Hotel for good.

She arrived back in Port Charlotte late Wednesday evening every bit as hollowed out from sea sickness as the day before. Feeling like forty miles of bad road, she took a cab back to the Osborn House, crawled into bed and resisted the impulse to moan and whine. Oh, where was Hazzard when she needed him anyway? Or better yet, Hattie. Or Mrs. Webster and Odetta? Odetta would make her broth and bring it to her in bed and Charlotte would heat a brick for her feet. They'd fuss over her and she'd pretend to find their attention irritating. Instead, she was in yet another hotel room, all alone, sick as a stray dog. And without her own dog, who was still with the O'Malleys. When she'd debarked the ferry she hadn't had the strength or the will to fetch him. If anyone asked her later she'd have denied that some whimpering and sniffling occurred in her room that night.

The next morning Kate was a new woman, albeit a hungry and thirsty woman. She dressed and hastened to the hotel dining room, grabbing up a newspaper along the way. She checked the advertisements just to be sure she remembered correctly. Kate smiled to herself. Mrs. Winslow conducted regular Thursday evening séances and, today was Thursday. She was about to leave her table when she saw Mr. Harcourt striding across the dining room towards her. She braced herself by pouring another cup of coffee.

He approached her table, his dark grey bowler in his hand. "Miss Warne, I must inquire about your progress on the case.

Mr. Lyon grows ever more anxious, as do I." His fat, wet tongue circled his lips like a questing slug.

Kate suppressed a shudder and motioned for Harcourt to sit. She wanted to tell him to leave her alone and wait for her to call on him, but Mr. Harcourt didn't seem inclined to take direction from a woman. Instead, she smiled and said, "I plan to solve the case this evening."

"How?" He lowered his brows and glowered at her.

"That is my business, Mr. Harcourt. You hired me, remember?"

"Exactly my point. I hired you. I deserve to be informed as much as I desire. And right now I want a report on your progress."

"No you do not," she said, correcting him with her gentle but firm voice. "You bought my services. You did not buy me." She glowered back at him.

He thwacked his hat upon the table and exclaimed, "You are a rude woman."

Kate stifled a laugh. She didn't like her client one bit, but she did owe him basic courtesy. "I may be rude, but your manners are also imperfect. By this time tomorrow, your Mr. Lyon ought to be safe from the consequences of his own foolishness."

Harcourt snorted and pulled back a chair to take a seat. "So you say."

She stood, forcing the wretched man to stay on his feet. "You are not questioning my word, are you?" She asked the question in the same mild tone she'd used throughout their conversation, but backed with just enough steel to give him pause.

He gripped his hat in both hands and shook his head. "No. No. I didn't mean to . . . ."

Kate interrupted his stammering. "How delightful to hear." She bobbed a small curtsy at him. "I shall meet with you and Mr. Lyon tomorrow morning. Shall we say ten o'clock?" Before he could respond, she sailed out of the dining room.

She considered her dislike for Mr. Harcourt all the way over to the O'Malley's. A Pinkerton detective didn't have to like the client but she rarely had such a visceral reaction to one. There was something about the man that grated at her, like sand in a sandwich, yet she'd never seen him do anything overtly awful. Still, he seemed like a man who kicked dogs when no one was looking.

When Kate arrived at the O'Malley house Monty bounced around the kitchen barking until she grabbed him up and allowed him to give her a hundred damp doggy kisses. Mr. O'Malley gave Kate and Monty a ride to the stable where they spent several hours lying about in Excelsior's stall, using him as a warm pillow. Kate spent the time thinking and napping in turn. Monty appeared to sleep more and cogitate less, though with dogs it was hard to tell the difference sometimes.

When the sky darkened Kate and Monty said goodbye to Excelsior and walked back to Osborn House. Monty gave his paws a thorough going over while Kate struggled into her best winter traveling dress and fixed her hair. Kate slipped his little coat on him, causing him great joy. She suspected his capering joy was less about the coat and more because the coat signaled she wouldn't leave him behind again. Monty's presence might

176

be helpful in controlling Le Compte should the Frenchman have the temerity to show himself this evening.

At 7 o'clock Kate once again knocked on Mrs. Winslow's door. Just as before, Mr. Bristol greeted her and led her to the parlor, with its large central table and chairs for ten people. Bristol excused himself, saying he had to prepare for the evening. The two gentlemen from the previous week were already in the room, sitting in a small seating area near the large, double windows. They stood when Kate entered and asked her to join them. The older and grayer of the two poured her a small sherry from the stocked sideboard before they sat down and returned to their conversation. Kate listened to them argue over whether the war would be over in four months or six. Both of them ignored the Union's debilitating loss to a superior Confederate Army at Bull Run the previous summer. Unable to stand their foolishness a minute longer, she excused herself and wandered about the room.

She circled the table and stopped before the window with the heavy drapes that abutted the cabinet. She gripped the thick fold of velvet and leaned forward, pretending to peer out the window. Instead, she looked behind the drapes, at the cabinet. Just as she suspected, the side panel had two small hinges along the front length. A person could step out, hidden by both the panel and the folds of fabric. She was about to check the floor under the table when she heard voices in the hallway. Mr. Bristol showed three older ladies into the room.

Mrs. Winslow appeared moments later, her entrance every bit as dramatic as the first time Kate had seen her. She circulated the room, pressing hands and speaking in a low, confidential voice with each séance attendee. Once again Mrs. Winslow's stunning beauty surprised Kate. Her dark hair, piled in a luxuriant mass at the back of her head, shone in the gaslight, setting off her ivory satin skin and perfect, pink mouth. Long dark lashes framed her mesmerizing eyes, captivating not only for their unusual color, but for the intensity of the lady's gaze.

When it was Kate's turn for attention the lady smiled and said, "I'm so glad to see you returned. I hoped you would. Tell me, what is it you hope to gain from your spirit encounter?" She grasped Kate's hands as she spoke and stared into her eyes like she was meeting an old and dear friend. Kate got the sense that when Mrs. Winslow looked at someone she really saw them. Were it not for her career as a spiritualist charlatan, blackmailer, and possible serial murderer, she would have made a fine detective.

Kate pretended to stammer. "As, um, um, as I explained before, I hope to contact my dear husband. I miss him so, which is not unexpected, but I also worry about him. He needed me to take care of him you see? He was so delicate. So sensitive."

"Did he enjoy poetry my dear," Mrs. Winslow asked, still pressing Kate's hands between her own.

Kate feigned excitement. "Yes! How did you know?" Mrs. Winslow let go of Kate's hands and waved one of her own about her head. "I sense spirits all around us, always. He is with us tonight." She paused as if listening.

"And your name dear?"

"Mrs. Barley. Mrs. Katherine Barley."

"I feel a great affinity with you, Mrs. Barley. Are you familiar with the concept of affinities?"

Kate shook her head.

"Spiritualists believe the spirit, or soul if you like, is not on-ly perpetual but it returns to this life repeatedly. Spirits find each other, life after life. Have you ever felt connected to someone you just met?"

Kate nodded, thinking she'd had that instant connection several times in her life. With both Hattie and Hazzard it had been like meeting someone she already knew. It had been disconcerting, but also reassuring.

"When one spirit recognizes another spirit from a previous life an affinity results. You and I are two such spirits for I had an affinity for you from the moment I met you."

"Did you?" Kate tried out her girlish squeal. It wasn't fantastic. She tried again. "Me too!"

Mrs. Winslow blinked her dark eyelashes over her purple eyes and smiled, exposing small, even, white teeth. "I knew you would. You are a sensitive soul."

Just as they were about to take their seats Le Compte burst into the room in a flurry of cold air and flying coattails. "Ma Cherie, you are ravishing tonight. The spirits will flock to you." He grasped Mrs. Winslow's hands, pecked kisses on them every few words. He looked up and saw Kate. His head reared back like a snake seeing a mongoose. Kate gave him a look of wide-eyed innocence but glanced down at Monty as she did. He saw the dog, blanched, then turned and laid his coat and hat on the back of the sofa.

When he turned around again Kate gave him her best school teacher glare, learned during her brief career at New York girls' school.

Any color left in his cheeks drained away and he swayed on his feet. Kate watched as he grabbed the nearest chair back. She felt a tiny bit bad. He was just too easy to frighten, but no one else seemed to notice.

Mr. Bristol vied with Le Compte for the honor of installing Mrs. Winslow in the cabinet, bumping and jostling each other in their eagerness to demonstrate their usefulness. Once again the lights went dark and instruments made dissonant noises. Glowing ectoplasm appeared, giving the evening variety and the ladies some thrills, which they expressed with squeals of delighted fright.

Once the gentlemen released Mrs. Winslow from the cabinet she performed some trance writing, which she interpreted as a love poem from Mrs. Barley's dead husband. Kate peered over the table at the paper. It looked like a page covered in scribbles.

Le Compte entertained them with an odd performance of clairvoyance. He pressed his hands to his eyes, pulled them off, blinked and repeated the procedure a dozen times, while the assembled ladies and gentlemen watched in utter fascination. He looked like he was having a fit. He claimed to see the spirits of both the gentleman's deceased wives while twitching and drooling like a lunatic. The gentlemen delighted in this development, though Kate couldn't understand why the wives of such ninnies would bother visiting their husbands once they'd escaped into the afterlife.

When all the dead husbands, wives, sisters and children had contacted their loved ones Mrs. Winslow threw herself back in her chair in a pose of utter exhaustion. Le Compte caught her look and did likewise. Kate stifled a laugh and glanced around the table. No one else seemed to find the spiritualists' performance at all unbelievable.

One by one the séance attendees buttoned up their coats and made their farewells to their host, each of them pressing money into her hand as they did. Kate loitered near the window, waiting for everyone to go. Finally, it was just Mrs. Winslow, Bristol, Le Compte, and Kate left. Mrs. Winslow appraised Kate with a cool eye and sent the men on their way, both men protesting their undying love and admiration.

When the gentlemen had finally removed themselves Mrs. Winslow turned to Kate. "Something troubles you, my dear?"

Kate snorted. "A great deal troubles me, Mrs. Winslow."

She ignored the change in Kate's tone. "Ellen. Please call me Ellen." Why don't you take a seat and I'll make tea? Then we girls can chat." She turned to go.

"I'm afraid this isn't a tea kind of chat." Kate's voice came out a good deal harsher and louder than she'd intended. She'd be damned if she'd sit around sipping tea with a blackmailer and murderer.

Mrs. Winslow turned back and found her own iron voice. "Please sit down. Whatever you have to say can wait the time it takes me to put together a tea tray." She glared at Kate with narrowed eyes and left the room.

A frisson of fear shivered up Kate's spine at Mrs. Winslow's tone. She wondered if her plan to confront Mrs. Winslow alone hadn't been a tad ill-considered. She pulled her revolver from her pocket and checked it before laying it in her lap. Then Kate settled back to wait for the woman she suspected was the Black Widow killer.

Chapter 18

January 20, 1862
Rochester, New York

Mrs. Winslow returned to the parlor laden with a silver tea tray atop which sat a steaming teapot with matching sugar bowl and cream pitcher. The ornate set looked out of place in the rented rooms, rather like a grand duchess in a seedy boarding house. She sat the tray on the table, poured two cups of tea and carried them over to the seating area. The whole time neither of them spoke.

Kate watched Mrs. Winslow take her seat. It was hard not to. She could see why gentlemen couldn't get enough of Mrs. W. She had the same indefinable thing Hattie had. Kate didn't know what it was, but she didn't have it. Oh, she was attractive enough, but that thing wasn't about looks alone. And she didn't mind not having it. If she did she'd be a less effective detective.

But this woman took advantage of her gift, using it to abuse others. She wasn't the first woman in world history to do so, but it infuriated Kate. It was too much like cheating. She tried to make her own way in the world through fairness and hard work. A lot of women worked hard. Women who used sex and manipulation to get what they needed, or worse, what they wanted, made women look bad. All women.

"Mrs. Winslow, I have some rather unpleasant news for you." Kate tried to look as if she regretted what she was about to say, but she suspected she failed quite badly.

Mrs. Winslow shifted in her chair as she reached for her teacup. "You can't have forgotten already? Call me Ellen, my dear."

"Oh, quit with the 'my dear' nonsense," Kate snapped. "You're no older than I am. And you're no spiritual authority. You're a fraud and not a very good one."

Mrs. Winslow's eyes widened. She sat down her cup with a clatter. "What is the meaning of this . . . this unwarranted attack? How dare you?"

Kate couldn't help herself. She laughed. "Are you kidding me, lady? That boogy-oogy stuff this evening. You might fool the poor saps who adore you, but you sure as heck don't fool me."

"Oh, my dear," Mrs. Winslow breathed. "I am sorry that I only briefly contacted your poor husband, but I assure you, I'll do better next time. The spirits are ever with me."

"I don't have a dead husband, you charlatan," Kate spat out. "I am an operative with the Pinkerton Detective Agency and I was hired to stop your blackmailing scheme."

"No husband? But I felt him so strongly. You heard him play upon my instruments yourself."

Kate noticed Mrs. Winslow ignored most of what she'd said. "Stop it. You've been caught. You and I both know everything that happened tonight was no more than trickery. Your cabinet is hinged on its side panel. You leave the cabinet and roam about the room producing effects, switching slates, that sort of nonsense, all under the cover of darkness. Then you return to the cabinet and pretend you were in there all along."

"I'm shocked to be attacked this way by a young woman. Spiritualism has many doubters but they are generally the sort of men invested in traditional religion and all its control of female spirituality. That you would assail me so . . . It is too shocking. I must ask you to go now." The lady pointed at her door to make her point.

Kate had to admit, Winslow was good. Just not good enough. "I am not some doubter. Pay attention. I said I am a Pinkerton Detective. Mrs. Winslow, if that is your name, you must abandon your act. Or would you like us to go over to the cabinet right now? Or how about we check the floor under your séance table?"

The lady deflated like a collapsed soufflé. She pulled a handkerchief from her sleeve and dabbed at her dry eyes. "Understand, we all use these tricks. I have a genuine gift, but it's not theatrical and it's not instantaneous and that's what people want."

Kate shook her head. "I don't care about the fakery. Not really. I grew up in the circus. What you do is not that different from circuses. You offer illusion and entertainment in return for payment. The real problem is that you use your séance table as a hunting ground for vulnerable men, whom you terrorize with bribery and blackmail."

Mrs. Winslow stared at Kate and then dropped her disguise of innocence like a woman dropping her clothing on the floor. Her posture and facial expression changed. Everything about her changed as she shifted from soft womanhood to

185

predator in the space of a few seconds. Kate almost recoiled, as one would from a poisonous snake. The transition reminded Kate of the Confederate spy Rose Greenhow, who could shift from lady to killer and back again in the space of seconds.

Mrs. Winslow gathered herself, picked up her teacup and took a deliberate sip. "How do you suppose I accomplish these evil deeds? Do you imagine these men I chose are innocent victims? Is any man innocent? Be honest."

"Some of them are innocent. Or maybe innocent is the wrong word. There are good men in the world. Too good for what you do." Kate said. "You encourage them to act in ways they would not without encouragement. You are a seducer of susceptible men."

"Nooooo!" Mrs. Winslow screamed and threw her teacup across the room, where it shattered against the wall. "Listen my dear, and listen carefully." She spat out her words, like poison pebbles. "Men are never innocent victims of my seductions or any woman's seductions. They have all the power. They take what they want and walk away, leaving the mess of women's lives behind them. Even the good ones do it. They sit in their chairs, preaching submissive womanhood, letting some downtrodden woman wait on them hand and foot and they call it love. Love! There can be no real love in any relationship so unequal."

Kate sat shocked at the lady's torrent of words. She'd had some of these same thoughts herself. She opened her mouth to object, to what she wasn't sure, but Mrs. Winslow kept talking.

"You see the truth of my words. I can see it in your eyes. Men use women's bodies and call themselves righteous if the woman is their wife. If the woman is not their wife, they say a bad woman seduced them. They take their pleasure and woe betide a woman who expects pleasure in return. Men declare her unnatural and unsuitable. And if an affair becomes public? The woman is labeled a harlot. And if a woman seeks to force a man to honor his false promises? Why, they label her a blackmailer. Women have no power in this society. No power to stop violence against our bodies, no power to make men honor their commitments, no power to earn a good living by ourselves. No man can be innocent in a system of such deep injustice. They are all guilty because they all enjoy the benefits."

Kate could only stare at the woman. Was she insane? Or just an astute observer?

"Look at you," Mrs. Winslow pointed her finger at Kate's face. "What choices did you have when you decided to make your own living? Could you train as a doctor or a lawyer? No, you could not. Was there any job available to you that wasn't menial and low paying? This job you do now? Are you taken seriously? Are you paid the same as your male colleagues?"

Kate shook her head. "The man who hired me treats me like an equal. So do some of my male colleagues."

Mrs. Winslow snorted. "Some. And what about the rest? Are you as safe as men are in the night? Can you vote to change the laws? No, you can not. And why? Because they say we are too weak. As if that's a good reason. If we are weak, don't we need more protection, not less? And why should men have the protections of citizenship and not women? Do not speak of the innocent man. Or the female seductress. Neither exists."

Kate stared at Mrs. Winslow, her mouth agape. "Your position is that poor Mr. Lyon or old Mr. Devereaux deserve their abuse because they are men?"

"Of course, you fool. They take what they want, with no regard for the cost." She made a dismissive sound. "You call yourself a detective but you are only a lap dog for powerful men and their lies. Did you even once ask yourself how Lyon and Devereaux came to be in their current situations? Did you never consider the woman to whom they'd made promises? Did you never ask yourself, why she would do it?"

It was Kate's turn to snort. "You do it because you are a wicked, evil creature. You cause misery because it suits you to do so."

Mrs. Winslow glared at Kate. "Wicked. Evil. Those are men's words for women they can not control. Why does it suit me to do what I do? Because I am wicked? Are you that simple?"

Kate felt her temper slip from her grasp. There was no justification for murder. "I don't know why you do it. I've been asking myself that question for years. Why would a woman murder? Because you are a stone cold killer Lily and I don't understand how you can live with yourself."

The color drained from Mrs. Winslow's face. "What did you call me?"

It took a moment for Kate to realize what she'd said. She hurried to correct her mistake. "I said I can't understand how you live with yourself."

Winslow shook her head. "No. Not that. You called me by another name. Lily."

Kate wished she could go back and bite her tongue. If Ellen Winslow was Lily Nettleton it did Kate's investigation no favors to notify the lady of her suspicions. But it was too late now. It was time to come clean. "Your real name is not Ellen Winslow. You are the notorious murderer Lily Nettleton."

The lady reared back her head, eyebrows arched. In a cold voice, she asked, "Preposterous! Why would you say such a thing?"

Kate held up two fingers. "Two things. First, you match physical descriptions of Lily Nettleton, from your age to your distinctive eye color. Second, it made little sense that Lily killed three men before her twentieth birthday and disappeared, to never do it again. A multiple murderer would be out there ruining lives. And here you are ruining men's lives. In short, you look like her and act like her."

Mrs. Winslow stood and turned her back on the séance table.

Kate lifted the gun from her lap and put it on the table.

Mrs. Winslow turned back toward Kate with the teapot in her hand, saw the gun and paused. Then she laughed. "Oh, my dear Mrs. Barley, if that is your name, I am no threat to you or to any woman."

She poured each of them more tea, returned the pot to the table and sat back down. "May I assume then, that you've investigated this Lily Nettleton person yourself?"

Kate nodded. "You were my first big case."

Mrs. Winslow shook her head. "I wasn't. This Lily person was. I am not she."

"I think you are."

"Let's leave that aside for a moment, shall we? Tell me about this investigation of yours. What did you discover about Lily's life and crimes? From the beginning, if you please."

Kate threw caution to the wind. "Almost six years ago in Kalamazoo, Michigan Lily Nettleton killed her father and her husband in the same night. She killed her husband first, then went to her parent's farm and killed her father. She left her mother and sister alive. And then . . . ."

Mrs. Winslow interrupted. "Not so fast. Did you talk to Lily's surviving family?"

"No. I tried, but Mrs. Nettleton wouldn't speak to me. The sheriff said she'd been traumatized by the experience. I never saw the sister, but she wasn't involved in the case in the first place so it didn't matter. The sheriff was clear about the details. He traced Lily as far as the train station in Battle Creek and after that to Fort Wayne. He lost her after that. I got a little further. I traced you to Detroit."

"You did?" Mrs. Winslow arched an eyebrow and took a sip of her tea. "What did you find in Detroit?"

"You seduced a minister, tricked him into buying you a load of clothes and jewelry. When you got what you wanted you drugged him, stole the household money and silver and disappeared again."

"Not me. Lily Nettleton." Mrs. Winslow smiled a small, closed mouth smile. "This Lily sounds like a nefarious character. Did the Detroit police tell you these things?"

"No," Kate admitted. "There was no police report. I found a hotel clerk who remembered Lily and sent me to an address, where I spoke to a woman who told me the story."

"And the Reverend?" Mrs. Winslow leaned forward, her face as eager as a dog about to eat.

"The woman said he'd moved west. Once Lily broke his heart."

Mrs. Winslow leaned back in her chair, clearly disappointed. "This Lily person becomes more sinister with each additional fact."

Kate nodded. "It gets worse. As I suspect you know."

She smiled. "Let us say I do not know."

"Fine. She went from Detroit to Cincinnati, where she convinced a rich widower to marry her. She killed him and once again absconded into the night. That's where I came in. The dead husband's son hired the Pinkertons to investigate his father's murder. Mr. Pinkerton put me on the case, thinking I'd have a better chance of catching Mrs. Gibson, which was Lily's name at the time. Your name, at the time."

"But you had no luck finding this husband killing monster?"

Kate gave Mrs. Winslow a hard look. "You're making fun of me, but it's not funny. Three men are dead. I traced Mrs. Gibson back to Detroit and Kalamazoo, discovering her original crimes and name, but I could not find her trail after Cincinnati. You eluded me."

"I'm sorry if I appear to be making light." Mrs. Winslow radiated sincerity. "It's just that I'm not surprised you couldn't find this killer. Your so-called investigation doesn't impress me as terribly thorough."

Kate leaned back in her chair, careful to keep her gun hand clear of her skirt. "How so?"

"Isn't it obvious dear?"

Kate shook her head, though she had to admit the lady had a point. There was an awful lot about the case she didn't know.

"Well, you know nothing about either marriage and thus nothing about the behavior of either husband. You seem to know nothing about this Detroit minister, but for his house-keeper's claims about the man's good character. And who is this housekeeper? Is she telling the truth? Is there any reason she might not?"

Kate wanted to yell 'caught you!' "I didn't say she was his housekeeper. How did you know?"

"I thought you were a detective dear. It's obvious, isn't it? If this woman was his mother you would have said so. You did not, so she must be the housekeeper. But let us return to the paltry nature of your investigation. You didn't even speak to Lily's mother or sister. You didn't speak to the authorities about the Reverend, you didn't check the Gibson son's story about his father's marriage. You traveled from place to place letting men lie to you. You know almost nothing."

Kate stood and walked to the window, her gun hand hanging forgotten by her side. She looked out for a moment. It was snowing again, soft swirls of white and grey that looked pretty until you had to step out in it. Then it would kill you if you weren't prepared for it. Kate thought about Mrs. Winslow's words. She wanted to argue, but the lady had a point. Her six-year-old investigation wasn't the same one she'd run today, that much was for sure. She'd rushed the investigation be-cause she'd been worried she'd lose the killer's trail. Which she had anyway. Kate heard the spiritualist shift in her chair. She turned and stared at her. The lady stared back.

After a long moment Kate spoke. "Who are you?"

Mrs. Winslow chuckled softly. "Are we to discuss philosophy then? Who are you, my dear? Detective? Wife? Lover? Daughter? Are you one person? Or many? And which is the real you? For now, let us say I am Ellen Winslow, Rochester spiritualist." She pointed at Kate. "Now. Ask me the question you really want to ask me."

Kate took a deep breath. "Are you Lily Nettleton?"

Mrs. Winslow smiled. "As I already told you, I am not she. But I may know the woman who was once her. I would share my information with you, but only if you conduct a real investigation. I think you can discover the truth of Lily Nettleton's past. When you do you shall return and tell me her story. If you get it right I will tell you what I know of her in the present. I will help you, but only if you rectify your mistakes."

Kate shook her head. "I can't retrace the old case until I clear my present case."

"Which is?"

Kate sighed. "I told you. A friend of Mr. Lyon's hired me to prevent you from suing the gentleman for breach of promise or otherwise causing him and his family social embarrassment."

Mrs. Winslow stood, stepped toward Kate and held out her hand. "You have my word, one woman to another, that I will cease my efforts against Mr. Lyon until you return. If your investigation takes longer you may request additional time. I want you to discover the truth of Lily's story."

"And Mr. Devereaux. I want him left alone too," Kate added, ignoring Mrs. Winslow's outstretched hand.

"How extraordinary. Is he also your client?"

"No. But I want him included in our deal. You leave those two men alone and I'll retrace my investigation. And if I find out you've violated our agreement I'll go straight to the Rochester authorities. You'll be in jail before you can blink." Then something occurred to Kate. "You're planning on running again, aren't you?"

Mrs. Winslow shook her head. "I'm done running. You have my word, one woman to another. If upon your return you still believe Lily Nettleton is a dangerous murderer I shall help you put her in jail. If, on the other hand, you return with a new understanding of Lily Nettleton, I want you to help her." She stretched out her hand again.

Kate looked into Ellen Winslow's amethyst eyes. Something in them made her trust the lady, though what it was she couldn't say. Kate transferred her revolver to her left hand and held out her right hand.

They shook on it. Ellen Winslow's hand was ice cold.

Back at her hotel room, Kate wrote a batch of letters. The first she wrote to Allan, explaining what she'd found so far and appraising him of the change in her investigation. She addressed that letter to Cincinnati but printed 'Please Forward' on it in the likelihood he'd left for Washington. She wrote a similar letter to Juba, knowing he'd share her news with everyone in the F Street house. Then she wrote to Hazzard at Fort Washington telling him she'd be gone longer than she'd expected. Writing it made her feel both closer and further away from him.

The final letter she wrote to Mr. Harcourt and Mr. Lyon. In it, she assured them both that Mr. Lyon no longer need fear a lawsuit from Mrs. Winslow, though she did not explain why. She asked the men to trust her in this matter and assured them she would soon be back to brief them on the case's details and that in the mean time they should not worry about the case. She folded and sealed the letter, hoping she wasn't making a calamitous mistake.

Chapter 19

*K*ate left Rochester two days later. She would have left the very next day, but the weather turned evil cold, with snow and wind that cut right through a person. Kate decided to send Excelsior back to Washington, rather than inflict the weather on his old bones. It took much of the day to make the arrangements, so Kate and Monty didn't leave Rochester until Wednesday morning.

They boarded the Erie Railroad to Dunkirk, New York, a town that seemed to exist for no other reason than to serve as a port for Lake Erie steamboats. They arrived in Dunkirk late in the afternoon, having missed the afternoon boat by less than an hour. Since the next boat didn't steam out of Dunkirk until the next morning they took a room in a ragged tavern home to more vermin than humans. It was Saturday night, so the place rang with song and hollering well into the night. Kate woke bleary-eyed and ready to strangle the next drunk she met. Monty bounded from the bed ready to take on the day, a sentiment he expressed by peeing on every frozen fence post, shrubbery and building corner he trotted past.

Suspecting it would do her no good to eat before crossing a body of water as fearsome as Lake Erie, Kate skipped breakfast. She ordered a bowl of oatmeal and a plate of sausages from the tavern keeper, which she stirred together and fed to her four-legged friend. Monty never got travel sick. Kate tried not to hold that against him.

Once aboard she headed straight for the mid-deck. The thermometer affixed to a deck wall said it was twenty degrees outside, but the wind made it seem much colder. Kate tried not to watch the waves, but it was almost impossible not to. Three to four-foot waves heaved the side-wheeled paddle steamer up and down and side to side in a manner Kate's innards found most unpleasant. A friendly steward dug a deck chair out of summer storage and found her a newspaper. He settled the chair into a corner, far back of the deck railing, and tucked a heavy travel rug around her legs. Kate considered marrying the man. Monty snuggled into the little tent her bent knees made and within the hour her stomach ceased its rebellion.

The newspaper's front page was awash with news of Mr. Lincoln's Special War Order No. 1, ordering the Army of the Potomac to seize Manassas Junction. She wondered if Hazzard would get his wish to go to battle. In his last letter, he said General McClellan's mood had turned dark. Kate suspected the Little Napoleon was angry at Mr. Lincoln's presuming to dictate orders to his generals.

When her fingers grew too cold to hold the newspaper she tucked it under her, put her hands in her pockets and leaned back in her chair. She wondered, not for the first time, why she was doing this. Why leave Washington and when everyone she held dear was there, including a certain artillery captain who might at any moment go to war. Why chase the Black Widow? And then, why leave her cozy Rochester hotel room for this heaving, freezing hell?

It was her own fault. She should have had answers to Mrs. Winslow's questions. Five years earlier Kate launched her investigation in Lily's early life and worked forward from there. She hoped this strategy, which reversed her first investigation, would help her find new evidence and see her old evidence in a new light. Not that she was ready to throw out her original conclusions about Lily Nettleton, but she conceded that her first investigation had not been her best work. Or it had been the best work of an inexperienced detective. Allan Pinkerton had never once treated her like a second-class detective because she was woman. Still, in his eagerness to prove the validity of his experiment with female operatives he may have had more confidence in her early work than warranted. Not that she was blaming Allan. No. She should have known she was in over her head. And maybe she had known. Maybe that's why the case haunted her these past five years.

It was a long, but not unpleasant morning. They stayed on deck in their lovely deck chair, removing themselves only once, to take a necessary break. Then the steamboat whistle blew a shrill note, signaling the end of the crossing. She'd already felt the boat slow and not one minute too soon. It hadn't been the worst boat trip she'd ever taken, but no one should have to cross Lake Erie in February. It had been longer and thus colder than the trip across Lake Ontario to Toronto. The steward told her they were lucky because Lake Erie was having a mild winter. Some years it was so cold for so long that the lake froze too hard for the steamships. This year they had plenty of open water and the patchy ice easily broke in the ship's forward thrust.

As the ship slowed for the lake's western shore and the Detroit dock Kate examined her train schedule. The Central Michigan Railroad had a 1:15 to Kalamazoo. She checked her watch. Almost Noon. She should make it. Meanwhile, she reviewed her strategy. The last time she'd been in Kalamazoo she's spoken to the sheriff and before that a man at the *Kalamazoo Gazette*. What were their names? She dug out the old case file, the one Allan handed over to her almost two weeks ago. There they were. Mr. Gibbs at the Gazette and Sheriff Miller. She'd start with them.

Kate watched Monty pee on a Kalamazoo light post, his green coat and black fur a stark contrast to the snowdrift lined streets. She rented a room at the Kalamazoo House on Main Street and ate a late dinner in the hotel's dining room. She shared her chicken and sweet potatoes with Monty, who'd parked himself under her chair. She wanted to sleep in this morning but Monty had other ideas. Once they were up and moving Kate admitted Monty had been right. She found a pastry shop selling warm fritters and bought two. Monty acted like fritters were his new favorite food and Kate agreed. They were filled with apple bits and were disgustingly delicious. After licking her fingers clean Kate headed back down Main Street the way she'd come. The courthouse and jail were on the same block, two blocks down from the hotel.

Kate and Monty entered the small jail building and looked around. She remembered the Sheriff's office was right inside the door. As she entered she saw Sheriff Miller, looking not one whit older than he'd looked five years before, though to be fair, he'd looked at least eighty years old then. He was one of those tall, rangy, nothing but sinew and bone New England types, all no-nonsense manners, and wisdom disguised by reticence. She introduced herself and reminded him they'd spoken once before.

"Why don't that beat the band," he asked, rubbing his hands through silvery hair so thin that Kate saw his pink scalp below. "I gotta tell ya' I thought you were funning' me back then. A lady detective. Did you ever catch that gal? The one that killed her pa and her man?" He motioned her to sit and poured two cups of coffee.

Kate sat and reached for the coffee cup, grateful for its warmth on her hands. "I might have. I'm not sure."

"Re-checking the case, are ya?" He watched her over his coffee cup.

"Yes, sir. I may have rushed my investigation the first time."

"Ayah. That happens. You gotta move fast on cases when they first break. We all do it."

"True, but there's a difference between fast and incomplete. Did you ever find her?"

"Nope. Never made a nickel's worth of headway on the durn case." He flung his feet up on his desk and leaned back in his wooden desk chair, causing some ominous creaking sounds. "Ya ever talk to Lily's Ma?"

Kate shook her head. "One of my oversights."

"Well, I don't see as how much she'd a done ya much good, not back then. She wouldn't say a word against Lily. Or the murders. She clammed up like a woman struck deaf mute." He shrugged. "But time heals some wounds, if not all

201

of them. I never heard her to string three words together, but you might have more luck. Still, that Mrs. Nettleton ain't one to run her mouth."

He grinned wide enough to show teeth. "Not like my wife and her friends, clucking and gossiping like a flock of fussy old birds day and night. Not that I pay it no mind, not after fifty years of wedded bliss." He dropped one eyelid in a wink. Kate winked back. He laughed and gave her directions to the Nettleton farm, advising her to take the omnibus south, to the edge of town and walk from there.

As they were about to leave Sheriff Miller noticed Monty. "Ain't you a sight? Never seen a little feller wearing a coat. Must be a big city thing." He rubbed Monty's head. "Not a bad idea though. You ain't got much hair, do ya pup? Wait till I tell the Missus. She'll think I'm telling one of my tall tales."

Kate emerged from the Sheriff's office and walked back to the hotel where she and Monty caught the city omnibus. Though not as gaily painted as Washington's omnibuses, it had glass windows that closed out the worst of the cold air. They passed block after block of small, wooden frame houses that looked snug and cozy. Kate found herself yearning for the kitchen at home with its bustle of friends and mouth-watering cooking smells. She heard herself sigh and stopped. If she'd done the job right the first time she'd be home right now.

At the south end of town, the omnibus turned around to go back. Several people got off with Kate, but they each walked west. Kate turned east, crossed a small stone bridge over a frozen creek and walked down the road. The sun on the snow made puddles of wet slush and water. Kate hopped over puddles left and right, trying in vain to keep her boots clean and dry. After about a half mile of puddle hopping, she came to a mailbox with 'Nettleton' painted on it. Kate turned down the road, toward the farmhouse. The place had a forlorn, neglected air about it, but a tendril of smoke drifted from the chimney, suggesting someone was home. Behind the small house stood a much larger barn, its white paint peeling in scabrous flakes. The place looked like a ghost farm.

A wan, pinched woman opened the door a scant three inches in answer to Kate's knock.

"Yes?" Her voice was rusty with disuse.

For a brief moment Kate thought she had the wrong house. This pale, shadow woman couldn't be related to the vivid Lily. How could she be? "Are you Mrs. Nettleton?" Kate used her softest, most reassuring voice, the same voice she used when trying to settle a spooked horse.

The woman nodded.

"May I come in for a moment? I'd like to ask you some questions." At the woman's obvious dismay, Kate added, "I swear I mean you no harm."

Mrs. Nettleton blinked several times and opened the door. She turned and walked away, leaving Kate to close the door behind her. The house's interior was as neat and lifeless as a museum. Kate gave Monty a 'be good' look and followed Mrs. Nettleton through the living room and into the kitchen. The lady sat at her table, shoulders hunched. She looked like a whipped dog.

Kate sat across from Mrs. Nettleton. Monty stationed himself next to Mrs. Nettleton's chair and watched her. She leaned down and patted his head. "I used to have a little dog," she said. "Before I married Mr. Nettleton. He poisoned my little Billy dog and never allowed a dog on the farm after that. I always wanted to get me a dog. It's so lonely here."

Mr. Nettleton sounded like a right bastard. He'd been dead for over six years and his wife hadn't gotten herself a new dog. Were men like Mr. Nettleton ever really gone? After a quiet moment, Kate spoke. "Mrs. Nettleton, I want to ask about your daughter Lily."

It was as if someone threw a switch in Mrs. Nettleton and woke her up. She straightened her shoulders and jutted her chin at Kate. "What business do you have with my Lily? Hasn't that girl suffered enough?" She stopped speaking and held a fist to her mouth.

Kate considered her options. Best not to admit she suspected Lily was a murdering fiend. "Have you heard from your daughter since the night she disappeared?"

The lady shook her head, fist still to her mouth.

"Do you know why she killed your husband?"

More head shaking.

"Perhaps someone else killed your husband?"

"Nooo," Mrs. Nettleton moaned

"So Lily killed him. You're sure."

The lady bit her lower lip and jerked her head in a yes. "My husband was a hard man. He expected his womenfolk to do their duty."

That was a strange answer. "Did Lily fail in her duty?"

Mrs. Nettleton pressed her thin lips together and stared down at the table.

Kate suppressed an urge to shake the woman. "Did they argue?"

Mrs. Nettleton didn't answer.

"Did she argue with her husband, Mr. Gosford?"

Nothing.

"Did they not get along?"

Still nothing.

"Mrs. Nettleton, I am trying to understand your daughter's case. It would be a great help if you would help me."

Mrs. Nettleton squared her shoulders again and stood. She walked across the kitchen, through the living room to the door. She opened it and stood there, cold air streaming past her.

Kate and Monty took the hint and left, no wiser than when they'd arrived.

After lunch Monty accompanied Kate to the offices of the *Kalamazoo Gazette*. Mr. Gibbs saw her from across the room and exclaimed, "The lady detective returns. To what do I owe this pleasure?" He stood, rolled down his sleeves and came around his desk toward her.

Kate explained what she needed and he agreed to fetch all his back copies from February and March, six years previous.

Mr. Gibbs hauled a box out from the back room and dropped it on his desk with a dusty thump. "You already looked at all this stuff. Can't you remember your own investigation?"

"Oh, I remember all right. But I missed something."

"What?" He cocked his head at her like a curious robin.

"I don't know. I'm hoping I'll know it when I see it."

He rubbed at his head. "Huh. Sounds like a snipe hunt. Glad to help though. You use my desk. I'm setting type today."

Three hours later, covered in dust and smeared in newsprint ink, Kate counted up what she'd learned. Nothing. Not one darn new thing. Well, one thing, one small thing unaccounted for in her first investigation.

She found Mr. Gibbs, clad in a heavy apron, leaned over his printing press with a screwdriver, muttering under his breath. She cleared her throat, which made him jerk his head up.

"I keep this old press together with gum and baling wire. You find anything?"

"Hard to tell. Can you answer a question?"

He sat his screwdriver down and wiped his hands on his apron. "Shoot."

"Do you have any idea what happened to Polly Nettleton? I went out to the family farm and spoke to Mrs. Nettleton, but Polly didn't seem to be there. Your articles say she was sixteen back then."

He nodded. "So she'd be in her twenties now. Hmmm. Hold on a second." He returned to his storage room and brought out a box that had 1858 written on its side. He dug through it, stirring up a cloud of dust as he did. "Here it is. Special Edition." He handed a one-page piece of newsprint to Kate. The headlines announced:

Public High School Opens

First in Michigan History

Kate stared at it, not sure why it was important.

"See that list of teachers? It's the far right column."

She scanned the list. There she was. Polly Nettleton, Mathematics

Mr. Gibbs took the paper from Kate. "I haven't seen her in a while, but the school would know if she's still here and if not, they might know where she is."

Kate sighed. It was a lead, but a thin one.

He pointed at his wall clock. "It's almost five o'clock. Won't be anyone over there now. They close at 3 o'clock in winter, so the kids can get home afore dark. But come 8 AM Miss Bird will be in the office. She'll get a kick out of you."

Kate helped Mr. Gibbs put the boxes back in his storeroom before leaving. The temperature had plummeted while she'd been inside, causing all the puddles to refreeze. Monty skipped right over them. Kate walked tight mincing steps for fear of losing her footing. A grim laugh escaped her. The case was like this walk, dark, slippery and none too comfortable.

Chapter 20

Jan. 22, 1862
Rochester, New York

At three in the morning, Ellen Winslow gave up on sleep. She might as well get out of bed and do something. Anything was better than lying there worrying. She pushed her feet into a pair of carpet slippers and pulled on her thick wool dressing gown. It wasn't the dressing gown she used for gentlemen visitors. That piece of ruffled frippery was the sort of thing men liked. And Lily hated it. Every time she put it on she felt like a whore. Not a high priced courtesan, which is what she'd become, but a common street whore, cheap and none too clean.

She lit a lamp and carried it down the hall to her kitchen. Rustling through her cupboards, she found her tea and teapot. She was careful not to make too much noise. If Mr. Bristol heard her he'd be over in a trice. She wasn't in the mood for his heavy-handed fawning. She dumped a spoonful of loose tea into her teapot and carried it into the parlor where a kettle of water simmered on the tiny coal stove. It was easier to buy her food already cooked so her kitchen stove sat there, unused and cold. Sometimes she thought about how it would be nice to have someone to cook for. Ma taught her to cook long ago in a faraway land, but there was no point now. No one expected a woman like her to be domestic anyway. Men didn't come to her for a home-cooked meal.

Lily sat in her usual seat at her séance table and poured herself a cup of tea. She looked around the room. There was her cabinet, her table of instruments, her bookshelves, all the trappings of a successful spiritualist. And she'd succeeded, there was no doubt of that. People flocked to her, men because she was young and attractive and women because she understood what they wanted. What they needed. Much of what she did was pure chicanery, but she'd been honest with Miss Warne. She had the gift. She was sure. But it was quiet and slow. Most people came to her for help, whether they admitted it or not. They wanted relief from their grey, mundane lives. They wanted the thrill of the unknown, a brush with death, but they wanted their danger controlled and safe.

But most of all, there were the mothers. They came for relief from the heartbreak and terror of losing a child. The mothers kept Lily in business. Mothers wanted contact with their lost babies and they wanted it right then. And they wanted conversations, not images and impressions. Which is all Lily ever got. Like the time she found the bees and the honey, she saw things in pictures. But that wasn't good enough for the people who came to her. So she made things up. Her act put food on the table and helped people in terrible pain. What was wrong with that?

She'd been eight years old the first time one of her visions happened. Back then Pa ignored her though he beat Ma all the time. He kept four woven bee keps in an open shed, about a quarter mile behind the barn in an open meadow. Lily loved to sit near the shed and watch the bees. The keps were thick, closed, dome-shaped baskets. Pa bought them from a nearby Hutterite colony each spring, then he'd use them to catch a bee swarm. They'd make honey in the keps all summer and then come fall Pa would take the bottom off the kep and take the honey. That would make the bees mad, but Pa would use a bunch of smoke to make the bees sleepy while he robbed them of their honey. When they woke up, they'd find their winter food missing and they'd leave. Every fall Pa sold that honey in town for cash money and started the whole cycle over again the following spring. Lily thought the system worked pretty well for Pa, but not so well for the bees.

Then one day a kep disappeared. Pa stomped and hollered around the yard, getting ready to beat on Ma. His fury and noise drove Lily to the cellar. She pushed herself into a dark, cool corner, pulled her knees up under her chin and waited for the storm to pass. She must have dozed off because she dreamed about the bees. When she woke up, she knew where to find the missing kep.

She'd hopped up, eager to tell Pa, so he'd quit with his growling and stomping. But standing in the dark, cool cellar it occurred to her that if she told him he'd think she was the thief. Then she'd be in for it. She gave the matter some thought. When she had an idea she went looking for Pa.

She found him up in the kitchen, Ma cowering in the corner. "Pa?" He rounded on her, arm ready to strike. Before he said or did anything she started to talk. "I been thinking about it Pa and bees would be hard to steal cause they'd be mad. And them keps are heavy this late in the season, full of honey as they are. So maybe it's nearby, you know, 'cause the thief had to get away from the mad bees."

211

Pa narrowed his eyes at her. Lily held her breath until he unloosed his fist. "That's a real good idea, Lily gal."

"Yep. And wouldn't they head for Deep Road? Cause they couldn't use our road?"

Pa agreed. The two of them set off to search. They found the kep sitting on a downed tree, just in front of the gully that ran along Deep Road. It was exactly how Lily had seen it in her head.

She'd never forgotten that day and not only because Pa hugged her and told her how smart she was. After that, she found that she could sometimes find lost things if she concentrated really hard. Sometimes she thought she could sense something else, like a person barely out of her sight range, but not always. She didn't tell anyone her secret, nor think it would ever amount to anything. Not until later. When she had her hard times.

One thing she'd learned through the hard times was that no one would take care of her. She relied on only herself. Men would say pretty things because they wanted her. Wanted to own her, control her and use her. Until they got bored and didn't want her anymore. Then a woman got thrown away like so much garbage.

But money bought safety. She learned to make a good living as a spiritualist. In fact, she could live off what she made doing readings and séances. But she didn't want to just get by. One thing life taught her was that the quiet times, the good times were only breaks between disasters. And disasters required a nest egg.

So she used men while they used her. And she put every penny she got from those men in a safe place. One day she'd

have enough money and she'd disappear again. She'd go looking for her baby, her baby who wasn't a baby anymore, but a
five-year-old child. She'd find her child one day. Somehow.
The money would help. People talked when you offered them
money. Then she'd go west, all the way to San Francisco.
They'd start over. She'd buy a house and support her child
herself. No more looking for a man to do it. She'd set up shop
as a spiritualist. There were always mothers who wanted to
talk to their dead children. She'd help those women and she'd
be a mother. And finally, she'd be safe.

Chapter 21

January 23, 1862
Kalamazoo and Battle Creek

The next morning Kate walked to Kalamazoo Union High School, having timed her arrival for a few minutes after when classes began. She left Monty in the hotel room on the premise that schools and dogs didn't mix well.

The building itself was a surprise. Public high schools were still controversial in most of the country and here, in this small town on the Michigan frontier stood a grand, two-story, brick school building. The tall, arched windows hinted at a well lit and healthy school at odds with her image of cramped, smoky country schoolhouses. Kate mounted the grand staircase and pulled open one of the two double doors. She found herself in a foyer with two sets of stairs, one going up and one going down. She chose up and at the top of the stairs found a door marked OFFICE.

Kate entered, expecting to find someone who looked like both a school teacher and a Miss Bird. Someone tall and slim, with glasses perched on the end of a beaky nose.

"How can I help you, my dear," came a voice from behind the counter.

Kate peered over the barrier, thinking the woman was on the floor for some inexplicable reason. Instead she found a tiny woman, no taller than a ten year old girl. The woman's head popped up, the face attached to it smiling like a friendly jack-in-the-box, complete with rosy pink circles on her cheeks. Miss Bird had a box behind the counter that made her much taller.

Kate tried not to smile. "Mr. Gibbs at the Gazette suggested I speak to a Miss Bird."

"I am she," the lady trilled. "In all my glory." Miss Bird leaned on the counter as if their exchange was the most fascinating thing that had ever happened to her. "And why did the lovely Mr. Gibbs suppose you need me?"

Kate held her hand out over the counter. Miss Bird took it. "My name is Kate Warne and I am an operative for the Pinkerton Detective Agency. I am in Kalamazoo on a case."

Miss Bird froze, mid-handshake. "You are a detective? Like in a novel?" She pronounced the word novel as if it had quite a few more o's in it than it did.

Kate couldn't resist. She laughed. "I am. It's pretty neat isn't it?"

Miss Bird leaned back in amazement. Kate worried she'd fall off her box. "I should say so. But there are more things in heaven and earth than are dreamt of in my philosophy." She tittered a little, then leaned forward again. "And you're detecting in little ole Kalamazoo?"

Kate nodded. "One of my first cases was the Lily Nettleton case."

Before she continued Miss Bird chimed in. "Oh, that was so awful. Heartbreaking really. Poor Polly. She worked here

216

for two years. Poor, poor Polly. Everywhere she went people would whisper about her crazy sister behind her back. And sometimes to her face. It was awful for the poor girl. Not that it wasn't awful for the husband and father, but still . . . ." Miss Bird's face fell

Kate nodded. "It's easier to feel sorry for the living."

"True. But it's more than that. I always thought there was something wrong with that family. Polly was a nice young woman, but she had something broken inside of her. She seemed disconnected like. And her mother, don't get me started on that Mrs. Nettleton. I don't like those pale, mealy-mouthed, weak women. They get people to do things for them by performing weakness. Only it's not a performance. I don't know. I don't understand it. It's a kind of manipulation if you ask me. But Mother was friends with Mrs. Nettleton before she married. Mother says she was different then. Mother was none too fond of Mr. Nettleton."

Kate nodded but didn't say anything. Miss Bird didn't seem to need her input.

"Now Polly, she isn't like her mother, but she isn't like Lily either. Lily was larger and brighter than most people, more vivid if you know what I mean. The way Mother talks, Mrs. Nettleton used to be like that, back before Mr. Nettleton broke her spirit. Polly though, well no sister could stand next to Lily and not be in her shadow.

"So where is Polly now?"

Miss Bird chuckled. "The girl showed some sense and left Kalamazoo. She's teaching down in Battle Creek. Nice town, nice folks and people there don't care so much that she's a Nettleton. I recommended her for the job myself, I'm that fond of the girl." Miss Bird pressed her lips together and shook

217

her head. "But she doesn't come back to visit. Too many bad memories, I expect." For the first time in their conversation, Miss Bird looked less than jolly.

Kate fetched Monty from the hotel and took the 12:15 train to Battle Creek. The town was only thirty miles from Kalamazoo and they made the trip in under two hours. A porter at the depot found her a cab and directed her driver to take her to the high school.

The cab driver stopped in front of a large, two-story wooden building. Kate paid him and asked him to wait.

She found the school office and spoke to the principle, a slim, spectacle-wearing man with none of Miss Bird's charm. He told her Miss Nettleton taught mathematics and had done so for several years now. He agreed to meet Kate after classes let out for the day and escort her to his math teacher's classroom.

Kate and Monty wiled away an hour in a tea shop on the town's main street. Kate ordered two roast beef sandwiches, one bowl of vegetable soup and one pot of tea. A shopkeeper, who looked like a Quaker grandmother, brought Monty a bowl of water along with the food. Guessing Kate didn't intend to eat two sandwiches herself she sat one sandwich before Monty, then stood back to admire the haste at which he consumed it. The grandmotherly woman and Kate had a friendly chat about dogs they'd known and loved.

Not for the first time, Kate noticed that traveling with Monty meant she was rarely without someone to talk to. She suspected most people wanted to talk to strangers but felt awkward about it. A little dog, especially one wearing a green wool coat, gave people a reason to talk to her. It was kind of nice.

At 3:30 Kate once more stood before the principal. She had Monty buttoned into her coat, his head sticking out like a weird canine appendage. He ignored her doggie accessory and led her upstream against the tide of boisterous students eager to leave school. As they crested the stairs a small scuffle between two boys broke out in the hall. The principal pushed Kate toward a door marked '204' before hustling off to intercede, muttering about how fights between teenage boys were not unlike dogfights, more sound and fury than real violence.

Kate opened the classroom door and poked her head in. A slim, brown-haired woman sat at the desk in the front of the room. "Excuse me, are you Miss Nettleton? Polly Nettleton?"

The young woman looked up, startled at Kate's voice.

The woman's resemblance to Ellen Winslow left Kate momentarily speechless. She remembered Miss Bird's description of Polly, as a shadow copy of her sister Lily, but that description did Polly a disservice. Where Lily's hair was lush and a gleaming sable brown so dark it looked black, Polly's was the soft brown of a Jersey cow. Behind wire-rimmed spectacles Polly's eyes were the color of storm clouds and her figure as lithe as a willow tree. Kate could see how Polly would pale in Lily's shadow, but only because Lily's beauty was so melodramatic and Polly's so quietly lovely.

The young woman put down her pen. "Can I help you?"

Kate introduced herself and asked a question that seemed more than a little redundant. "Are you Polly Nettleton?"

"I am." The pretty teacher gripped her desk with both hands, her fingers white with pressure.

"I'm sorry to interrupt your work," Kate said. "But I am hoping to ask you some questions about your sister Lily."

"Lily? Why?" The young woman squeaked when she spoke. She jerked herself to her feet, knocking her chair back in her haste.

Kate hurried around the desk and grabbed the back of Miss Nettleton's chair to keep it from spilling her over. "Careful." She waited a moment and then added, "I'm not here to harm you. I first investigated your sister's case back in '57 and I missed something. I'm looking for the truth and I'm hoping you can help me find it."

Miss Nettleton made a dismissive sound. "The truth? No one has ever wanted the truth about Lily. People just want to point fingers and feel superior."

Kate pulled one of the student chairs over to Miss Nettleton's desk. She unbuttoned her coat, releasing Monty to explore the classroom. "Would you tell me the truth? About your sister and the murders?"

Miss Nettleton yanked open one of her bottom drawers. She drew out a cookie tin and a metal plate and put them on the desk. "You might as well call me Polly." She put some cookies on the plate and offered it to Kate, then she tossed one to Monty, who caught it and swallowed it with no noticeable chewing. "I swore I'd never talk about Lily."

Kate took a cookie and bit into it, congratulating herself on her un-Monty-like restraint. Oatmeal Raisin. Her favorite. She said so.

"Mine too," Polly said. "Ma makes them for me. She brings cookies when she visits."

"I met your mother yesterday to ask her some questions. She didn't say much."

"Strangers frighten Ma. And she can't talk about anything important. She just can't. Pa beat her voice out of her."

"Your father beat your mother?" Kate wasn't surprised. Mrs. Nettleton seemed too much like an abused animal.

Polly fiddled with the cookie plate for a moment, then took a deep breath and spoke. "I might as well tell you everything. She's long gone and you'll never find her. Not Lily. She has a streak of iron in her Ma and I don't have." She looked up at Kate, her eyes pleading. "I've never spoken to anyone about any of this."

Kate wondered. Should she tell this young woman she suspected Lily was in Rochester? But if she did, Polly might not talk. But Kate might be able to use what Polly told her to convict Lily of murder. "I can't make any promises of secrecy or anything like that."

"I understand. Yes, Pa beat Ma. He beat us all, but he beat Ma the worst. Pa liked everything just so and he made sure none of us ever met his standard, but Ma set him off him the worst. He made sure pretty much everything she did was wrong. He liked it that way. Him the Lord of the Farm, his women all frightened subjects, scurrying around trying to please him. It was the only thing that made him happy."

Kate nodded again. "I've met men like that. My ex-husband used to hit me. He'd get this funny look on his face like he was happy and mad at the same time."

"Yeah. I've seen that face. Pa had it too." Polly looked down at her lap.

Kate waited.

Polly wrang her hands like a wet dishrag. "What I'm about to tell you is awful. Ma and I have never talked about that night. Or anything else that matters."

Kate waited some more. The clock ticked in the background, seeming as loud as a series of gunshots.

Polly spoke, not looking up from her lap. "When Lily was about fourteen, she filled out. You know what I mean." Polly cupped hands out in front of her chest.

Kate nodded.

"Pa gave her own room. He emptied Ma's upstairs storage room to do it. At first, Lily was happy, but after a while, she wasn't. It was like the life dripped out of her, little by little. And she wouldn't tell me what was wrong. Then one night Pa came to my room. He wanted to . . . ." Lily stopped. She hunched her shoulders and pressed her lips together, as if to stop up the words in her mouth.

Kate's heart broke for this girl and her sister. "I know what he wanted Polly. You don't have to say it."

"The thing is," Polly looked up, catching Kate's eyes. "Lily stopped him. She came into my room and she stopped him. He said he was tired of her. Tired of how she always fought him, not like a real woman who understood her duty. Polly said she'd quit fighting him, but only if he left me alone."

Kate waited a moment. What did one say in moments like this? "Did he leave you alone after that?"

Tears leaked down Polly's face in mute rivulets. "She protected me and I let her. So I wouldn't have to. So she had to. I'm so ashamed."

Kate wanted to throw something at the wall, break something valuable. Instead, she patted Polly's hand. "You have nothing to be ashamed of. Neither does your sister." Polly opened her top desk drawer and drew out a handkerchief. She rubbed her face with it, scrubbing at herself like she was trying to remove a pesky stain. "There's more. Lily ran away to marry Mr. Gosford. I guess she had to get away from home. But she left Pa a note. I found it. She said if he touched me she'd come back and kill him. He must have believed her because he never did. Touch me, I mean. Then one night, the doctor came to the door. He said Lily had lost her baby and needed our help. We got in the wagon and drove right over there, Ma, Pa and me, even though it was snowing to beat the band."

Polly paused again. She had the handkerchief squeezed in one hand, her fingers white with the tightness of her grip. "Mr. Gosford was in a temper when we got there. He was so much like Pa it scared me. He was angry with Lily and yelling at all of us. Said she'd failed at her sacred duty to make him a son. He asked the doctor how long before she'd be breeding again. That's what he called it. Breeding. The doctor said Lily was in a delicate condition and needed some rest. Mr. Gosford got so mad he yelled at Pa. Said Pa sold him bad stock."

Kate interrupted. "Bad stock?"

Lily nodded. "Like Lily was a milk cow or plow horse. He wanted his money back. See, Mr. Gosford paid Pa for Lily. And he was right mad that she wouldn't be doing her wifely duties. Pa said he bought her fair and square, but Mr. Gosford said he'd bought her for sons and for the pleasure of her. He said now he was used to it and had to have it. I didn't understand what he was saying. Not then. So Pa says to him, I'll leave you Polly to fill in for Lily while she gets better. I figured Pa was leaving me to help Lily with the chores, cooking and

223

churning and the like. Then Pa says he'll need more money though, on account of me being a virgin. I remember I looked at Ma while they were talking but she just stood there looking at her feet. She never said a word. No. Not Ma."

Polly looked out the window and sighed. "She only once stood up for us and by then it was too late."

Polly stopped talking. The clock ticked in the background.

A part of Kate wanted Polly to continue the story and another part of her wished Polly would quit talking.

The clock ticked and then Polly spoke again. "So Ma and Pa left. Left me with Mr. Gosford. Soon as they left he was on me. I screamed and pushed him away. That must have woken Lily cause he had me on the table and was . . . . Ah . . . Having his way with me when he jerked and fell to the floor. And there she was behind him, our old cast iron skillet in her hands, her nightgown all bloody cause she hit him so hard it splattered his brains. She leaned over and whacked him twice more. To be sure I guess. After that, she cut him some. His thing. She cut his thing." Polly looked down at her lap, unable to go on.

Kate had seen the Sheriff's report. At the time she believed the mutilation was the work of an evil woman. Now she thought it was too bad the bastard hadn't been alive when Lily cut his pecker off. It would have served him right.

Polly slumped in her chair, as exhausted as if she'd had a hard day's work. Which Kate guessed she had.

"Lily helped me clean myself up and then we rode home. Ma was sitting there at the table like she was waiting for us. Lily told me to stay downstairs with Ma. She grabbed ma's fry pan and took it upstairs. When she came back downstairs, the

224

pan had blood all over it. She bashed in Pa's head, same as she did Mr. Gosford's."

Kate shifted in her chair. She'd heard a lot of stories during her career as a Pinkerton, but never anything this horrifying. Nothing even came close. Shame flooded through her. She'd been sure Lily killed for financial gain and because she was a bad woman. And of course, the Sheriff didn't know any better. People didn't talk about this stuff, did they? How many families held such horrors? How many women never said a word?

Polly wiped her face with her handkerchief again. "And then Ma did the only right thing she ever did for us. She gave Lily the money. Pa's money. I suspect it was the money Mr. Gosford paid for Lily. And Ma told Lily to go. Me and Ma waited a day before we rode to town and told the Sheriff. And we pretended we hadn't heard about Lily's husband. It took another day for the Sheriff to figure out he was dead. By then Lily was long gone and we were free of Pa."

The expression of fierce joy on Polly's face made Kate want to weep.

Chapter 22

January 23, 1862
Rochester, New York

"Billy is with us now," Lily announced to the table, using her best mysterious voice. "My dear boy, your mother is here. Would you like to speak to her?" She waited for a long moment, stiffened for a moment, before slumping into a shrunken, smaller version of herself. "Mama?" Lily's voice was high pitched and childish.

A soft brown wren of a woman leaned forward, careful not to break the circle of hands. "Billy? Is that you dear?"

"Yes, Mama."

"Are you all right, baby?"

"Oh yes, Mama. There are ever so many children to play with. And the games are grand."

"Do you miss me, Billy?" The mother's voice quavered.

"No, Mama. Because I am always with you. I watch over you and I love you every day."

Mrs. Lewis let out a quiet sob, lifted her chin and smiled.

Lily tipped up her left eyelid and took a quick peek at Mrs. Lewis. The poor woman. She'd been through so much. She'd given birth to five children and lost two in infancy. Then last summer her four-year-old son Billy died, a victim of yellow fever. That the woman managed to get out of bed and take care of her remaining two children was a source of eternal wonder to Lily.

"Mama?"

"Yes, dear?"

"I am always with you. I wish with all my heart you would not be sad every day. You used to sing around the house. If you would sing once more I would hear you."

"I'll try baby, I will. I miss you baby, but if you're happy then Mama's not so sad. Not anymore."

Kate peeked at Mrs. Lewis. She looked as relieved as she sounded.

Lily straightened her spine and opened her eyes. In her own voice, she announced, "The connection has broken." She sounded like a woman waking from a long sleep. "Did he come through Mrs. Lewis?"

The four ladies nodded with happy enthusiasm. Mrs. Lewis beamed at Lily. "It's as you said, Mrs. Winslow. He's there, in the afterlife, but he's here too. With me."

The ladies still held each other's hands. It was as if they were afraid to let go, afraid to lose their connection. These poor mothers of dead children. Was there anything sadder? "Death is not an end, but a change in being. Remember the tenets of spiritualism say we can communicate with the spirits because the soul continues to exist after the body no longer does."

"I wish I had the skill to talk to my Billy like you do Mrs. Winslow." Mrs. Lewis's voice shook again, as she were about to cry.

Lily smiled at her. "Oh, but you can Mrs. Lewis. You can talk to him every day if you wish though I recommend you speak to your living daughters and Mr. Lewis as well. You won't hear Billy's answers. But you know your Billy, so you can imagine his answers as you talk to him. And remember, I don't talk to Billy. I channel him. He talks to you because he wants to. I am the instrument. Don't you see? If you were the instrument, you'd be no use to him. He wants to talk to you, not me."

An older woman, her dark hair shot through with grey strands said, "I talk to Janet every day, Mrs. Lewis and she hears me. I am sure of it."

Lily smiled at the older woman. "You have great faith Mrs. Armbruster and a soul that continues to learn and accept new things. We should all strive to continue to learn about our world and accept that which can be known, by any means, both material and spiritual."

The ladies murmured their assent, squeezing each other's hands as they did.

Lily wasn't sure that everything she said made sense, but she didn't care much either way. Three Wednesdays a month she held these special séances just for mothers. She helped them with their grief and their fear for their dead children's souls. Their ministers and priests couldn't help them, nor did their families because they didn't understand a woman's grief. If they had, the women wouldn't be here.

Sometimes a lady would ask to bring her husband to the Wednesday circle, but Lily always said no. These evenings were for mothers. In her heart of hearts, she felt sure no man grieved the death of a child, not like mothers did. In Lily's experience, men faked most of their feelings. They had to because they had so few feelings outside their own self-interest.

Sure she was faking too. Billy didn't really come to her tonight. Their children never did. Lily didn't know if the dead children were in the afterlife or just gone. Part of her didn't much care either way. Her business was with the living, not the dead. She helped mothers no one else helped. Because no one had ever helped her.

Chapter 23

January 24-25, 1862
Detroit, Michigan

*K*ate returned to Detroit with a new view of the Black Widow case. She struggled to comprehend the horror that had been the Nettleton women's lives. It was also clear to Kate that in marrying Gosford Lily had gone from the frying pan into the fire. That was the problem with all these high-flown ideas about womanhood. The upholders of the social convention would have it that women were too delicate for equality, delicate being a code word for weak and inferior. Instead, or so the theory went, husbands protected a woman's rights. Which was all well and nice for the women who wanted to be only wives and mothers and had sober, kind husbands to support them. But what about women who wanted an education or a profession? Or women married to tyrants?

And how many women were married to scoundrels and wife beaters? Wasn't a system of male superiority a system that encouraged the abuse of women? How many men were strong enough to resist the temptation to abuse their power? It was why, though she loved and admired Hazzard, she didn't want to be his wife. Even if he continued to treat her as his equal, the law said he would own her and everything that was hers. Legally he'd be her master. Kate felt sure he'd be a kind master, but benevolent slavery was still slavery.

And what of the men who were not benevolent? The men like Mr. Nettleton and Mr. Gosford? The law said they were within their rights to treat their wives and children anyway they pleased. And though the law frowned upon incest, a wife couldn't testify against her husband, nor could children. So both the law and social custom sanctioned what had happened to Lily. Certainly, the Sheriff hadn't asked a lot of questions. And neither had she for that matter. And why not? Why had it been so easy for her to believe Lily was a monster?

Kate found herself almost as angry at Mrs. Nettleton as she was at Mr. Nettleton and Mr. Gosford. She should have protected her daughters. Part of Kate wanted to go back to Mrs. Nettleton's door and tell her how awful she was. Another part of her recognized Mrs. Nettleton as yet another victim of a system in which women didn't have much of a chance.

Kate continued contemplating these questions as she moved through the Detroit train station. The city omnibus line took her from the port terminal to the Michigan Exchange Hotel, dropping her right at the hotel's gleaming double doors.

Her room was nearly as fancy as the Osborn House in Rochester, lacking only an in-room water closet. The sheets were snow white, the mattress soft and accommodating and management didn't mind adding a small dog to their guest list. The hotel also had a well-run dining room. Kate and Monty ate a monumental dinner of squab, roast potatoes, Brussels sprouts and bread pudding. Kate ate hers from a china plate at the table and Monty gobbled his from a bowl under the table.

While she ate dinner, she perused the newspaper for war news. In Tennessee, the Confederates had surrendered Fort Henry, which from the article's tone Kate guessed was a great victory for the Union. Also, Mr. Lincoln had refused the King of Siam's offer of a dozen war elephants. The Newspaper quoted the president as having said, "United States geography does not favor the multiplication of the elephant." Kate mind boggled at the image of elephants on a modern battlefield. She'd known elephants in the circus, including the great Lallah Rookh, and never found them to be creatures that enjoyed loud sounds like explosions or gunshots. Elephants, for all their size, were gentle, peace-loving creatures. Thank goodness Mr. Lincoln had declined the King's offer.

The next morning Kate examined her case notes one more time. She'd read and reread them so many times she had them committed to memory, but she checked them once more. She noted the address she had for the Reverend Bland's housekeeper, fastened on Monty's coat and together they set off to conquer the day.

Kate showed the address to a waiting cabman who took her across town. The trip took only a few minutes, but given the temperature, Kate thought the cab fare was money well spent. An extra dollar convinced the cabbie to wait for her.

This house bore only a passing resemblance to the neat little dove grey cottage she'd visited years before. Beneath the snow the paint peeled in scabrous flakes, revealing glimpses of a disreputable green paint underneath. Kate picked her way up the icy walk and knocked on the door. Inside a dog barked and a child yelled. Monty growled. Kate shushed him and waited. A woman with a baby on her hip opened the door.

"Yes?" she asked, glancing back over her shoulder. Shrieks came from inside the house. She hollered, "You all be quiet for a wee minute." The baby grinned a single toothed smile at Kate.

"I'm sorry to bother you. I'm looking for Mrs. Cawley. Does she still live here?"

"Oh, heavens no," the woman said, pushing a wisp of loose hair off her forehead with the back of her hand. "My Johnny bought this house over a year ago." She looked over her shoulder again and yelled, "Junior, you let go of your sister's hair right now."

Before the woman closed the door Kate asked, "Do you know where she is now?"

The lady scrunched her eyes closed. "She left a forwarding address for mail. I'll go see if I can find it." She closed the door, leaving Kate standing on the frozen stoop. Kate turned around and looked at her cab driver. He shrugged his shoulders at her in an unspoken question. She held up her mitten-covered hand to suggest she'd be quick.

It was five cold minutes before the door opened again. The woman still had the pink-cheeked baby on her hip. "Here," she said, thrusting a scrap of paper at her and slammed the door shut once more.

Thinking it could be worse, Kate returned to the cab. She held the scrap of paper up to her driver. "Can you take me here?"

He took the paper from her and glanced at it. "I can. You sure you want to?"

234

"Why not?"

He shook his head. "That's Dark Town. I don't like to take my horse down there."

Kate held up two silver dollars. He changed his mind.

Her driver took her and Monty to Lafayette Street, where dark-skinned men and women did indeed fill the sidewalks. The people Kate saw seemed to be neatly dressed and minding their own business. She saw a prosperous-looking smithy, a busy cooperage, two churches and several boarding houses that looked old, but not particularly run down. Her cabman stopped in front of one such house.

Kate hopped out. "If you wait, there's another dollar in it for you." She marched off, not waiting for his reply. Either he'd wait or he wouldn't and she gained nothing by appearing weak and needy.

She knocked on the boarding house door. This time a lady she recognized opened the door. "Mrs. Cawley?"

"And what if I am?" The lady gripped the door like she feared Kate would steal it from her.

"I'm Kate Warne," she started.

Before she could continue Mrs. Cawley threw open the door. "I remember you now. You're that lady detective. You're letting the cold in." She stood back and opened the door wider.

Kate stepped into the house, Monty right behind her. The air was redolent of boiled cabbage and stale beer.

Mrs. Cawley motioned for Kate to follow her. They walked down the hall to the kitchen which was warmer if even more redolent of cabbage. "I've come down in the world since we last met, haven't I?"

Kate appraised Mrs. Cawley. Where once she'd been merely stout, now she was run to fat. Her skin appeared blotchy and her hands reddened and rough, her hair grey and fly away.

Mrs. Cawley pulled out a wooden kitchen chair for Kate. "No need to say so dear. I've got a mirror. It was that devil Bland what brought me to this. May he burn in hell."

Kate startled at the lady's vehemence. "Reverend Bland?"

The lady snorted. "Reverend, my arse. He were no more a man of God than any other whore monger and card cheat. Why your little dog there's more of a gentleman than the young master."

Kate couldn't contain her astonishment. "The last time we spoke you sang his praises to the heavens."

"He were still paying me in those days, wasn't he? Little bastard run out on me like he did all his women. Serves me right I suppose. I don't owe him my loyalty and lies, not no more."

"What happened?" Kate tried to sound like an eager gossip.

"Well, it was like this." She settled back in her chair to tell her story. "Young Edwin was always a scoundrel. When he was a lad he got himself thrown out of Harvard for cheating. His mother brought him home, believing his tale of innocence, but he gambled and drank away his allowance. She, being a pious woman, cut him off without a penny. So the scoundrel announced he'd given up his life of sin and to prove it he enrolled in seminary school and then got himself ordained. His fool of a Mama forgave him everything. She gave

236

him a big allowance which he used to recommence his life of whoring and drinking and gambling."

"Where did you come into this scheme?"

"Ah, well. He had to keep his vices secret from his mama and anyone who might tell her. So he figured that it was more discrete to set up a little house to keep his whores in. And paying me was cheaper than paying the bordellos. He'd find a desperate young woman and seduce her into living there with him, with me as the housekeeper you see. So he saved money and had all the pleasure he wanted. Plus, he liked ruining them. He'd tell them he loved them and that he wanted to marry them. When they asked when he'd say as soon as his mother died and left him his fortune. And the fools would believe him. He'd have his fun and when he got tired of 'em he'd disappear west for a few months. I'd disappear right after him, go visit my sister in Buffalo and the poor things would wake up to an empty house. A few weeks of that and they'd pack their bags and go. Then I'd come home and he'd start it all over again with a new girl."

"That's terrible," Kate said without thinking.

"Ain't it though?" Mrs. Cawley's agreement came out sounding cheerfully admiring. "He was a rascally man. But in the end, it caught up to him. After your young miss, his mother caught wind of his schemes. She rewrote her will again and cut him without a penny though he didn't know it till after she died. He and I held out for a while, him always sure she'd die and he'd inherit the lot. But the old biddy up and kicked off and left it all to the Methodists. Can you believe that?"

She chuckled in glee. "He didn't get one red cent. Oh, he was angry at that. He blamed that girl. He thought she'd told his mother. He stomped around this house for days saying he'd get his revenge on her. I never seen him like that before. Ooooweee, he were mad."

Mrs. Cawley sat back in her chair with a satisfied thump. The tale of her master's downfall disturbed her not one whit.

Kate marveled that this woman would tell a story like this and not feel one tiny bit of shame or regret. "What happened to him?"

"Doan know. He up and disappeared one day—stuck me with all the household bills. Running from his debts, no doubt. I sold that little house, though it weren't rightly mine to sell, and bought this place. It ain't much, but it provides me with an income and the colored folk 'round here are right nice to me. So it didn't turn out all that bad for Mother Cawley after all."

"What can you tell me about Lily Nettleton?"

"Who?"

"Lily Nettleton. The girl."

"Oh, her. She said she her name was Lily Winslow. Or that's what she told the young master and me."

Kate nearly peed herself. "Winslow? She was calling herself Winslow?"

"Yeah. Didn't I say that before?" To Mrs. Cawley's credit, she looked mystified at this line of questioning.

"No. You never mentioned a last name."

The lady grinned at Kate. "Back then I mighta not a tole you on purpose. I was still thinking the young master was my meal ticket."

Kate smiled back at Mrs. Cawley to show her there were no hard feelings. And to be honest, the lady's ebullient approach to chicanery was the tiniest bit charming. "So, back to the question. What can you tell me about Lily?" What she didn't add was, 'that you didn't tell me before.'

"I felt sorry for the girl, to tell the truth. The young master could hardly keep his hands off her and nature took its course. She caught pregnant. When that happened Edwin told his usual tale about having to go minister out west, but how he'd be back soon and they'd be married. Most of 'em believed him, but that Lily saw right through him. I don't think she ever believed his nonsense. I'd catch her looking at him sometimes with this look. It were hard to describe, but I remember thinking she was on to him from the start."

Kate was still processing the part about Lily being pregnant. "What happened to the baby?"

Mrs. Cawley shook her head. "No idea. The girl didn't miss but one of her courses and announced she was pregnant. She were gone not long after that. Drugged me and the young master and stole off into the night with the household silver and my house money to boot. And let me tell you, Edwin was furious. He'd never had one of his gals get the best of him afore." Mrs. Cawley's eyes widened in delight at this admission.

"What did he do?"

"Well, like I said, he raged around the house blaming the girl. He kept saying when his mother died and he got all her loot he'd go looking for the girl and teach her a lesson. Then his mother died for real and he didn't get one red cent. He were stupid if you ask me. His old mother would a been mad if he'd married Lily, but grandbabies have a way of mending fences. And that girl woulda helped out. Like I said, she was a smart one and she'd a made friends with the old lady. I think that's why the young master kept that girl away from his mother. He was afraid they'd like each other."

"But if he wanted the money why not marry the girl and let her soften up his mother?"

"Ah," she said with a dismissive wave. "Edwin wasn't the settling down kind. He were a rascal good and proper. He liked his freedom and doing what he wanted. His mother gave him everything, let him do and say whatever he wanted. He got so he thought all of life ought to be like that. Why, when he found himself disinherited he came near unglued. I feared for his sanity. He swore he'd get back all the property that girl stole from him and he'd teach her a lesson."

Kate tapped the table, mostly to keep herself from tapping the side of Mrs. Cawley's head. She didn't seem quite so charming now.

"So he took advantage of her, lied to her, got what he wanted, impregnated her and abandoned her? And you helped him?" Kate meant to keep her voice even but heard her voice get loud.

Mrs. Cawley stared open-mouthed at Kate.

"Thank you for the truth." Kate pushed her chair back with a jerk and stood. Monty bounced to his feet. "And may God have mercy on your soul."

Kate scooped up Monty and marched out Mrs. Cawley's boarding house, slamming the door behind her as she stomped away. It was stupid and childish. And not as satisfying as she'd have liked. When she got back to her hotel room, Kate threw herself on the bed and tried not to cry for a girl who'd been betrayed over and over again by the very people who should have protected her.

Chapter 24

January 26-27, 1862
Cincinnati, Ohio

While she rode the train Kate did the math, checking the old case file for dates. Alexander Gibson's second wife, whoever she was, killed him six months after Lily Winslow left Detroit and the care of Reverend Bland. She stared at the dates. Was it possible that Lily was already pregnant when she married Gibson? No one ever mentioned a pregnancy, not the Gibson's son who'd hired them, not any of the hotel employees, no one. She must have lost the baby, either by accident or design, before or soon after she married Gibson.

The alternative was too ominous. If Lily carried the baby to term, what happened to it? More worrisome, at least as far as Kate's investigation was concerned, why had no one ever mentioned that Mr. Gibson's accused murderer and wife was pregnant. It would have required a massive cover-up, one orchestrated by the Gibson's heirs. And why do that?

When she arrived in Cincinnati Kate checked into Gibson House, more because she was familiar with the hotel than because she might get any useful answers from anyone at the hotel. If Alexander Gibson's son forced his employees into silence about his step-mother's condition five years ago, they weren't likely to talk now.

Her first impulse was to re-interview everyone who'd been at the hotel in '57. It wasn't a good impulse. She needed more information. Something she could use as a pry bar. She needed to turn this case on its head. What if she started with the premise that Lily had been pregnant when she left the young reverend?

Kate checked her reflection in the mirror. The brown dress looked a little travel weary but it would have to do. "What would she have done, huh Monty?"

Monty cocked his head at Kate.

"Well, you're a man-dog, so it's not a fair question." Kate bit her lower lip and looked at Monty. "If I were pregnant with one man's baby and married to another, I'd not leave anything to chance. I'd find myself a midwife who would help me with the pregnancy and the husband. Right?"

Monty didn't have an opinion either way. She stood and pushed back her shoulders. "Well, pup, it's a big job. We best get started.

He stared at her.

"You're right. Breakfast first."

By mid-day, Kate's feet hurt and her whole body ached with cold. She'd trudged around the city for hours in below zero weather. To make matters worse, the wind cut through her new coat like a knife through warm butter. Every time she was outside she'd button Monty into her coat, but the bitter cold made a mockery of their efforts to stay warm.

She started her day at the city library where a grumpy librarian showed her the shelf that held city directories. Kate took down the 1857 directory and copied the name of every midwife into her little notebook. Next, she checked those names against last year's city directory, adding addresses to the names.

Once she left the library, Kate hired a cabman to drive her from address to address. She sat in converted parlors and clinic waiting rooms with dozens of pregnant women, many of them towing wailing children. After her third midwife, the combined infant misery had Kate considering a liquid lunch. It got worse when they ventured into Cincinnati's poorer neighborhoods, where the women looked increasingly overwhelmed and the children increasingly ragged.

She worked her list until it grew dark, feeling more downhearted every time someone said no to her. Too cold and too tired to go on, she admitted defeat and had the cabman take her back to the hotel. She and Monty walked straight to the dining room where she had soup and a double brandy and he had a bowl of water and a piece of turkey. She'd crossed nine midwives off her list today, with three more still to go. She wondered if she was wasting her time. There was no evidence Lily had been pregnant in Cincinnati. All she had was the word of a woman whose word wasn't worth much. Still, it felt right to her. Any healthy young woman might get pregnant in that situation. And the pregnancy might explain the spectacular implosion of her second marriage.

Kate finished her soup and went to bed.

The next morning she set out again. She'd made it through the Rs yesterday with a visit to Mrs. Reston's clinic. She had Mrs. Schmidt, Mrs. Telford and Mrs. Wallis left.

A hansom cab driver drove Kate to the heart of Cincinnati's Little Germany. They passed storefronts that sold sausages, rye bread, pastries, and pickled cabbage. There seemed to be a brewery on every corner, each sending yeasty aromas into the air. Kate's stomach rumbled. She promised herself she'd stop at a bakery after the next clinic and buy herself a treat. Monty agreed with her idea, or at least the set of his ears when she said 'cookie' suggested as much.

Kate and Monty entered a small storefront marked only by a small paper sign in the window that said

Mrs. Schmidt's Cottage

Midwifery & Ladies Medicine

There were two ladies, both hugely pregnant, in the waiting room, but no clerk. The room didn't even have a desk. It contained only a dozen chairs and, in one corner, a basket of worn toys. Kate took a seat near the tiny coal stove, unbuttoned her coat and released Monty. He sniffed his way around the room and having found no abandoned sausages, crawled under her chair for a nap. Kate curled and uncurled her toes in her damp boots, trying to warm up her feet while she waited. After about ten minutes a young woman stepped through the door at the back of the room. She wiped her hands on her clean, white apron and pulled a notebook from the apron pocket. "Mrs. Abel?"

One of the pregnant ladies heaved herself to her feet. Kate stepped up to the young woman. "I'm sorry to interrupt. I see that you're busy, but I wonder if Mrs. Schmidt might spare a moment to answer a few questions for me? I promise it won't take over five minutes."

244

The girl, as blond and blue-eyed as a Swiss milkmaid, gave Kate an up and down glance that made it clear she suspected nothing but the worst. "I'll ask her." The two of them disappeared down the hall, forcing Kate to return to her chair. Why hadn't she brought a book along? She decided that if she failed here, she'd go to a bookstore and buy something to read. Then she'd go back to her hotel room, snuggle into bed and read the rest of this miserable day away.

A short, heavyset woman, her hair hidden under a voluminous white kerchief, bustled into the waiting room. She seemed like the sort of person who left tiny whirlwinds in her wake wherever she went. "Someone has a question, ja?"

Kate stood. "I do, Mrs. Schmidt."

"Vat do you need?"

"I'm looking for a woman. She would have been pregnant in the spring of 1857. Twenty years old, dark hair, blue, blue eyes. A beautiful young woman married to a rich old man."

Mrs. Schmidt grabbed a handful of her apron and wrung it in her hands. She glanced around and shook her head. "Nein. No woman like dat. Nein." She shook her head so that her kerchief flapped back and forth, turned and fled the room.

Kate looked at the pregnant woman sitting four chairs over.

The lady smiled at Kate. "Mrs. Schmidt is a terrible liar isn't she?"

Kate nodded. "That she is. I think I'll wait." So she did. The girl assistant returned to the waiting room, trailed by two pregnant ladies who left the clinic. The last waiting woman followed the blond assistant out of the room. She saw Kate waiting, but she pretended not to. Another half hour passed. The assistant returned, followed by the last pregnant lady.

245

That lady winked at Kate on her way out, but the assistant ignored her. Kate held her seat. They'd have to contend with her sooner or later.

The light outside failed while Kate waited. Her stomach growled. Monty stared out the window. Kate suspected he was looking for a sausage shop. Finally the inside door opened.

Mrs. Schmidt poked her head out, saw Kate sitting there and shook her head. "I vant you to go avay."

Kate stood. "I need your help."

She shook head. "I von't hurt dat poor girl. Ist no gut."

"I understand. I'm trying to help her too. Could you at least tell me if she had a baby or if you helped her with, you know, the other."

Mrs. Schmidt sighed and turned around. "Follow me. We talk in mine office."

Kate followed the woman down the hall to a small room, crowded with a desk, two tall wooden filing cabinets, a table and two chairs. Mrs. Schmidt motioned Kate to a chair. The German woman dropped into the chair like a woman whose legs wouldn't hold her up one second longer.

Kate waited.

"You have an honest face. And you're nicht ein man. I vill trust you. Dis poor girl, she came to me. I vill never forget her. She vas hard used by her man." She shook her head. "Zuch a terrible thing."

"So she had the baby?"

"Yes. For all de good it did her." Mrs. Schmidt paused again, gathered herself and launched into her tale. When she'd first met Lily the young woman had been calling herself Lillian Gibson or Mrs. Alexander Gibson. She came to Mrs.

246

Schmidt because she was pregnant with another man's child. The newly minted Mrs. Gibson wanted to pass the baby off as her husband's and needed a midwife's help to do it.

This deception didn't bother Mrs. Schmidt one bit. "I see vat the men do to vimmen. Is hard enough to be voman in dis world, ven de men make all da rules for de vimmen. Dose old rich men, day marry pretty girls like dis Lily and dats all good for dem, but vat of de girls?" Mrs. Schmidt shook her head. "I care not for dese rich men who take vat dey vant."

Kate nearly agreed but reminded herself that Alexander had ended up dead and no one deserved that. Well, almost no one. Had Lily's father and first husband deserved death? Was that anyway for a Pinkerton operative to think? Kate suspected not.

Mrs. Schmidt said the problem came when Lily went into labor a month early, which the husband thought was three months early. He'd ignored her pleas to call Mrs. Schmidt and called his doctor instead. The doctor delivered the baby and knew. Which is where the whole plan unraveled. The doctor had a frank talk with Mr. Gibson. Enraged at being cuckolded, Mr. Gibson ordered his second wife sequestered from the staff and from her baby. The next day he presented her with divorce and adoption papers. He told Lily he would not let her keep the baby because he would not have a bastard out in the world with his name.

"So he took her baby away from her and gave it away?"

"Ja, dat's vat da poor girl told me. And ve never did find it," the lady half whispered. "Awful man to steal a mother's child. He deserve vat she did."

In spite of herself, Kate agreed. Mr. Gibson could have let Lily keep her baby. The same lawyer that drew up adoption

247

papers could have instead drawn up papers that signed away the baby's right to the Gibson name and fortune. No, Mr. Gibson took the baby away from Lily for the sheer, cruel pleasure of punishing a woman who disappointed him.

"So what happened?"

"The poor girl, she came to me. After. She vas bleeding and bleeding and, vat you say? Hysterical. She cry and cry and cry."

Mrs. Schmidt explained that Lily had some postpartum complications most probably caused by the doctor's refusal to treat her after he saw the baby. Mrs. Schmidt put Lillian in a friend's boarding house and visited her each day. This friend, a Mrs. Becker, tried to find the baby. She'd checked the Catholic orphanage run by the nuns and the Methodist orphanage just outside of town, but with no luck. No one had a new baby. It didn't help their search that Lillian had never seen the baby, so she couldn't describe it. She didn't even know if she'd had a girl or a boy. Mrs. Schmidt suspected the baby was a boy because Mr. Gibson and been so adamant that no bastard child carry his name. Men didn't get that worked up about girl's names.

"And no one ever came looking for Mrs. Gibson?"

Mrs. Schmidt smiled a grim smile. "Oh, da police, day came and dey asked, but I did not tell. Ever body in da Rhine knew da story of da poor girl and no von tell. Das Deutchers, ve are tender about de babies and de mothers." She shook her head some more, a mulish look on her face.

"In the Rhine?" Kate was confused. Last time she checked she was in Cincinnati.

Mrs. Schmidt waved her arm over her head. "Dis neigh-borhood. Ober den Rhine. You see, Den Rhine is a river in Deutschland and we call dat canal da Rhine. So we are Ober den Rhine."

"You're saying you all hid Lily from the authorities?"

"Ja." She said it like it was obvious anyone would have done the same. "Vouldn't you kill a man who took your baby? Vouldn't anyone?"

Kate nodded. She'd wanted to kill the woman responsible for kidnapping her friend Juba and he was an adult man. She couldn't even begin to imagine how she'd respond if someone took her baby from her. Or maybe she could. And that was the problem.

Kate and Monty checked out of Gibson House that after-noon. They moved down the street to the National Hotel, much to the Gibson House desk clerk's dismay. Kate didn't care. Clearly, Alexander Gibson's son had known about the baby and he'd lied about it. Worse, the son must have forced his employees to lie to the police. He probably threatened them with their jobs. Whatever he'd done, they'd all covered up the truth and in the process made Lily worse than she was.

Though Kate hated to admit it, the judicial system would not have treated Lily any differently if the Gibsons hadn't lied about the baby. Polite society had no pity for women who broke the bounds of respectability. But just what did respecta-ble society propose women like Lily do? Abused by her father and then by her husband, she'd killed to defend herself and her little sister in a world where no one had defended them. Men raped and beat women all the time and no one said boo about it. And a woman pregnant out of wedlock faced ruinous social and economic recrimination. No wonder Lily went looking for a husband after Reverend Bland betrayed her. What choice had she had?

Kate sat in bed in her new hotel room and considered all she'd learned. Really, it had been so much clearer when she'd known less. Lily had been the Black Widow, an evil woman killing innocent men. It was a black and white tale. Maybe that was the problem. People wanted to think good and evil were sharply different. But people weren't that simple.

Kate remembered the Countess, a woman she'd killed last spring, who'd tortured and maimed people for reasons of her own. She'd seemed entirely evil, but maybe she wasn't. Had the Countess any redeeming characteristics? Someone she loved? Some good she did in the world? Kate didn't know. And if she did, did that make killing her a moral offense? Maybe it was, but Kate knew if she had to do it again she wouldn't do anything different. The Countess needed to be put down, much like you had to shoot a rabid dog so it wouldn't hurt anyone.

Kate rubbed one of Monty's silky ears between her thumb and forefinger. What was a Pinkerton detective's job? Was her prime directive to uphold the law? Because if it was the latter, her duty was clear. The law said murdering your rapist, or your sister's rapist was still murder. Murdering a man who stole your child was illegal too. The law didn't even recognize a woman's right to her own children. Children belonged to their fathers. But she was a private detective, not a policeman. Of course, the police didn't hire women, and wasn't that part of the problem too? Men made the entire justice system, for men and white men at that.

If Lily Nettleton and Ellen Winslow were the same person, and Kate would now bet Monty's right paw they were, she'd tried to do the right thing. Her first husband abused her, the second man never intended to marry her and the third reneged on his marriage the first time she disappointed him. So she'd become a murderer. And a spiritualist. Kate thought it was a stupid job, but it was a job open to women and one that allowed for some female authority and power.

So, back to the original question. Did a Pinkerton detective have a responsibility to turn Ellen Winslow over to the authorities as a triple murderer? Or did Kate bear some responsibility, as a private detective and as a woman, to form her own judgments about Lily's moral transgressions? Kate wished Hattie were here to help her clarify this mess. Or Charlotte, or Odetta, or Louisa. This problem called for was one of their kitchen table conferences, but one with just the ladies. One needed other women for these sorts of things.

It was well past midnight when Kate turned down the lamp and snuggled into her blankets. And even then, sleep did not come till near dawn.

Chapter 25

January 27, 1862
Rochester, New York

A knock so forceful it rattled the door startled Lily out of her morning reverie. She put her teacup down and stood. The pounding came again. It was probably Bristol though he rarely knocked. She checked her hair in the little mirror she kept by the door. The door boomed yet again. She pulled it open, ready to chastise whoever stood on the other side. It was, after all, not yet 9 in the morning.

"You Mrs. Ellen Winslow?" The man who asked wore a rough checked coat and a disreputable bowler.

She nodded, unsure what this man was doing at her door.

He held a large brown envelope out to her.

She stared at his red, roughened hands. He thrust the envelope toward her. Without thinking, she took it.

"You've been served," he barked. He turned and stomped down the stairs.

Lily peered after him. What had just happened?

She heard the downstairs front door slam. She closed her own door and leaned against it. After a few long moments Lily took the envelope over to her séance table and sat. She stared at it. Whatever it was, it wasn't good. After a long moment, she popped the sealing wax with her thumbnail and opened the envelope.

She pulled out a sheaf of papers. The top one it read, *From the Law Offices of Milton Waxford, Esq.*

Milton Waxford? She leaned over the papers. *"Under Ohio Penal Code 158 Mrs. Ellen Winslow is accused of common barratry."* She scanned down the page.

"Whereas Mrs. Ellen Winslow has attempted to bring about fraudulent lawsuits, for the purpose of profit, thus encouraging groundless litigation for no better purpose than financial gain and general harassment to the defense. In the courts she is accused by Mr. Abelard Lyon of the crime of barratry. She is to present herself to the court February 6 to answer charges against her person."

Lily stared at the paper in her hand. Abelard was suing her? Men didn't sue her. She sued them. Or she threatened to. And barratry? What was that? She scanned her bookshelf, pulled out her dictionary and paged through the Bs. There it was.

Barratry (n.) 1 Archaic, fraud or gross negligence of a ship's master or crew at the expense of its owners or users. 2. Legal, vexatious or fraudulent litigation or incitement to vexing and fraudulent litigation.

She set the dictionary down and stared blankly out the window. She hadn't defrauded a naval crew that much was sure. But she also hadn't brought her suit against Abelard. She'd promised Miss Warne she'd wait and so she had. They couldn't prosecute her for something she hadn't done, could they? This had to be a mistake.

Maybe Miss Warne hadn't been clear in her letter to Mr. Lyon. Maybe he was heading her off, suing her before she could sue him. It was a smart move, but unnecessary. So this was a mistake. It had to be. She'd go to Abelard's office and explain it to him.

A nauseating worry plagued Lily as she dressed. She tried to dismiss it, but it plucked at her composure as she chose her outfit for the day. She needed to look enticing, but respectable. Abelard wouldn't want her in his office looking like a siren. She chose a light pinkish lavender dress of lightweight wool. The dress had royal purple embroidery around the hem and cuffs, with a matching wide ribbon around her waist. A bow at the small of her back gave the ensemble a piquant femininity. She pulled on her blue velvet coat and chose a deep purple bonnet with a lavender lining. Lily stepped back from her swivel mirror and examined her reflection. Her dark lashes and brows stood out against her pale skin, her eyes flashing purple-blue as they always did when she wore this coat. She nodded to herself. Dressed for battle, she braved the winter day.

Lily stepped into the Arcade, marveling as she always did at its architecture. She could pretend to be a city sophisticate all she wanted, but the wonders offered by Detroit, Cincinnati and Rochester astounded the Kalamazoo farm girl she still was inside. As she walked past the shops, with their glittering merchandise in the windows, she found it all impressed her less than it used to. None of this meant anything if you were alone and lonely.

She'd never been to Abelard's office before but he'd told her where it was. On the second floor she found a door marked by a discreet sign for Lyon Enterprises. Butterflies made a jumble of her stomach as she pushed open the door and entered the office. A man with a head full of dark blond hair sat at the desk. He looked up from his paperwork as she entered.

Lily froze. "You," she whispered. He looked both the same and different. He had the same too-long hair and storm grey eyes, though he'd traded in his waxed mustache for a beard one shade darker than the hair on his head. He looked like a shopworn version of the man she'd known years ago.

He threw down his pen and stood, leaning across his desk at her, his eyes narrowed like an adder about to strike. "Ah, my little harlot. The years have been good to you." His eyes traveled up and down her body, just as they had when they'd first met.

Lily forced the words out. "You are Mr. Lyon's assistant? You are Harcourt?"

He laughed. It came out as a low, mean sound. "Of course I am you, stupid whore." He licked his lips and laughed again.

Lily felt her knees go weak. She looked around for a chair before she remembered herself. She would not sit in the presence of the Reverend Edwin Bland. Here was the man who'd seduced her and tried to abandon her. A long moment passed. Lily's mind whirled. The pieces fell into place. She turned and fled the office.

Heart pounding, Lily lurched for the stairs. Her skirts slowed her down until she hoisted them in one hand. Behind her she heard a door slam, then footsteps on the stairs. Once at the bottom of the staircase she ran for the building's back entrance. The door opened on to a narrow alley, thick with snow that no one had shoveled.

256

Lily realized her mistake as soon as the door closed behind her. She should have gone into the Arcade's main hall and headed for the Exchange Street exit. There were people there. Too late now. She'd trapped herself in this alley and HE was behind her. She picked her way down the alley, careful not to slip in the icy snow. She looked back over her shoulder. Edwin Bland was there, only ten feet back, a look of gleeful fury on his face. It occurred to her she'd seen that look before, on her father's face just before he beat her mother.

She slipped on a patch of ice and fell to her knees. Bland seized her arm and pulled her to her feet. Lily tried to pull away but his grip was like an iron band. He yanked her sideways and slammed her back against the wall. It felt like a block of ice against her back.

"Not so fast you bitch," he hissed. His voice was rancid with hate.

Lily's brain skittered in terror. "Why?" It was all she could say.

He shook so hard her head bounced of the wall. "You ruined me you worthless bitch. You told my mother about us and she cut me off without a penny. And you stole from me. No one takes my things. No one."

He pulled her away from the wall and slammed her back once again. Her head bounced off the brick again. "Did you think I'd let you get away with it?"

She whipped her head from side to side. "I didn't. I never spoke to your mother. I never even met her."

"As if I'd believe a word out of your lying mouth. Do you take me for a fool?" He pushed his mouth against hers, grinding his lips and teeth over hers. His body pressed into hers as he did. She could feel his excitement through her coat. He

257

pushed his tongue into her mouth, then pulled away and slapped her. "You foul harlot," he half-shouted at her. "Look what you made me do." His hand grabbed her breast through her coat and squeezed.

His hand felt like an animal's claw, digging into her. "Please," she whimpered. "I never talked to your mother. Not once. I swear."

"You did, you lying bitch. She cut me off without a penny. Which is exactly what you wanted."

Lily's mind raced. Someone must have seen them together. It wasn't like they'd been careful. But there was no point saying so. He'd made up his mind. And now he'd found her.

Bland's face flushed with excitement as he thrust his hard groin at her. "Why did you do it?"

She shook her head again. "I was pregnant. Desperate. You were leaving."

"Of course I was leaving you stupid cow. What else could I do? Take a pregnant whore home to Mother?" He pushed against her again, once, twice, three times.

"I'm what you made me," she cried. "You wanted me. You said you loved me."

"That's how the game is played." He snorted and scrabbled at her skirts. "Of course I wanted you. What red-blooded man wouldn't? And then you ruined me. So I will ruin you. I've already begun. You'll learn not to betray me. When you have nothing left you'll beg me to take you back." He pressed a palm against the center of her chest and held her against the wall while he pulled her skirt up.

Lily wrenched herself sideways and screamed, half in fear, half in anger. This couldn't be happening. Not to her. She wouldn't let him. Not anymore. Lily kicked at her old lover, striking his knee with her right foot. He squealed as his knee buckled. He let go of her and crumpled to the ground. Lily took off running.

She ran out of the alley, onto Exchange Street and right into traffic. A horse screamed. Lily looked up, saw flashing hooves and threw herself backward. She fell in the gutter, cold slush soaking her skirts.

"You all right miss?" Lily looked up to see a gray-bearded face hovering over her. "You gotta be more careful. I almost kilt you."

She nearly laughed as he pulled her to her feet. "A man tried to rob me."

"Where? Who?" He pulled his cap off and looked around.

She shook her head. "He's long gone. Could you get me out of here?"

The wagon driver helped her into his wagon and clucked the team into motion. After a brief argument, he agreed to drop her at a nearby police station. He watched as she entered the building. After he drove away Lily walked out of the police station. She spoke to no one.

On her way home Lily stopped at Western Union office. She prayed her telegram would reach Miss Warne in time.

Chapter 26

The next day dawned not at all. At 7 AM it was lighter than night, but not by much. Outside her window, she could see it snowing with an implacable steadiness that worried Kate. The sooner she got out of Cincinnati and back to Rochester, the sooner she finished this case, the sooner she could go home, where it wasn't so cold. She crawled out of bed, used the chamber pot and then stood before her window watching it snow. Monty jumped back into bed, a strategy for dealing with the day Kate decided to emulate. They snuggled back under the covers, Monty curled up against the small of Kate's back and didn't stir again until two hours later.

Kate rang for the maid and ordered a pot of coffee and two bowls of oatmeal. Kate threw on her coat and a hat and took Monty outside where he hurriedly peed on a wagon wheel. They both thought it was too cold to linger outside. While she waited for breakfast, Kate examined her city directory once more. There were four Beckers listed, but Mrs. Schmidt said she wanted Sarah Becker. There was a lady with that name on Thirteenth Street in Little Germany or, as Mrs.

Schmidt called it, the Over-the-Rhine. Kate checked the directory map again. It was a long walk from her hotel to Mrs. Becker's boarding house. She wished she'd brought Excelsior with her, but one look out the window reminded her that her old boy was better off in Washington. She'd have to take another hansom cab.

An hour later the cabman let her off at her destination. Monty bounced out of the cab after Kate and conducted some doggy business in the street. He hated it when Kate watched him, so she examined boarding house instead. It was a two-story, sturdy, workmanlike house, with narrow, shuttered windows and a welcoming porch that ran along the entire front of the house. Kate hustled up the walk. Someone had shoveled it, but long enough ago that the path had in an inch or two of snow in it. A young woman with skin the color of coffee opened the door. She was wearing a voluminous white apron and holding a broom. She bobbed her head at Kate. "Yes, Ma'am?"

"Is Mrs. Becker in?"

The girl nodded. "She's in the kitchen. You best come in."

Kate stomped the snow off her boots and followed the girl down a narrow hall, Monty hot on her heels. They walked through a green baize door not unlike the door that led to the kitchen in her Washington house. They entered a room thick with warm, steamy air. It was laundry day. A woman stood at one of the washtubs, elbow deep in the grey wash water. She'd braided her grey hair and pinned it into a crown on top her head. Even splashed with wash water the woman looked like a benevolent queen. "Are you looking for a room dear?"

Kate shook her head. "No, Ma'am. Are you Mrs. Becker?"

"Goodness me. Where are my manners?" The lady abandoned whatever garment she'd been washing, wiped her hands on her apron and stepped towards Kate. She pulled out a kitchen chair. "I am Mrs. Anna Becker, proprietress of this rooming house. Set a spell why don't you. It's a nasty day, for sure. Your poor little doggy must be froze through." She bent and rubbed Monty's ears like a lady who understood dog ears. He leaned into her and made a little doggy moan. When she stopped, he settled himself under the table and prepared to take a nap.

Kate watched the lady make friends with Monty. Unlike Mrs. Schmidt, Mrs. Becker had only the faintest German accent. Kate held out her hand to the woman and said, "I'm Kate Warne. I'm a detective working for the Pinkertons. Mrs. Schmidt said I should talk to you."

"Really? A lady Pinkerton? Don't that just make your day, Juney?"

The girl who'd let Kate in smiled at Mrs. Becker. "I never heard such a thing." She stared at Kate a moment before turning her attention to Mrs. Becker once more. "You want me to do the walk again Mrs. B? Or work on the towels? That way you can talk to this here detective lady."

"You're a good lass Juney. Give the walk another pass, would you? Can't have the boarders wading through snow when they get home. Bundle up now. Don't forget your hat."

Mrs. Becker watched Juney go, then turned back to Kate. "Now what can I help you with? Miss Warne was it?" She wore a large wooden cross on a string around her neck, which swung to and fro when she moved.

"It was. Is, I mean. I'm looking for a girl named Lily Nettleton. You and Mrs. Schmidt knew her as Lily Gibson. And

263

before you say you don't remember her, Mrs. Schmidt told me about you."

"Lily? Have you seen her? Is she all right?" Mrs. Becker popped up, grabbed two coffee mugs and poured them each a cup without missing a beat. "I sure miss that girl. I know what she did, but I never had a bit of trouble out of her and she was here for months. The poor girl was sicker than a dog. And you have never seen a woman so sad as poor Lily, what with her missing baby and all. You heard about that, right?"

Kate nodded. "Mrs. Schmidt told me about the baby and the way you two hid Lily from the authorities."

Mrs. Becker frowned at Kate. "You're not here to cause trouble, are you? Because if you are I'll say it's all a lie."

Kate held up her hands in surrender. "No trouble. I admire you for helping her. I was up half the night and somewhere past midnight I decided that if someone took my baby I'd kill them too. It wasn't murder. Not really."

"Why do you say that?"

Kate smiled. Mrs. Becker was testing her. "Because Mr. Gibson owed his wife some loyalty. He owed her some understanding and he owed her love. That doesn't mean he had to stay married to her or take the baby as his own, but he didn't even talk to her about it. He never gave her a chance. He didn't love her, not really. She was a shiny new thing to him and when she wasn't shiny and new anymore, he threw her away. And he used her baby against her. And now there's a baby out there without its mother."

Mrs. Becker jerked her chin at Kate. "And a mother without her baby, a baby she wanted."

Kate heaved a sigh. The two women regarded each other. After a moment Kate spoke. "Mrs. Schmidt says you looked for the baby?"

"I did. I visited to the Catholics twice. They run the St. Aloysius Orphanage, but they said both times they had no new babies. It's quite a large place, but the sisters seemed touched by the story and eager to help me get the baby back to its mother. The Methodists have a foundling home too, the German Orphan Home. They didn't want to talk, at least not to me, but one of Mrs. Schmidt's ladies had a contact in the place who dug through the records." She shook her head. "I kept asking every few weeks, supposing Mr. Gibson put the baby out with a wet nurse. But no baby ever turned up, at least not one the right age. Oh, except over at the colored orphanage and Lily assured me the baby's father was white. Not that I care you understand, but it would help with knowing where to look. The Catholics and Methodists might have taken a colored baby, but it's not likely."

Kate stared wide-eyed at Mrs. Becker. "You would have looked for a colored baby born to a white woman?"

She snorted and grabbed her cross. "Judge not lest ye be judged, that's what Mathew said. And he knew Jesus."

"Most religious people are not so tolerant."

"Most religious people forget to read their Bible. Or they just read the parts they like. Too busy being self-righteous if you ask me. Jesus wasn't a self-righteous man. I try to emulate him though I fall short every day."

Kate thought Mrs. Becker was doing just fine, but she wasn't about to argue with her.

"I dream about Lily and that missing baby all the time. A few weeks after she left it occurred to me that I didn't check

265

the reformatories and poor houses. They're for wayward children and the indigent poor. If this Mr. Gibson hated that baby he might have given it to one of those places. I almost started looking again, but what good would it do? I never heard from Lily again, not after she left. Not that I blame her. I'd want to forget if I were her." Mrs. Becker sipped her coffee and looked out the window at the snow.

"What do you know about those places?"

"Not much. There's the City Work House, out by Camp Washington. And next door, the House of Refuge, which sounds nice but it's no more than a jail for young people. When they first opened it, oh about ten years ago, they called it the House of Correction."

Kate pursed her lips and tapped the table top. "It doesn't sound like a likely place to find a baby does it?"

"No, but that baby ended up somewhere. Unless that nasty man killed it and I don't think he did. He was a coward. A mean coward, but a coward nonetheless. City officials send homeless children to the workhouse. And the ones they say are criminals? Off they go to this House of Refuge." Mrs. Becker swept her arm toward the kitchen window. It was snowing with the same implacable steadiness as when Kate first woke up. "Can you imagine being out there, with no home, no parents to take care of you?"

Kate looked out the window and shook her head. She considered her gang of Irregulars, as she called them. Street children who did odd jobs for her in return for lunch each day. Washington was plenty cold in winter, but nothing like these northern cities.

266

Silence lay between the two women for a few moments before Mrs. Becker spoke again. "I'll tell you something. Lily regretted killing Mr. Gibson, though he had it coming. In the four months we took care of her she convinced herself he would have softened and told her where her baby was." She shook her head. "He was never going to tell her. He was proud and unyielding by nature and used to getting his way on account of his money and sex. And he'd have had to admit he made a mistake. Men like that are never wrong. Never."

Kate left Mrs. Becker's house to find the hansom cab hadn't waited for her. She and Monty looked down the street and then back at Mrs. Becker's house. The snow made the day quiet. There was, as far as she could tell, no cabs on the street. She could go back inside, but she didn't know what that would accomplish. She had work to do and hanging around Mrs. Becker's warm kitchen wouldn't accomplish anything.

So she and Monty walked back to the hotel. On another day it might have been a pleasant walk, but not today. Her boots slipped on the packed snow as her feet slowly turned to blocks of ice. Her skirts got heavier and heavier with crusted snow, making each step harder than the one before. Kate kept her head down in an effort to keep the snow off her face and watch her footing. The walk turned into an endless trudge through a white tunnel of biting silver cold. After a few blocks, she tucked Monty into her coat, though he was so snow encrusted it was like putting a block of ice against her torso.

By the time Kate stumbled through the front door of the National Hotel, she felt half dead. The doorman grabbed her by the elbow and guided her inside to one of the soft lobby chairs. He left her there, returning a moment later with a hot brick for her feet and a pot of tea for the rest of her. He also promised to send a late lunch up to her room in half an hour. Monty stayed tucked into her coat.

Kate sipped her tea, feeling grateful for good hotels. She made a simple plan. Warm up, change shoes and then check the reformatory and workhouse for Lily's missing baby.

She was about to go up to her room when a pimply clerk walked up to her. He held out a telegram envelope. "This came for you Ma'am, forwarded over from Gibson House." He snapped his heels to together with a little bow and scurried off.

Jan. 28

Rochester, NY

Have no right to, but need you to return to Rochester post haste. Harcourt is Rev. Bland & he means to destroy me. Need your help. Badly.

Lily E. Winslow

Kate stared at the scrap of paper in her hand. Harcourt is Bland? And Lily Winslow? Was Ellen Winslow signaling she was Lily Nettleton? Kate frowned and thought about it. Then the pieces fell into place. She pushed herself out of the lobby chair and trudged upstairs to pack.

Before Kate left Cincinnati, she sent two telegrams and wrote one letter. The first telegram was to Lily telling her she was on her way. She sent a second telegram to Mrs. Becker, asking her to call at the Union Hotel for a letter. The letter Kate left at the hotel's front desk included a detailed set of instructions. Kate had little doubt that Mrs. Becker would do what Kate asked.

Chapter 27

January 29-February 3, 1862
Rochester, New York

It took Kate the better part of that night and next day to travel back to Rochester, the five hundred mile journey slowed by snow and ice on the train tracks. She staggered off the train well past dinner time, her stomach cramping with hunger, her head bleary from lack of sleep. Monty wasn't much happier, having spent most of the train ride huddled by her side trying to keep warm. That he peed on only one light pole worried Kate a great deal. A short cab ride took them to Osborn House where she'd left her large travel trunk. She engaged the same room she'd had almost two weeks ago. The clerk helped her send a telegram to Lily Winslow telling her Kate would call on her at 10 o'clock the next morning.

Ten hour's sleep in a soft bed in a warm, unmoving room and a full stomach considerably improved Kate's mood. Having access to more clothes than her carpet bag could carry also helped, as did a breakfast of waffles, sausages and eggs, though Monty ate most of the sausages. Best of all, the snow had stopped and the morning dawned bright and clear, the sun making the snow sparkle like it was strewn with tiny diamonds.

They enjoyed the blue sky and brisk but not biting air as they walked to Lily's boarding house, passing the stable where Excelsior had stayed. Monty wanted to explore the building so Kate gave him a few moments to check the stable's interior. He returned, looking undaunted by Excelsior's absence and they walked on. Kate reflected that people could learn a lot from dogs. They lived in the moment and accepted things as they were, sparing little energy for what was not to be.

As Kate walked up the boarding house's steps the large front door opened. It was Lily.

"Thank God you're here. I've been waiting." She let Kate and Monty in and led them up to her rooms. She glanced at Mr. Bristol's door and over her shoulder said to Kate, "I've sent him to Claude. They'll take my clients between them." At Kate's blank look Lily added, "Claude is Le Compte."

"Oh, right. I forgot."

Lily closed and locked the door. "I've got hot water. Would you like tea or coffee?"

Once they settled themselves over a pot of tea Kate had to ask. "What in heavens name is going on?"

"How much did you figure out?"

"Well, you're Lily Nettleton, not Ellen Winslow, or perhaps more to the point, you are both women at the same time."

Lily nodded, fiddling with the sugar tongs as she did. "I think legally my name is Lily Gibson." She handed Kate the summons. "They mean to have me in court next Thursday."

Kate examined the paper with a frown, then looked up at Lily. "If Harcourt is your Reverend Bland, then he set you up. And he used the Pinkertons to get revenge upon you." This thought made Kate angrier than she liked to admit.

Still fiddling with the sugar, Lily asked, "And what did you learn on your trip west? Will you still help them prosecute me?" Her voice dribbled away to a whisper as she spoke.

Kate sighed. "Mrs. Winslow, I owe you an apology. For my shoddy first investigation and for the part I have played in what's happening to you now."

The tongs stilled. "You might as well call me Lily. But not Nettleton. I'm Lily Winslow now." A pause hung between them. "And what did you discover that changed your mind?"

Kate told Lily about Kalamazoo, and how she spoke to the sheriff, the man who ran the newspaper and Lily's sister.

"You found Polly?" Lily looked up at Kate. "How is she?"

"She's doing well. Lonely if I had to guess, but she's teaching math in Battle Creek and it suits her."

"Oh, that's good." There was real pleasure in Lily's voice as she spoke.

"She'd like to see you. Your mother probably would too."

"Probably?"

Kate told her how shrunken and frightened her mother seemed. Before Lily could ask questions about her mother Kate also told her Polly's story.

Afterward Lily could only sigh and stare at the table, her forefinger making little circles on the shiny surface. "Poor Polly. I did my best for her, but it wasn't good enough."

"Oh, I don't know," Kate said, her voice a good deal harder than she'd intended. "You stopped both awful men from hurting another woman. I'd like to dig them both up and kick their corpses."

Lily looked up at Kate, her purple-blue eyes shining. "You don't know the half of it." Lily paused, fiddled with the tongs again, then set them aside and told Kate what her life had been like with her father. And then she talked about her life as Mrs. Gosford.

"Your sister said your father sold you to this farmer," Kate said.

Lily shrugged. "I was his to sell."

"Or so he thought."

"No." Lily shook her head. "Not only in his head. According to the law."

"That didn't mean he could sell you though. Slavery's illegal in Michigan, isn't it?"

Lily shrugged again. "It's not that simple. People say it is, but every woman married to a brute knows better. So do the children. I sure know better. How do you think Mr. Gibson legally took my baby? Because according to the law it was his baby, not mine."

Kate wasn't sure what to say. Part of her wanted to hug Lily, but Lily wasn't a hugging sort of woman. And until recently Kate had been trying to put her in jail for being a triple murderer.

Instead, Kate took a deep breath and continued her tale. She told the story of how she went looking for Mrs. Cawley in Detroit and how the lady changed her story about Edwin Bland."

Lily smiled a tight, mirthless smile. "So he did to her what he did to me. Serves her right."

272

"He got his comeuppance when his mother cut him out of her will."

Lily sat her cup down so abruptly it clanked against its saucer. "He blames me for that."

Kate looked up from her tea to see Lily's face had lost its color. "He does? How do you know?"

Lily jerked her head as if to ward off a blow. "I'll explain after you finish your story."

Kate shifted her story to Cincinnati and how she found Mrs. Schmidt, who led her to Mrs. Becker. "I'm so sorry Lily. I can't imagine what it would be like to lose a baby like that."

"It's the not knowing that's so awful. It's why I save all my money. Money will loosen tongues where pity for a mother will not."

Kate said nothing about Mrs. Becker's idea about new places to look for the baby. Nor did she tell Lily she'd left the lady some investigative instructions before she came to Rochester. There was no reason to get this woman's hopes up if it all came to nothing. "Lily, I'm going to be honest with you." Kate paused and forced herself to go on. "I'm still troubled over Mr. Gibson's murder." She held up her hand as Lily opened her mouth to protest. "I'm not saying he was a good man, nor am I saying he didn't deserve your wrath, but Lily, you've got three murders on your hands. That's a lot of bodies and it troubles me. It should trouble you."

Lily stared at Kate. "Whether it troubles me is my business, not yours. What will you do about it?"

Kate looked at her. "Nothing right now. The world is a better place without men like those three. I'm not sure you or I should be judge and executioner, but no one else would." Kate opened her hands and spread them before her. "I will

273

help you. Because you've gotten a rotten deal from this world and it's time for you to quit paying for the sins of others."

Lily burst into tears. She stood, paused and then fled the room. Kate got up and stirred up the coal stove. Then she dumped the cold tea and rinsed out the pot. After about twenty minutes Lily returned. She stood in the doorway between the parlor and her bedroom. "What do we do now?"

Kate poured hot water into the teapot and sat it on the table. "Are you going to tell me how you found out about Mr. Harcourt."

Lily first showed Kate the legal papers she'd been served two mornings previous. Then she explained how she'd decided to talk to Mr. Lyon on the premise that he'd made a mistake about her intentions. She described walking into Lyon's office and finding the Reverend Edwin Bland was also Mr. Harcourt.

"So you'd never met Harcourt before this?"

Lily shook her head. "In retrospect, it's clear that wasn't an accident, but at the time I thought nothing of it."

Lily told Kate how Bland chased her into the alley and assaulted her and how she escaped. "Right after that, I sent you the telegram. I took a chance you'd be at Gibson House."

"I wasn't. After I found out the entire family and hotel staff conspired to keep your pregnancy secret I was so angry I changed hotels. A clerk at the Gibson forwarded the telegram."

"The staff was always efficient," Lily said with a grim smile. "The thing is, it now all makes perfect sense. Abelard, I mean Mr. Lyon, came to me on Harcourt's recommendation. When he, Mr. Lyon that is, told me how much Mr. Harcourt admired me I didn't recognize the name, but that's not unusual. Many people use a false name when visiting a spiritualist. Abelard also said Mr. Harcourt encouraged him to court me. Harcourt told him it was high time his boss quit grieving for his wife and find a new one. Then, after months of close attention, Abelard turned cold and would not see me. I'm sure Harcourt, or Bland, or whatever we're supposed to call him now, turned Abelard against me."

Kate nodded in agreement. "It makes sense. He's convinced you caused his downfall and wants revenge. So he manipulates a rich man, using what he knows of you both to spur the rich man on."

Kate paused. What she had to say next troubled her. "He knows you're Lily Nettleton. Why travel all the way to Cincinnati to hire my agency when there are detectives in Rochester? He must have known the Pinkertons had the original Lily Nettleton case."

Lily stared at Kate, her face pale as the snow outside. "So he knew you'd investigated Lily Nettleton and connect Mrs. Winslow to her?"

"It makes sense. He described you so Allan couldn't help but connect you to the old case. It's either that or it's a big coincidence and no detective likes coincidences."

"Why not just tell the authorities where I am and let the law have me?"

Kate tapped the papers Lily had left sitting on the table. "Here's what I think. He's using this lawsuit and the Pinkertons to expose you as Lily Nettleton. They'll use the evidence I collected to expose you, both as a charlatan and as a triple murderer. Harcourt-Bland is counting on a dramatic court-

275

room scene to put you in jail, thus avoiding an investigation which might expose him."

"Isn't he worried I'll expose something in court?"

Kate shook her head. "He knows you can't expose him without exposing yourself. And once the court knows you killed your father and two husbands no one will care what you say next. You'll be the Black Widow. If you're lucky, you go to jail for the rest of your life. If you're not lucky, they'll hang you. Either way, he gets his revenge."

"But I ask again, why this elaborate charade? Why not just give me to the police?"

Kate shook her head. "I'm not sure. I suspect he doesn't want to reveal himself. Which means we need to ask why. Why does he not want anyone to know he's Edwin Bland? What does Edwin Bland have to hide that's so big he can't go to the police about a triple murderer?"

Lily's eyes widened. "I think I know. I bet he killed his mother. He must have. He hated the way she tried to control him. He hated being dependent upon her and felt entitled to her money. It's all he talked about—what he'd do when she died and he got all the money."

Kate considered the idea. "Let's see. After you left he had money trouble and not long after she conveniently died. He didn't know she'd disinherited him until after the reading of the will. And he blames you for that. So, does that mean he killed her?"

Lily chewed at her lower lip. "You said you don't like coincidences and she died just when he needed the money most."

"That's a good theory. I'll see if I can get a Pinkerton operative to go to Detroit and check the mother's death certificate."

"We should do it ourselves, not trust someone else. Too many people have lied about all this."

Kate shook her head again. "It would take at least twenty-four hours to get there and another twenty-four to get back. Maybe more in this weather. And another day to find out what we need to know. And meanwhile, we're not getting ready for court. We don't have time for that. Not if the trial is set for next Thursday. I can have a Pinkerton operative in Detroit by late tomorrow."

Lily agreed but Kate could tell she really wanted to storm off to Detroit.

"In the meantime," Kate said, "We'll find you a lawyer and get ready for court. Mr. Harcourt/Bland has had months to plan his revenge so we're way behind."

After some argument, Lily agreed to hire Kate for trial preparation and a lawyer for the courtroom. This deal was a compromise because Lily wanted to represent herself. Kate told her in no uncertain terms how stupid her idea was. "They have all the information I gave them. They have a file about Mr. Devereaux and Le Compte. They know how you faked your séances and that you've got a shady past as a bouncer."

They were sitting at Lily's séance table making lists while outside the brilliant sunshine melted snow and ice. "You're only chance of winning, as far as I can see, is presenting yourself as the innocent victim of bullying men. That and if they call me I have to keep my mouth shut about your identity.

They won't ask me. Why would they? Harcourt's counting on me volunteering the information."

Lily believed Devereaux wouldn't testify. "He's terrified of his wife. As well he should be. She knows he's a monster. You want to know what I bribe him with? I caught him with a girl, a child no older than ten. I took her away from him and sent her back to her family. I've got proof and if he does it again I can turn him into the authorities."

Kate put down her cup and gaped at Lily. "I got nothing right, did I? Though it makes me feel better about accepting your money. Here I was worried you were paying me with dirty cash."

"I do what I have to do." Her voice turned iron hard as she spoke. "I should have turned Devereaux over to the authorities. Instead, I scare the daylights of him every chance I get. Which is why he won't want to testify. And he's Canadian so the American courts can't force him to appear."

Kate pointed at her. "That's the version of you the judge and jury need never see. That streak of cold iron you have in you—it's fine to show it to me but not in the courtroom. Strong women make most men nervous and some men just plain angry. Which is why you can't defend yourself. You need to appear defenseless and vulnerable. They need to feel sorry for you and want to protect you. Which is why you need a big strong lawyer to defend you."

"I don't want to spend the money. Not on this nonsense. I'm spending enough on you and I'm saving what I have left to look for my child."

Kate held her tongue about the child. There was no purpose in getting Lily hopes up. "A lawyer is not nonsense. This is life and death business. And remember, if you're found guilty or worse, exposed as the Black Widow, you'll never find your child. We need to take advantage of your greatest asset—men find you irresistible."

"It's stupid," Lily scoffed.

"No, it's not. I'm attractive, but nowhere near in your category." Kate held up her hand to forestall Lily's denial. "It's true. Still, I'm willing to trade on my looks if it gets me what I want. I've made a career of fooling men, either by getting them to tell me things they wouldn't tell another man or by allowing them to underestimate me." Kate stopped and cocked her head. "We'll use that same impulse to your advantage. Because trust me Lily, you will need every advantage you can get."

"Fine." Lily threw her hands in the air. "I'll hire a damn lawyer. Where do we find this paragon of masculine legal protection?"

Kate picked up a pen and tapped it on the table. "We need someone who believes in spiritualism. A true believer, not a dabbler. This trial might end up being an argument about the legitimacy of spiritualism. If spiritualism is legitimate, then you are legitimate, and vice versa. Do you have a lawyer who comes to your séances?"

Lily smiled. "No, but I have a female client whose husband is a lawyer. I've helped her with the death of her son. The husband wrote me a lovely note of appreciation and included a tidy sum of money."

"Let's go see him today. You can give him his money back in return for his services in court. We'll do all the leg work and use him for court. That should save you considerable money."

Later that day they engaged the services of Oscar Lewis, grateful husband, lawyer and a true believer in Mrs. Winslow, Spiritualist, Mesmerist and Channeler of the Dead. They also paid a call on Mrs. Lewis, who promised to gather the lady troops. Then they went to work on Lily's defense.

Monday morning Kate received a large packet of papers in the mail from Detroit. She and Lily took the packet to Lawyer Lewis's office and locked it in his office safe.

Chapter 28

February 6, 1862
Rochester, New York

Three men sat at the prosecution table, Mr. Lyon, his lawyer Mr. Calderwood and the ubiquitous Mr. Harcourt. Lyon and Calderwood whispered to each other while Harcourt busied himself making notes. Kate guessed his notes were only scribbles so he could pretend to not see his ex-mistress.

The prosecution thought Kate was working for them and until Calderwood rested his case Kate wouldn't disabuse them of that notion. She didn't feel one bit bad about the lie either. Harcourt had used the Pinkertons and herself to do his dirty work. He'd lied to both Allan and Kate about his identity, his motives and the facts of the case. And she'd done what they'd paid her to do, investigate Ellen Winslow the spiritualist. No, she didn't feel even the tiniest bit bad about lying to these men. She drew the line at lying under oath, but she didn't think it would come to that.

Lily sat at the defense table next to Mr. Lewis. Lily's job was to wear her prettiest gowns, keep her eyes wide and innocent and sniff delicately into a handkerchief anytime someone maligned her character. Kate tried not to look over at Lily because each time she did she could feel a small smile cresting her lips.

The judge gaveled court into session and Lyon's lawyer, Mr. Calderwood, called Dr. Hubbard to the stand. Kate knew they'd call him, but still her stomach sank. She'd given them Hubbard and she regretted it. As expected, Hubbard provided testimony on the fakery of spiritualism. He related his story about his brother's suicide, causing both the gallery and the all-male jury to glare at Mrs. Winslow. Hubbard reiterated that all spiritualism was "humbug," an opinion Kate privately agreed with. He concluded his testimony by offering his opinion that Mrs. Winslow as a 'bouncer,' who moved from city to city fleecing unsuspecting men and women until she wore out her welcome.

Without rising from his seat Lawyer Lewis asked, "How much were you paid for your testimony today Dr. Hubbard?"

Hubbard huffed and puffed but admitted he'd been paid ten dollars for his time. Lewis then made Hubbard admit that he debunked Spiritualists for money, information he'd gotten from Kate, who hadn't forgotten Hubbard had only talked to her after she paid him $5. Lewis finished his cross-examination by asking Hubbard if he hadn't once been a spiritualist himself.

Knowing the prosecution would call him, Kate looked into Hubbard's background the week before the trial. A neighbor told her that when Hubbard first graduated from medical school, he couldn't make a living as a doctor and so had turned to spiritualism. Old newspaper advertisements backed up this claim. He repudiated spiritualism only after his brother's self-murder.

Kate watched with relish as Lewis dismantled Hubbard's testimony. Hubbard himself helped Lily's case by becoming angry and red faced under questioning. He wasn't a man accustomed to being contradicted and finished his time on the stand looking like a man who bullied pretty women.

Mr. Calderwood next called Mrs. Evalina Gray. Kate watched Lily slump her shoulders and pick up her handkerchief.

A slim young woman approached the witness box. She wore a dress slightly too tight and too shiny to be respectable. Kate recognized the style. She used it herself when pretending to be a woman of dubious reputation. Mrs. Gray took her chair and looked around the courtroom with wide-eyed delight.

Mr. Calderwood approached her and, after confirming her name, asked her if she knew the defendant.

"Oh, yes," Mrs. Gray said in a breathy, high-pitched voice. "She taught me everything I know. We used to share rooms. In Terre Haute."

The lawyer questioned Mrs. Gray at length about her apprenticeship under Mrs. Winslow.

The more the young lady talked the worse it got. She revealed that Mrs. Winslow had not been Mrs. Winslow in Terre Haute, but Mrs. Mercer. Mrs. Gray spoke about the tricks she'd learned and how Mrs. Mercer had advised her to marry a rich man. "Why, when I met Daddy, I mean Mr. Gray, Mrs. Mercer couldn't have been more helpful. She knew right away that Daddy would love me so much he would let me do whatever I pleased. And he does!" She sat back in her chair, her face glowing with delight. She did not seem to notice the growing disapproval on the faces of the men in the room.

When Calderwood asked her what sorts of things Daddy let her do she happily explained.

"Why, for example, if I want him out of the way for a few days all I have to say is 'Daddy, you don't look well. Take a rest in the country and I'll write you when I want you to come back.' He makes a long face, but he goes. He's never made a rumpus in my life. Mrs. Mercer," she nodded at Lily, "I mean Mrs. Winslow was ever so right about marrying a rich old man. Mr. Gray and I have a very accommodating marriage. He accommodates me and I accommodate myself." Her laugh tinkled through the courtroom. The men in the jury box looked less than impressed.

Mr. Lewis tried to interrupt Mrs. Gray's testimony with objection after objection, pointing out that her story had little to do with the case they were trying, but Judge Townsend overruled him each time.

Mr. Calderwood asked her if she'd ever traveled with Mrs. Winslow.

"Oh, yes. We'd take these sweeps through the small towns in Ohio and Indiana. People in small towns will pay almost any amount to be humbugged. It's better than their boring lives you see? We made a bundle of money. An absolute bundle." She bounced in her chair as she told this story.

The more she talked, the worse it got, her glib tongue pounding nail after nail into Lily's coffin.

It was clear to Kate that Mrs. Evalina Gray was a lady who'd substituted good sense and self-restraint for self-interest and attention seeking. Kate hadn't had the time before the trial to get anything damning on her, so Mr. Lewis didn't have much to counter her story. In cross examination he got her to admit that she'd lived with Mrs. Winslow for less than six months and that she'd had no contact with her for almost two years. It was something, but not much.

After an hour break for lunch the prosecution called Mr. Claude Le Compte to the stand. The natty little Frenchman smiled across the courtroom at Lily and Kate. Kate knew he intended to be as unhelpful as possible to Lyon's case. He had, in fact, offered to perjure himself and deny any relationship with his beloved Mrs. Winslow. Kate urged him to tell the truth, explaining that Harcourt and Lyon had her report and if he lied they'd use it against him.

Kate watched Le Compte step up to the stand. To her dismay, he wore his favorite lavender trousers and purple checked coat. Lyon's lawyer kept Le Compte's testimony short by asking simple, direct questions. Le Compte professed his professional admiration for Mrs. Winslow, but he also made it clear the lady had allowed him the physical delights of the marriage bed without actual marriage. Every man on the jury acted as if they'd never heard of anything more scandalous than extra-marital relations, though Kate had little doubt that most, if not all, had more than a passing knowledge of illicit fornication.

The more Le Compte described Lily and her work the worse he made her case, what with his French accent, lavender pants and obvious infatuation. Lewis's cross examination attempted to limit the damage by encouraging Le Compte to speak about all the widows and grieving mothers Lily helped, but the damage had been done. By the time Lewis dismissed him the jury could hardly look at him. Blithely unaware of their contempt, Le Compte beamed at Lily as he strode out of the courtroom, walking stick swinging at his side. Kate held her breath until he left the courtroom, afraid he'd undertake one of his dashing demonstrations of affection before he left.

Mr. Lyon took the stand next. Lily sat up a little straighter and smiled at him though it didn't appear Mr. Lyon even saw his ex-paramour. He looked only at his lawyer Mr. Calderwood.

Calderwood began with questions about the death of Mrs. Lyon, making it clear his client was a grieving widower. He next questioned Mr. Lyon about his business and considerable personal wealth before moving on to a discussion of Mr. Lyon's relationship with Mrs. Winslow. Mr. Lyon admitted that he had intended to marry Mrs. Winslow, but that his assistant Mr. Harcourt helped him see the folly of this plan. Lyon also spun a tale about how Mrs. Winslow became angry and threatened him with violence when he withdrew his proposal of marriage. By the time Lyon finished his testimony every man on the jury felt sorry for the old man.

For his cross examination Mr. Lewis approached the witness stand, a sheaf of papers in his hand. He studied them for a few moments and then looked up at Mr. Lyon, seeming almost surprised to find him there.

Kate hid a smile. The theater lost a performer when Mr. Lewis went to law school.

"Mr. Lyon," Lewis said with a small bow. "I wonder if you could help me."

Mr. Lyon's grizzled whiskers quivered as he said, "If I can."

Lewis approached held the papers out to Mr. Lyon. "This is a copy of the lawsuit that occasioned this trial. I wonder if you could show me where it says Mrs. Winslow sued you for breach of promise?"

Lyon took the papers, but spared them not a glance. "Well she never did, so it's not here."

"How extraordinary." He glanced at the jury, then back at Lyon. "Perhaps you could show me where she sued you for something else? Anything else?"

Lyon shook his head. "She never sued me."

Mr. Lewis reared back his head in a look of pure astonishment. "Not even one little lawsuit? I confess myself confused Mr. Lyon. This court has charged Mrs. Winslow with barratry at your behest, correct?"

Lyon stared at Lewis, eyes wide, mouth agape.

Lewis persisted. "Well? You allege she has maliciously pursued you with legal suits, correct?"

"She did." Lyon stuck out his lower lip and thumped his walking stick for emphasis.

"Then again, I call upon you to help me. Perhaps I misunderstand the legal meaning of barratry. What is it?"

Lyon sputtered. "You know perfectly well what it is."

"I'm not sure I do. I thought it was the legal means whereby one could stop persons engaging in frivolous and malicious lawsuits against another person or corporate entity. But you say Mrs. Winslow has never brought a case against you. Do you see why I'm confused?"

"She threatened to sue me," Lyon nearly shrieked. "I was a happily married man for forty-two years and then my dear Minerva died and Mrs. Winslow caught me in her net. She is not half of the woman Minerva was. Or one-quarter. She

287

tried to get me to marry her. To set herself up in my dear, departed Minerva's place."

"She did? Have you any proof?" Lyon scratched at his head as he turned back to the defense table. He rifled through the papers there. "I don't see anything like that here."

"She threatened me when I changed my mind and wouldn't marry her. She is a wicked, frightening creature." Lyon glared at Lily.

"This little woman?" Lewis pointed toward Lily. "You contend she frightened you?"

Lily batted her black eyelashes over her sapphire eyes and heaved her bosoms a little. Several men in the jury box smiled at her.

"She did," Lyon squealed.

Kate heard one a juror snort. Then someone laughed, which made several more men laugh.

The judge banged his gavel on his desk. "Stop that at once," he shouted.

The jurors went quiet, but they continued to look amused.

Lewis turned toward the judge and waved his hand toward Lyon. "I'm done with this witness your honor."

Lyon thumped his way out of the witness box and took his seat. His shoulders slumped like a tired old man.

His lawyer leaned over to him. They whispered back and forth, then the lawyer pushed himself to his feet. "I call Miss Kate Warne to the stand."

Kate took her place in the witness box. Her heart felt like it would explode from her chest. Kate identified herself as a Pinkerton operative and described how she came to be working the case. Calderwood next asked her a series of questions about her investigation.

"You followed Mrs. Winslow on several occasions did you not?"

"I did."

"What did you discover?"

"Mrs. Winslow was having an affair with Mr. Le Compte. They met in bars and hotel rooms."

Calderwood raised his eyebrows as if he hadn't known what she'd say. "For what purpose?"

Kate returned his surprise. "Do you mean to tell me Mr. Calderwood that you do not understand what men and women do in hotel rooms? And you need me to explain?"

Several of the men in the jury box chuckled and exchanged amused glances.

Calderwood puffed up his chest in indignation. "I mean to be clear. Let me ask this, did you discover Mrs. Winslow in inappropriate relationships with men other than Mr. Le Compte?"

Kate wasn't about to discuss Mr. Devereaux in open court. Lily had been right. He'd refused a court summons. And he and Lily had not been having an affair so Kate didn't have to lie. "No. Just Mr. Le Compte. And Mr. Lyon of course."

The jury laughed again.

"What else did you find out about Mrs. Winslow?"

Kate knew a fishing expedition when she saw one. "A good many things. Could you be more specific?"

"Is she a real spiritualist?"

Kate shrugged. "I don't know if such a creature exists. Does it matter? I thought she was on trial for barratry, not fraud."

Mr. Calderwood tried again. "What did your investigation uncover about Mrs. Winslow's wrong doings?"

"I'm not sure what you want Mr. Calderwood, but I'll tell you what I didn't find. I found no evidence Mrs. Winslow was suing or planned to sue Mr. Lyon. Mr. Lyon did make her an offer of marriage and withdrew it, so she has a case for breach of promise, though she has not pursued that case. Perhaps because after I discovered the affair with Mr. Le Compte she would never win such a case."

As Kate spoke Mr. Calderwood's eyes narrowed and his face flushed with anger. "Miss Warne, I insist you cooperate."

Kate tried not to smile. "I've answered every one of your questions."

Calderwood threw his arms in the air and bellowed, "You are not telling the court everything you know!"

Mr. Lewis leapt to his feet with an objection. The judge directed Calderwood to move on. Kate sat in the witness box and watched it all.

Calderwood stood before her, shoulders slumped. "Do you have anything else to tell the court?"

Kate shook her head. "No, Sir."

He dismissed her. Kate took her seat behind the prosecution table once more, careful to not spare even one glance at Lily.

Mr. Calderwood leaned over and whispered in Harcourt's ear again. Harcourt whispered back. Calderwood straightened up and said, "Your honor, I've one more witness before I rest my case, but it's getting late and my witness would prefer to testify tomorrow."

Harcourt sat there looking smug.

Kate's heart sped up. It was just as she suspected.

The judge nodded. "We'll reconvene in the morning. Nine sharp."

He banged his gavel and left the room.

Lily and Mr. Lewis stood, as did everyone else.

Lily turned back to Kate, her face bleak. "That was awful."

Mr. Lewis patted Lily on the back. "It went about as we planned. They haven't proven their case. It's just like I said when you hired me, they have no intention of proving your guilt. The point is to ruin your reputation."

Lily glanced at Kate again. Mr. Lewis didn't know she'd once been Edwin Bland's mistress and that Harcourt was Edwin Bland. Nor did he know about the murders.

"Tomorrow we'll call our witnesses and before I'm done, the jury will believe you are being victimized by an unprincipled bully."

"Because I am," Lily said with fierce determination.

Lewis smiled at her. "What you are and are not is of no concern to me. My only concern is what the jury thinks you are." He looked over at Kate. "Is it time?"

Kate nodded. Lily grinned.

He handed her the packet of papers he'd taken from his safe that morning.

She gestured toward the courtroom door. "You two get out of here. I'll meet you outside."

After they turned to go, Kate stepped over to the prosecution table where Harcourt was packing a leather satchel. Mr. Lyon and his lawyer were waiting for him. "Mr. Harcourt? I wonder if I could have a word in private? She leaned in close to him and whispered, "Or should I call you Mr. Bland?"

He jerked his head up, his eyes wide, mouth open, then turned and motioned for the other two men to go on without him. He turned back to Kate.

"That's right. Lily told me." She threw a large envelope on the table in front of him. "If you take the stand tomorrow, I'll take the originals of the those documents to the Cincinnati police."

He snatched the envelope off the table, tore it open and shuffled through the papers. "What is this," he hissed, his eyes narrow and angry in his bloated face.

Kate thought he looked like an over-fed, cornered rat. "The top sheet is from the Detroit coroner. It says someone poisoned Mrs. Amelia Bland with arsenic. The second piece of paper is the testimony from a Detroit chemist saying he sold rat poison containing arsenic to an Edwin Bland. The third is a copy of your mother's last will. The one where she cut her son off without a penny."

Harcourt tore the sheaf of papers in half and threw them on the desk. "How dare you?" He grabbed for Kate's arm.

She stepped back, slipping her dagger out of her sleeve as she did and held it in front of her. No one could see it but Harcourt and herself. "Don't touch me. I am not some defenseless woman you can assault in an alley." She put every bit of loathing she felt into her voice. It turned out to be quite a bit of loathing.

The blood drained from his face. He staggered back a step. "You didn't let me finish." Kate stepped toward him, knife still in hand. "The last piece of paper is an affidavit from Mrs. Cawley attesting to an inappropriate relationship with at least three young women." Kate nodded at the papers on the table.

"And those are fair hand copies you idiot. We locked the originals where you can't get them." She took another step toward Harcourt, and then another until they were toe to toe. She let the dagger touch him, just to the left of his groin. "You take the stand tomorrow and I'll come after you. I'll burn you down. And then I'll have you arrested and tried for murder. And once I expose you as a man who'd poison his own mother do you think it will matter what you say about Lily? Do you think anyone will listen to you?" She leaned into him, noting his bloodless face and unblinking eyes, before she turned on her heel and walked away.

Kate pushed through the courtroom doors into the cold afternoon air feeling better than she'd felt for weeks. She found Lily waiting outside in the cold for her.

"Did it work?"

Kate beamed at Lily. "It did and it was a lot of fun."

"Mr. Lewis wanted to get home to his wife," Lily said with a half smile. "How about you and I get dinner? Or pick up something and take it back to my place?" Before Kate could say anything she added, "I don't feel like being alone."

"A little celebration would do us good," Kate said, buttoning up her coat and tying her scarf tight around her head. "But only if we fetch Monty first."

An hour later they were installed in Lily's rooms, a coal fire glowing red in the parlor stove and four small meat pies reheating on top. Kate sprawled on the sofa thinking about the trial, though as the buttery scent of pastry filled the room she thought rather more about the pies. Monty snoozed on the room's largest armchair, emitting small doggy snores. He'd gobbled his pie as soon as they entered the apartment.

Kate could hear, but not see Lily behind her, pouring them each a large brandy and complaining about Mr. Lyon. "That old weasel, he never talked about his wife. He didn't miss her at all. I asked him about her once, but he said she was the past and I was his future. The old hypocrite."

A loud crash startled Kate out of her doze. As she realized the sound was window glass breaking she saw a flash of red fly over the sofa. Behind her came a scream. For a second Kate thought Lily had dropped one or both of the brandy glasses, but she remembered the sound of the window breaking. Something red rolled under the large armchair. Before it could come to a stop the chair exploded with a roar and a flash of blinding incandescent light.

Monty's small body flew across the room, propelled by a wave of hot air. He smacked into the wall and fell to the floor like a sack of hammers. Kate pushed herself to her feet, hardly noticing the jagged splinter of wood embedded in the back of her hand. Behind her Lily screamed again. Kate staggered over to the small, crumpled form lying across the room.

As she knelt next to Monty, Kate heard Lily speaking, her words muddy and indistinct through the loud ringing in her ears. Kate held her fingers to the little dog's chest. His fur was so soft, so silky. She waited. Please. She begged a god she hardly believed in. Please. His chest rose, then fell. She knelt there next to him, numb and confused. She felt cold air on her back but paid it no mind. Please.

After a universe of time passed, Lily appeared at her side, a silver platter large enough for a roast goose in her hands. She looked at Kate, nodded once, and together they slid the tray under Monty's small body and lifted him to the table. Cold air filled the room as the curtains billowed against the night air. Kate used two fingers to palpate Monty's tiny body. One of his forelegs bent where it should not and a trickle of blood leaked from one nostril, but otherwise he seemed intact. Kate looked at Lily. She saw Lily's lips move, but she could hear no words.

Lily leaned in to the side of Kate's face and tried again. "I've sent Mr. Bristol for the police. And a doctor."

Kate stared at her.

Lily hollered into Kate's ear. "The doctor has terriers."

Kate nodded her understanding. She turned and surveyed the room. The explosion had reduced Monty's chair to a pile of upholstered rubble that sagged through a hole in the floorboards. The window behind the chair had disappeared, leaving surprisingly little glass behind. Kate guessed most of it was outside in the snow, blown there by the force of the blast. She shivered and realized how cold the room had become.

What had done this? She walked over to the wrecked chair, careful to circumvent the hole in the floor. What had she seen? That flash of red. What was it?

She decided she didn't care and turned back to Monty, still lying on his silver tray upon the table, like a capon served for dinner. Lily left the room, returned with a wool shawl. She wrapped it around Kate's shoulders and left again. Kate pulled the shawl off and tucked it around Monty, careful not to bump his floppy front leg. Lily returned with the tea kettle and canning jar. She poured hot water into the jar, wrapped it in a tea towel and snugged it against Monty's back. Then she picked up Monty's tray and gestured at Kate to follow her. They went down a short hall and turned into a comfortable room of soft blues and lavenders. Lily lay the tray upon a double bed, wrapped Kate in another shawl and left again. Kate sat down on the bed next to her dog and waited.

Two hours later the police and the doctor had all come and gone. The doctor, a tall scarecrow of a man with a soft, deep voice, examined Monty and splinted his leg.

"That's all I can do, miss," he said with obvious regret. "Either he's in shock and will wake up none the worse for wear, or the bomb scrambled his insides and he's dying." He grabbed Kate's hand and patted it as he spoke. "For what it's worth, I don't think he's got internal injuries. His abdomen feels normal. But with creatures this small it's hard to tell. All we can do is keep him warm and wait."

The police found the remnants of a glass flask, corked and sealed with red sealing wax. Neither of them had seen the man who threw it, though Lily said she caught a glimpse of a black coated man fleeing down the hall. That confused Kate, who was sure the bomb had come through the window. Lily said someone threw open the door to her rooms and hurled something in. Together they established that the bomb had come through the front door, but that it had bounced off the window, cracked the glass, which broke and fell seconds before the explosion.

One of the policemen, a mustachioed fellow with a thick Irish accent, sniffed the bottle shards and proclaimed it had once been filled with nitroglycerine. "Funny stuff," he said. "Sometimes it blows when barely jostled, sometimes it doesn't even when thrown. A bottle this size could have blown the whole house apart or done nothing at all."

Kate thought about the moment between when the bottle hit the carpet and when it bounced under the chair. "So whoever threw this had no guarantee it would explode?"

The policeman, whose name tag identified him as Mr. O'Rourke, scratched his head. "Well, I don't rightly know. A wagon full of the stuff blew up in California two weeks back. Newspapers been full of stories about the dangers of nitroglycerine, how volatile it is and all that fear mongering the press likes to print and people like to read. Could be your thrower thought he had a sure thing with his little bottle."

He joined a bevy of policemen who swarmed Lily's rooms, each more shocked than the last that someone would try to blow up two women and one small dog. A senior officer, one Inspector Smythe, questioned Lily, but with no evidence and no witnesses Kate knew his investigation would have no where to go.

Officer O'Rourke promised to find a man to replace the window the next day, but insisted Kate and Lily vacate the premises for the time being. Kate hated to move Monty, but she had to agree with O'Rourke. Lily's apartment wasn't safe, not with a bomb throwing assassin out there somewhere. Plus, Lily's bedroom didn't have a fireplace or coal stove, so there was no way to keep the room warm. They bundled themselves up, refilled Monty's hot water bottle and climbed into a hansom cab one of the police officers scared up. O'Rourke carried Monty and handed him up to Lily while Kate directed their cabbie to Osborn house.

Once they were rolling Kate turned to Lily. "You think it was Mr. Harcourt-Bland?"

Lily pressed a soft kiss to Monty's exposed nose and lifted her face to look at Kate. "Who else?"

297

Peg A. Lamphier

Kate met Lily's gaze. Who else indeed?

Chapter 29

February 7, 1862
Rochester, New York

*L*ily leaned over the courtroom rail and whisper at
Kate. "Just how is this a jury of my peers?"

Kate glanced over at the jury and shook her
head. Twelve men. Prosperous, respectable, suit wearing
white men. "And the judge," she whispered back.

This morning Kate took a seat behind Lily and Mr. Lewis.
The men at the prosecution table pretended not to see her
defection and Kate was too tired to care either way. She'd
been up most of the night keeping watch over Monty. He'd
still been unconscious when she left for court this morning.

"I begin to think Mrs. Stanton is right." Lily said, still in
her low voice.

"About women's suffrage?" Kate's mind scrambled and
caught Lily's meaning. If women could vote they'd be able to
serve on juries.

Lily nodded.

Before Kate could answer, Lawyer Lewis shot a lawyerly
stare over his shoulder. Kate tried not to laugh, but she got the
message. From his seat high on the bench Judge Norris glared

at them, his bushy eyebrows drawn together so they made one slashing line across his face.

The moment the judge gaveled court into session Mr. Calderwood declared he had no other witnesses and wished to rest his case. Kate had expected him to do just that, but it was a great relief to hear him say it. She assumed that Harcourt-Bland's failed bombing would keep him from taking the stand, but a man who would throw nitroglycerine at women and dogs wasn't a man who would always do the rational thing.

Mr. Lewis began his defense with a parade of ladies, each the mother of a dead child. Each woman testified to Lily's skill as a spiritualist and general good character. Lawyer Lewis's strategy seemed to be working. The prosecution dare not cross examine the bereaved mothers for fear of seeming coldhearted, nor did the judge interfere much in their testimony.

Kate checked her watch. Twenty minutes to twelve. Surely the judge would take a lunch break after this witness. Kate snapped her pocket watch closed, and held it in her hand, wishing Hazzard was with her and not four hundred miles away. He'd given her the watch last summer, the same evening he gave her the pearl handled Colt revolver. Hazzard wasn't a man for useless gifts. If Monty died, she'd use the revolver on Harcourt-Bland, make no mistake.

She glanced over at the jury. They seemed as impatient for lunch as she. Lily glanced over her shoulder at Kate. Picking up on the general impatience for a hot meal, Lawyer Lewis finished his examination of Mrs. Clay, a well dressed woman who described the peace she found after Mrs. Winslow helped her in the wake of her four-year-old daughter's death.

Kate wondered how these women did it. How does a parent survive the death of a child? She was nearly undone by Monty's travail and he was a dog and was, as far as she knew, still alive.

After Mrs. Clay left the stand, the judge called a lunch recess, stipulating they should reconvene at 2 PM. Kate stood, both eager to check on Monty and dreading it at the same time. What if he'd died all alone, while she sat here listening to testimony? Maybe she should have stayed with him? No. She had a job to do, wounded dog or not.

Kate tried to catch Harcourt-Bland's eye before she left. On the way into court this morning she'd found him and grabbed his elbow. He staggered when he saw Kate.

"Didn't expect me, did you?" she whispered.

Blood drained from his face, leaving him as white as new snow. He didn't answer her. In fact his mouth seemed frozen half open.

She leaned in and whispered, "If my dog dies I will kill you and dump your body where no one will ever find it." She released his elbow with a shove and he stumbled away.

Now Mr. Harcourt-Bland took considerable care to keep his head down as they left court, which both pleased and irritated Kate. Mr. Lewis caught up with her on her way out of the courtroom, Lily right behind him. "The judge has agreed to meet with the police inspector and myself at lunch time."

Kate shook her head. "He'll say there's no evidence."

"That's what I said," Lily said.

He shook his head. "Doesn't matter. I want the judge to know. It'll be on his mind when he instructs the jury. I'll see you both back here at two. Lily, Mr. Clay tells me he's taking you and his wife to lunch. He wanted to insist you go too

301

Kate, but I told him I needed you for an errand. So you better get out of here before he calls me a liar. I know you want to check on your little fellow." He bustled off, their knight errant in a black frock coat.

Kate turned to go, but Lily put a hand on her arm. "I know you're in a hurry, but I didn't get to say this last night or this morning. I'm more sorry than you can know."

"About what?"

"Your dog," Lily said with an urgent tone. "If I hadn't brought you back to my rooms, if I'd been braver and not needed company, he'd be fine right now."

"Did you throw the bomb? No? Then it's not your fault. This is how they get away with shit." Kate caught her voice rising as she spoke. She hated this kind of thing.

Lily looked confused.

Kate got herself under control. "Bad men. Bad people. They do what they do and leave wreckage in their wake and the people who have to clean it up always feel guilty, like there was something they should have done to stop it." Kate shook her head. "It makes me tired." She shook off Lily's hand and fled the courtroom.

Back at the hotel room Kate found Monty unchanged. His nose and tongue looked dry, so she wetted a handkerchief and used it to squeeze water into his mouth. She thought she saw him swallow, but she wasn't sure. Then she dabbed rose oil on his nose, which caused a definite nose twitch. After that she lay on the bed next to him for about an hour, stroking his velvety ears and telling him what a good dog he was. His back paws twitched once or twice, as if he were chasing three legged cats in his dreams. But still he slept on, which worried Kate a great deal more than she cared to admit.

Once back at the courthouse Kate looked for Mr. Lewis. She found him across the room, near the jury box and raised an eyebrow in silent question. He shook his head.

"I didn't think so," Kate said, half to herself. As she turned to her seat, she saw Le Compte sitting in the back of the courtroom. He gave her a fluttery little finger wave that made Kate smile in spite of herself. He was a weasel, but a loyal and charming weasel nonetheless.

Mr. Lewis took his seat and turned to face Kate, who was once again sitting behind the defense table. "The judge is disinclined to believe the bomb was anything more than a disgruntled customer. In fact the judge is less than enamored with our client." He looked up as the judge entered the courtroom. "Here he is. Back to our seats before we make him crankier."

They only had two witnesses after lunch. Mr. Lewis first called Mrs. Amy Post. Kate watched the lady approach the stand with interest. She'd interviewed Mrs. Post two days before and found her fierce intelligence and unswerving moral compass fascinating. Mrs. Post and her husband had been leaders of a variety of Rochester reform movements the last twenty years, though in Kate's opinion their most important work was in the abolition movement. Mrs. Post enjoyed a personal relationship with luminaries like Frederick Douglass, Sojourner Truth and William Lloyd Garrison. Mrs. Post was also a staunch supporter of women's rights. She'd shown Kate her signed copy of the Seneca Falls Declaration, where fourteen years ago over a hundred women and men first met to demand women have equal rights. Kate had hardly dared touch the document. Mrs. Post was also a firm believer in Spiritualism, or at least a firm believer in a religious tolerance that included spiritualism as a legitimate avenue to the divine.

Whippet thin and straight backed, Mrs. Post carried but did not lean on her cane as she made her way into the witness box. She wore a plain black dress adorned only with the snow white collar and cuffs of a Quaker. She took the stand and gazed around the room like an aged queen surveying her kingdom. Which, Kate realized, was exactly what she was in Rochester.

After the usual introductory questions Mr. Lewis got down to it. "Mrs. Post, did you ever have occasion to investigate a spiritualist?"

"I suspect everyone in this room knows I did Sir," she said with a snap in her voice.

Several people in the room laughed. The judge banged his gavel until the tittering quieted.

"Could you remind us of the circumstances of your investigation and its conclusions?"

The old lady nodded. "Certainly." She launched into an explanation of her rather famous investigation of the Fox sisters, two girls who'd caused a national sensation some fourteen years before. The girls claimed they could communicate with the dead through a system of questions that spirits supposedly answered in raps. These spirit rappings generated an immense amount of controversy. The Posts took the girls into their home and after examining the phenomenon declared the girl's spiritual communications were real.

As Kate listened to the Mrs. Post's testimony she couldn't help but think humbuggery could fool even otherwise rational people. The problem was that the basic theory of spiritualism aligned with Christian beliefs in the soul and the afterlife. Spiritualist used those beliefs, combined with the understandable human desire to communicate with dead loved ones and a natural curiosity about what comes next, to accomplish their goals, which were often money collecting. Though, if one were fair, a lot of churches did much the same and called it religion.

Once Mr. Lewis finished with Mrs. Post, Mr. Calderwood had a go at her, but the lady would not move off her testimony. A lifetime of moral rectitude had taught her not to doubt herself when confronted with skeptical authority figures, be it in matters of women's rights, slavery or spiritualism. When she left the stand, she paused in front of the defense table and nodded at Lily before leaving the courtroom. Her demonstration did not go unnoticed by the men in the jury box.

Kate steeled herself for the final push. They had only one more witness to call.

Lawyer Lewis stood and announced, "The defense calls Mrs. Ellen Winslow."

Lily stood and approached the witness box. Every eye on the room followed her progress across the front of the courtroom and for good reason. Lily wore a tailored grayish lavender dress cut to suggest a wide lapel, military coat. Pewter buttons ran in an angle across the bodice and down the front of the dress, to a hem piped with a thin line of black cording. It was a plain enough dress, one that would have made most women disappear. On Lily it did quite the opposite. The coloring and lack of fluff suggested respectable, half-mourning, while the impeccable cut and fit of the dress highlighted her figure. When Kate had first seen Lily this morning,

305

she'd regarded her own serviceable navy blue wool dress with a jaundiced eye. Then she reminded herself that it traveled well and that she, not Lily, had a handsome artillery captain waiting for her at home.

Mr. Lewis began by questioning Lily about her life before Rochester. Lily lied with aplomb, inventing a story of a happy childhood in Ohio and an early marriage to a fictitious Mr. Winslow. In all fairness Mr. Lewis didn't know she was lying. Lily gained considerable sympathy from the male jurors with her wrenching tale of the imaginary Mr. Winslow's death and her subsequent discovery of his considerable debt, which left her a pauper widow. Kate felt a moment of doubt as she watched Lily tell lie after lie while on the stand and under oath. Then she remembered her recent investigation. And last night's bomb.

"So you became a medium to support yourself," Lewis asked.

"Well, yes that," Lily said, "but also I have a gift." She told the story of how she found a bee hive when she was a child before describing the manner in which she developed and refined her clairvoyant talents."

"And you did this for profit?"

"Well, yes. I had debts, remember? And my papa said one must always pay one's debts. But also to help people. Like the ladies you heard from this morning. So many people grieve the loss of a loved one. But grief is too small a word for what mothers feel. I try to help them by contacting their lost children."

Lewis reared back his head in mock disbelief. "You can't expect us to believe you contact the dead Mrs. Winslow."

"But I can. All people of faith believe in things unseen. It is the essence of faith. Spiritualism is not at odds with Christianity. I am a Christian myself. That is why I believe death is not the end, but a beginning. Of what, we do not know, but a beginning nonetheless. And if we have souls and most of us in the room believe we do, then those souls go somewhere after death. We speak of passing on, don't we? And if our souls go somewhere, might not a trained intermediary contact them? And that's what I am. A conduit."

Kate watched the men in the jury. They couldn't keep their eyes off Mrs. Winslow. She was beautiful, soft spoken, submissive and sentimental. In short, she represented a male fantasy of womanhood and one every bit as fake as Mrs. Winslow herself.

"And did you use this power to manipulate Mr. Lyon into marriage?"

Lily shook her head and responded in a patient voice, just as they'd practiced. "No, it's not like that. I can hear the dead. I can't force the living to do my bidding."

"Did you threaten to sue Mr. Lyon for breach of promise when he failed to make good on his promise of marriage?"

Lily shook her head again. "You have it all wrong. He asked me to marry him, but later withdrew his offer. I believe Mr. Lyon loves his wife still, though she is beyond the veil. I admired him for that, so I released him without rancor."

Mr. Lewis leveled a stern look at Lily. "Come now. You never sued Mr. Lyon?"

"He said I did not in this very court. Yesterday."

"You never threatened to sue Mr. Lyon?"

"I did not," Lily said in a quavering voice. Her eyes filled with unshed tears. "I believe his assistant Mr. Harcourt told him I did, but I did not."

"And why would Mr. Harcourt lie?" Lewis turned and looked at Harcourt-Bland, thus ensuring the jury did as well. The man's face paled from pinkish-red to a yellow-white. His eyes blinked and slid from side to side. Kate almost laughed. It was as if the fool was giving a seminar in how to act guilty.

Lewis turned away from Harcourt-Bland, pulled his handkerchief from his pocket and offered it to Lily. "Question withdrawn."

When Lewis finished with Lily, Mr. Calderwood thumped over to stand before her.

"Mrs. Winslow, if that is your real name, isn't it true you've changed your name several times?"

She crumpled Lewis's handkerchief in her hand and nodded. "Many mediums do."

"And why would that be? To better fleece your victims?"

Lily widened her eyes in shock. "No, not at all. Say I leave Rochester and move my business to Buffalo. But when I arrive there is a Mrs. Winslow, or even a Mr. Winslow, or a Winslet or a Winter, already in business there. I would change my name to mark myself as a different medium from those with similar names." She ignored the lawyer and offered the jury a small smile. "It's harmless."

Calderwood snorted. "So you say. In my experience respectable women do not change their names willy nilly."

Mr. Lewis objected. The judge waved Caldwell forward to his next question.

"And you continue to claim Mr. Lyon, a wealthy business man and a respected member of Rochester society, made an offer of marriage to a woman such as yourself?"

Lily fluttered her dark eyelashes as if to keep back tears. "He did, but it doesn't matter. I released him from his promise. He loves his wife. I already explained all that."

"So you say. Then why are we here?"

"Because your client is suing me and you served me papers demanding my presence," Lily said, indignation in her every word.

Laughter erupted in the courtroom.

The judge once again banged his gavel and glared around the courtroom.

Kate looked over at the prosecution table. Mr. Lyon stared at the table top. Had he begun to regret this farce?

Mr. Calderwood glared at Lily. "You know what I mean. If there is no cause for this suit, we would not be in court."

"Isn't that exactly what court is for? To decide if there is a cause?"

The lawyer flung his hands in the air. "I say you are a hussy of the lowest sort, Madame, no better than a common harlot." He half-yelled his last words.

Lewis leapt to his feat. "Objection your honor."

The courtroom erupted into a noisy gabble.

The judge gaveled the room back into submission.

Calderwood waved Lily away and slunk back to his table.

Still on his feet, Lewis waited for the courtroom to quiet and announced, "The defense rests."

Chapter 30

February 7, 1862
Rochester, New York

M r. Lewis flashed Kate and Lily a triumphant smile as he turned to his seat. Kate had to agree with his unspoken assessment of the case. The prosecution had not made their case and the jury knew it. And then disaster struck.

Judge Townsend used his gavel to bring the courtroom to attention. He glared around the room before turning to the jury. "Gentlemen of the jury, it is now my duty to instruct you on your deliberations. The cause, in this case, requires little discussion or disagreement. Given how clear your course is I ask you to make haste. Rochester can little stand the attention a lengthy deliberation would bring. Even one more day of a trial this distasteful would be too much."

Kate stared at the judge. What was he doing? She glanced over at the jury. Their faces suggested they were wondering much the same.

Judge Townsend tugged at the front of his voluminous robe and continued his speech. "I see you are uncomfortable with my comments, but let me assure you it is the policy of all courts to seek justice as swiftly as possible. You must be guided only by the evidence and the law, not by emotion. If you do so, you will have the everlasting thanks of the right-minded men of this community." The judge paused and glared at the room where murmurs arose like butterflies on a breeze. He waited for the room to quiet.

Lily turned around and glanced at Kate, her eyes wide with worry. Kate shrugged and looked at Mr. Lewis. He sat unmoving, his face white with anxiety.

When Townsend continued, he raised his voice to a near bellow. "The defendant's counsel wants you to be lenient with her because she is attractive and young. But you must see what she is. Her lawyer has suggested one of the most esteemed men of this community would make an offer of marriage to a woman. He would also have you believe a viper such as she would release him from his promise. Does this make sense? We know he is a man of character and we know she is a person who has gone from city to city defrauding good men."

Kate wanted to grab Lily and flee the courtroom rather than listen to this blatant misuse of judicial power. Instead, she sat pinned in her chair.

"Consider these facts: she operates under aliases, consorts with foreigners and shared her home with lewd women. And yet she asks you to take serious the notion that a gentleman would marry her. No man on this jury would consider a relationship with this woman. Her claim the plaintiff did so is an outrage."

He paused again and fiddled with his robe. Kate began to hope he'd finished his diatribe, but he spoke again.

"You have also heard testimony that the defendant is unchaste. If there was a marriage contract her impurity would render that contract null and void. No man can be held accountable for promises he makes to an unchaste woman."

Kate snorted to herself. What about the man who made the woman unchaste? Heaven forbid society hold any man to the same strict sexual standard as women.

"She is a woman with no shame, keen shrewdness and a wicked nature, developed in depravity to a level seldom seen in this court. The vilest, lowest prostitute is better than this woman, yet she aspires to a respectable man's name and fortune."

By the time he got to the end of his sentence, Judge Townsend was bellowing again. Red-faced and sweating, he looked like a man standing on the edge of sanity.

"Gentlemen of the jury, before you is a woman who has left a trail of evil machinations over this land. You must convict her or bring shame to yourselves, this court and the decent citizens of this county." He banged his gavel one more time, stood and swept from the courtroom in a flurry of black robes and moral indignation.

The jury seemed too stunned to move. The bailiff opened the gate at their enclosure. They walked out, as quiet as lambs to slaughter. Kate watched Lily watch them go. When the courtroom door closed behind the twelfth man Lily burst into tears. Kate didn't blame her. Lawyer Lewis patted her on the back while throwing helpless looks over his shoulder.Kate had no idea what to do.

Behind her, people made sounds like they were leaving the courtroom. She glanced over at the prosecution table. Harcourt shook Mr. Lyon and Mr. Calderwood's hands. When

Harcourt stepped back to allow Lyon to shake Calderwood's hand he glanced in Lily's direction. Kate recoiled at the nasty, gloating of expression on his face. She almost expected him to rub his hands together and twirl his mustaches in a theatrical pantomime of evil. Kate's mind spun like a whirly-gig. There was something going on her. But what?

Kate stood and waited for Harcourt to leave the court-room, but just then the bailiff pushed open the door at the side of the courtroom and announced, "The jury is coming back."

It hadn't been even five minutes. Kate felt a nauseating sense of dread.

The judge took his seat while the twelve jurors filed back into the jury box. They kept their heads down.

The judge harrumphed and fidgeted in his seat before pounding his gavel once again. "Has the jury reached a verdict?"

From the jury box a tall, spectacle wearing man in a black frock coat stood. "We have your honor."

"Will you read it, sir?"

The man nodded, careful to keep his eye on the judge. He took a slip of paper from his front, inside coat pocket, unfolded it and held it before him. "We the jury find the defendant, Mrs. Ellen Winslow, guilty of barratry. We also find her guilty of fraud."

The nearly empty courtroom was silent while the judge glared at Lily. "The defendant will rise."

Lily stood, back straight, chin up. Kate realized she admired Lily. She was a hard woman to break.

"In light of your unwillingness to admit your guilt, I sentence you to the maximum punishment. You are to serve six years in the Female Wing of Auburn Prison for your crimes. May you use your time there to reflect upon your transgressions and mend your ways."

Judge Townsend excused the jury after thanking them for their service. He slammed his gavel down one last time and left the courtroom.

The bailiff approached Lily with a look of pity on his face. "Come now miss. I have to take you to the cells."

Mr. Lewis stopped the bailiff from taking hold of Lily's elbow. "I'll file an appeal first thing in the morning."

Lily smiled, first at Mr. Lewis and then Kate. Her purple-blue eyes glimmered behind her black eyelashes but she did not cry. Then the bailiff took her away.

Kate stormed down the courthouse hallway, her boot heels thumping on the marble floor in most satisfying manner. She'd planned to leave court today and hurry back to her hotel room to check on Monty, but no. Instead, this had to happen. Either he was better or he was not. Right now there was nothing to be done about it either way. This perversion of justice had to be her priority. And the maid had promised to check on the little bugger.

Dammit. In her capacity as a Pinkerton detective, she'd sat in on several trials and she'd never seen anything like what happened in court today. True, judges instructed juries, but in all of Kate's experience, their instructions were on matters of law, not invective filled directions on how the jury should rule. The judge's instruction had the stench of corruption upon it. She'd go to his office and provoke him into some kind of admission. It wasn't her best plan, but she was too angry to come up with a better one.

She found the door to the judge's chambers and stepped inside. There was a small anteroom where a clerk would sit, but no one was there. There was a door behind the clerk's desk. Kate assumed that led to the judge's chambers. She was about to knock when voices came through the door. Loud voices. Two men yelling at each other. Unable to resist, Kate pressed her ear against the door.

A voice she recognized as Judge Thompson's yelled, "Dammit, I've done what you asked and I expect my money!"

Another voice spoke up, though all Kate could hear was a low murmur.

"Pay me or I'll void the sentence," came Thompson's voice, loud and angry.

The other voice spoke. Then the judge yelled, "You have one hour."

Kate pressed her ear harder against the door, only to hear the thump of boot heels. She dashed for the window and its voluminous black velvet curtains. She slid behind a long velvet panel, thanking the powers above she'd worn her navy blue dress today and not a lighter color. She heard the door open and peeked around the velvet in time to see a man striding across the anteroom. There was no mistaking his dark blond hair and thick torso.

Kate waited for a count of five before she followed Harcourt-Bland. He left the courthouse and walked toward the Arcade and the offices of Lyon Enterprises. Daylight had given way to the dim light of early evening, but she kept well back of him. By his bouncing stride and the jaunty way he swung his walking stick, Kate guessed he was feeling good about his day in spite of the judge's threats. He surprised her by walking right past the Arcade building. He crossed the street and turned into a stone building in the middle of the next block.

Kate hurried up to the building and peered at the doors. In gold leaf print, they read 'Commercial Bank.' She crossed back across the street and stood in front of a milliner's shop, pretending fascination with the spring bonnets on display. After about fifteen minutes Harcourt-Bland exited the bank and walked back the way he'd come. Kate followed him, tamping down the impulse to get up behind him, stick her gun in his back. She'd like to take him some dark place and rid the world of him.

Instead, she followed him back to the courthouse, but let him enter that building alone. Even if she caught Judge Townsend and Mr. Harcourt-Bland in a cash exchange it would be their word against hers. No one would believe Mr. Lyon's assistant had bribed the judge to direct a guilty verdict against Mrs. Winslow. Or at least no one with power. Like no one would believe he'd thrown the bomb. Powerful men didn't murder women and dogs, or so people liked to tell themselves.

No, there was no use appealing to the authorities. She'd have to take authority into her own hands. She left the courthouse and walked back to the hotel. By the time she arrived she had a plan.

Chapter 31

February 7-8, 1862
Rochester, New York

*B*ack at the hotel Kate found two pieces of good news waiting for her. First, Monty was awake and limping around the bed on his splinted leg. There was some barking and licking and capering about, most of it performed by a small black and white whirlwind. Kate did swing the little dog up into her arms and dance him around the room.

Second, she found a letter from Cincinnati on the floor, where it had been slipped under the door. She read its contents, suppressed a yelp joy and hugged Monty again instead. He wriggled and washed her face with his warm tongue. She didn't care what people said, doggy kisses were among the best kisses in the world.

She took Monty outside for a quick visit of lamp poles and returned to the room to order a roast beef dinner sent to the room. After sharing dinner they snuggled into bed with a notebook and pen. Kate made a list and Monty napped, his splinted leg poking out into the air until Kate slid the end of a pillow under it.

Peg A. Lamphier

The next morning Kate awoke at dawn. She dressed in her plain brown wool dress and borrowed a ragged coat from one of the maids.

Outside, the sky was just turning from black to a pale blue dawn. Kate's plan assumed the city jailers would be moving Lily to the women's prison in upstate New York in the immediate future. The jail was in the courthouse basement though she only suspected the exterior door was at the back of the building. She'd come and gone from the courthouse the last two days and not once seen a jailer or a paddy wagon.

Kate made her way to the courthouse, Monty tip tapping alongside her. In the back alley she found what she expected, one box wagon with a barred door at its rear and one back entrance guarded by one policeman. She sashayed up to the guard, grinning like a mad woman. "Oh, ain't you a handsome one?" She laid a mitten covered hand on the young man's chest.

He removed her hand, but smiled as he did. "You don't fool me you little minx. What do you want?"

Kate pushed out her lower lip into a pout. "Is dat wicked woman in here? Da one from yesterday?"

"That she is darlin'." He bent and ruffled Monty's ears.

"She comin' out today. So I kin git a gander at 'er?" Kate swung her shoulders from side to side, like a winsome child begging candy.

"Tomorrow morning darlin', real early like. We drive prisoners out at 5 in the morning, before the decent folk is up and about."

"Oooheee, I wish I might see," Kate squealed. "They say she's real good lookin' but badder than bad."

320

The guard agreed that Lily was indeed a most nefarious woman. "But not near so pretty as yourself darlin'."

She tipped up on her toes and pressed a kiss on the man's stubbly cheek. "I'd like to see the wicked tart but that's too early for the likes o' me. Too bad." Kate turned on her heel and sashayed away, putting an extra swing in her hoop skirt as she did.

Back at the hotel she wiped down her lock picks, cleaned her pistol, oiled her dagger and took Monty out to run errands. She ended up carrying him most of the time, but she wasn't ready to let him out of her sight just yet. They stopped at a rooming house several blocks from the jail and reserved a room for one week, beginning tomorrow. Next they found a hardware store. After she'd made her purchases there the hardware clerk directed them to a second-hand store where Kate bought a grubby black coat.

Shopping complete, they returned to Osborn House. Kate arranged to check out of the hotel the next day and the clerk agreed to forward her trunks to the address she provided him. After lunch Kate spent the day lounging in the bed reading Harriet Jacobs' autobiography of her life as a woman who'd escaped slavery. Monty's soft snores bothered Kate not one bit.

The next morning they were up so early there was no doorman to see them off. Kate let Monty pee on an Osborn House light pole for the last time, his tiny body making a big shadow in the gaslight. She tucked Monty into her second-hand coat and strode down the sidewalk, a small canvas bag bouncing off her hip as she walked. There was no place for a little dog with a broken foreleg in tonight's plans—but if her plan worked she wouldn't be returning to Osborn House.

The city was quiet and cold. She snuggled Monty up under her chin, glad for his warmth and reviewed her plan. So much could go wrong. Once Lily was inside the Auburn Prison she'd be under heavy guard for six years. Unless Mr. Lewis's appeal succeeded, which seemed unlikely considering Harcourt-Bland's malevolence, Lyon's money, and Judge Townsend's corruption.

Kate frowned at the courthouse as she walked past it and once again walked around the back of the building. The prison wagon stood near the back door, but this time there was no guard. That made sense. With the jail locked up tight at night, there was no need to watch the door.

Keeping to the shadows, Kate edged down the alley toward the wagon. It loomed in the dark, like a great, wicked beast. No wonder they called police wagons Black Marias. It was a formidable and forbidding carriage, with its plain black box and barred rear door. Kate noted the front wheels were about half the size of the rear wheels, probably because the reinforced box and iron door at the rear required sturdier wheels. This meant the front wheels would have smaller, easier to manage hub nuts. She checked around the alley one more time, before skittering around to the Black Maria's far side. Kate squatted before the front wheel. Her nose wrinkled against the smell of urine that rose on the cold air. Clearly, the jailers and policemen used the wall behind the wagon as a bathroom. Monty's nose twitched in a fit of sniffing, but otherwise he staid still inside her coat.

Kate pulled a lightweight ball-peen hammer from the bag, along with an adjustable wrench. She worked the head of the tool into the wheel's hub housing and got a grip on the hub nut. An image of Hazzard popped into her head, squatting before a wagon wheel not all that different from the one in front of her. Everything she knew about sabotaging wagon wheels she learned from him. They'd been traveling incognito in a medicine show wagon and used a broken wheel as an excuse to stop in front of a planation that needed investigating.

The wrench slipped when Kate tried to tighten the wrench teeth. Swearing, she stripped off her gloves and used her thumb to tighten the wrench on the wheel nut. As she suspected, the nut was cranked down hard. She peered around the wheel, checking for company. Nothing. She picked up the hammer and tapped the wrench. It didn't budge. Worse, it made a loud tinging sound. She grabbed one of her gloves, laid it across the wrench and hit it again. It bumped down a notch. She tapped away until the nut felt loose, then pulled the wrench out of the hub housing and tried to turn the nut with her fingers. *Crap, it was cold.* She put her gloves on and tried again.

Once she'd unscrewed the nut Kate slipped it in her bag, along with the tools. She was about to stand when she heard footsteps echoed up the alley. Someone whistled. Kate froze, crouched behind the wagon wheel, cursing the poor cover. A man in a police uniform walked down the alley. He stopped whistling and walking at the same time. Kate's heart stuttered. This had to be the worst hiding place ever.

She placed a gloved hand on Monty's head and watched the policeman. He fumbled in his pockets and seconds later a lit match illuminated his face. The man held the match to a cigar, puffed a few times and headed for the door to the jail. He pulled out a key, unlocked the door and disappeared.

When her heart had slowed sufficiently, Kate stripped her gloves off again and stepped to the rear of the wagon. Pulling her lock pick set from her pocket, Kate eyed the lock on the Black Maria's barred door. What it lacked in grace it made up for in heavy ugliness. Kate smiled at the lock. People thought the bigger and heavier the lock the more effective it would be, but it was the small, finely crafted locks that were a real bear to pick. Kate slipped her pick locks back into her pocket and fished out her skeleton keys. She tried one, then another. The third key, one with a simple cross on the end, popped the lock right open. Kate grinned and re-locked it. Monty, sensing her excitement, tipped his head up and licked her chin.

"Fun's over. Now we to wait," she whispered to him.

She'd scouted the area yesterday, noting that the most likely route out of town was straight up Exchange Street to West Avenue and from there east out of town. Auburn was only sixty miles away on a road that went due east, through farm country and a string of small towns. Still, she wanted to get Lily out of the wagon before it ever left Rochester. Cities were easier to hide in than open countryside.

Kate walked a little way up Exchange Street, stopping under a gas lamp to check her watch. It was half past 4 o'clock. She waited in a tiny church that was only marginally warmer inside than outside. She let Monty out of her coat to sniff around the pews after first giving him a stern talking to about the impropriety of peeing in a church.

While she waited Kate made a mental list of things that could go wrong. The wagon might take another route and she'd miss it. The wheel might fall off before the Black Maria left the alley, or it might not fall off at all. The wagon could have two policemen on it, making the escape twice as dangerous. The driver might catch her or both of them. Lily could refuse to escape. Kate smiled at that. Now she was worrying for worry's sake. Lily, with her disdain for rules and respectability, would go with her as surely as night followed the day. The wheel would most likely fall off after the wagon turned onto West Avenue. And they wouldn't pay two men to move one woman to prison. But logic had no place in the cold as her watch ticked away the minutes.

At 5 o'clock she snapped her watch shut, tucked Monty back in her coat and left the church. On her way out she silently thanked the minister that left it open all night for the use of lost souls. And for what she was about to do she should surely count herself as one such soul. Pinkerton operatives weren't supposed to break convicted felons out of police custody.

She moved down off the church steps and into the dark recess of street-level doorway. Kate waited and shivered. The cold made each minute seem like an hour. Finally it came, the clip-clop of a horse's hooves and the rumble of iron-clad wheels on frozen cobblestones sounded in the frigid pre-dawn air. The Black Maria hove into view. Kate waited for it to roll past, relieved to see it had only one man aboard, the driver.

Surely Lily rode in the back, unseen, locked up like a rabid animal. Kate followed the wagon up the street, counting on the fact that the driver wouldn't look back. And if he did he'd see only a lone woman on the sidewalk. The front passenger side wheel wobbled. Not a lot, but it had a definite wobble. Kate squeezed Monty in anticipation.

325

The wagon turned onto West Avenue. The wheel wobble increased as the Black Maria crossed the bridge. They passed Osborn House. The wheel began to move in a most satisfying manner. The wagon passed down a dark stretch of street, an empty lot on one side and another church on the other side. There the wheel gave up its struggle and slipped off the axel. The Maria's front axel hit the frozen street with a thump and screeched as the metal axel cap scraped on the cobblestones. The wheel rolled up the street several yards, slowed and flopped over. From inside the wagon came a woman's high-pitched scream. Kate nearly laughed in relief. It was Lily.

The Black Maria thunked to a halt with a jangle of harness buckles and the neighing of a confused horse. Kate scampered up behind a tree trunk and peeked around. The driver came around the far side of the wagon and pulled his hat off. He looked at the axel, then at the wheel. He scratched his head and put his hat back before turning to retrieve the wheel.

Kate bolted up to the rear of the Black Maria. Lily was at the door, her hands clutching the bars. Kate put her forefinger to her lips with her left hand while she used her right hand to slide the skeleton key into the lock. The lock popped open with a soft snick. Lily grinned as Kate pulled the door open. The hinges screeched. Kate castigated herself for not considering the damned hinges. Too late now.

"Hey," the driver yelled. His voice was half indignant, half confused.

Lily threw herself onto the dark street and they ran.

Kate never again wished she'd worn men's clothing as much as she did then. She'd worn a dress thinking if the police caught her she might talk herself out of arrest but now she thought she'd made a mistake. Clutching Monty with one arm to her chest, she bolted toward the church, Lily hard on her heels. She caught the words 'St. John's' on a sign before they were past it and heading for the back of the building.

Behind them the driver hollered at the top of his lungs, though Kate could not make out individual words. They rounded the church's rear corner and ran smack dab into an iron fence. The thing had to be at least seven feet high and it stretched out into the dark. Inside the fence there were tombstones and small, stone buildings.

Kate grabbed Lily's hand and pulled her up to the fence. "Up an over."

Lily put her foot on the bottom crossbar and grabbed the top bar. She leaped up. Kate put both her hands on Lily's narrow rear end and shoved with everything she had. Lily sailed up, up, up and fell with a thud on the other side. She swore and scrambled to her feet. Kate pulled Monty out of her coat and shoved him through the fence railings, into Lily's arms.

Kate looked up at the fence. There was no one to help her, but a childhood in the circus had given her more strength and agility than most women. She shoved the keys into a skirt pocket, hiked up her skirts and climbed. She was up and over in a trice.

Lily put Monty on the ground and grabbed at Kate's arm. "We're trapped."

Kate pushed Lily away and pointed at a small stone building at the cemetery's center. She leaned down to scoop up her dog, but he slipped her grasp and threw himself at the fence. His leg cast clinked against a bar and then he was through.

"Monty, come," Kate hissed, patting her thigh as she did.

327

From the front of the church the driver hollered again. This time Kate heard the words. "I'll get you!"

Monty glanced at Kate, turned and hop, skipped away. He ran toward the street, his little cast a white blur against the dark. Kate wanted to call him back, but didn't dare yell. *Dammit, dammit, dammit.*

She turned and looked for Lily, but she'd had already taken off across the cemetery. Kate looked once more for Monty, but he'd disappeared. She ran, feeling helpless and terrible as she did. She caught up with Lily and pushed her down behind a double tombstone. A man screamed. It was a high pitched, blood-curdling screech of pain. The sound came again, echoing on the night air.

Kate peered over the tombstone to see Monty running back to her, so fast he was a blur of dark and light shadow, like the stuff of hope unlooked for. He wriggled through the bars and scrambled over to them. Leaping the last few feet, Monty threw himself into Kate's waiting arms. Kate held him against her chest so hard she could feel his tiny heart thumping behind his ribs. He wriggled out of her arms, leapt to the ground and peered around the tombstone, growling as he did.

Kate wanted to shake the little dog for scaring her, but Lily laughed out loud in delight. She grabbed Kate's shoulder. "Let's go." She pointed at the mausoleum behind them. "You too, Monty," she said with mock severity.

Keeping low, the three of them sprinted across the cemetery, zigzagging between tombstones. As she ran, Kate pulled her skeleton keys out of her pocket. They snagged on her wool skirt and slipped from her fingers. Before she could come to a full stop Monty had scooped up the key ring in his teeth. They arrived at the mausoleum only seconds behind Lily.

Kate grabbed the simplest key in her ring, a straight, thin piece of white metal with a hook on the end of it. With a hasty prayer, she pushed the slender key in and turned. Or tried to. It didn't budge. She tried the next key, this one with an axe-shaped head. In it went. Kate held her breath and turned. The lock clicked open. She pulled the door open and the three of them slid inside the crypt. Cold damp air closed around them. A plain, stone catafalque stood in the middle of the tiny room. Five empty coffin slots yawned into the grey. The sixth slot contained a lone coffin. Kate shut the wooden door with a soft thump, leaving them in unrelieved blackness. They collapsed against a wall, leaning against each other, everyone breathing hard. Monty slathered Kate's face with kisses. Kate felt Lily shake like she was laughing.

Kate leaned into Lily. She was laughing. Silently, but laughing.

Lily made a choked sound and giggled. "Did you see the name on the mausoleum?"

Kate shook her head. She'd been too busy messing with the keys to do any reading.

"Lyon," Lily said in a solemn tone. She giggled again.

Kate stifled a laugh of her own. "You're kidding? Lyon?"

Lily nodded. "If I had to guess I'd say we're hiding with the first and only Mrs. Abelard Lyon."

Snorts of laughter echoed in the tiny chamber for several long, lovely minutes.

They hid in Mrs. Lyon's tomb until grey light crept under the mausoleum door. Kate ventured out of the cemetery to find the sky lightening in the east. She walked out to the street

329

and looked for the Black Maria. It was gone. Nor did she see any policemen. The search for the missing prisoner appeared less than robust. Kate stood on the sidewalk and pondered the quiet street. If she had to guess she'd say Judge Townsend was none too happy right now. He wouldn't be eager to see either Mrs. Winslow or her detective for fear they might reveal his corruption. Which was exactly the response Kate hoped for when she planned Lily's escape.

She fetched Lily and Monty from the Lyon mausoleum and took them to the rooming house, only six blocks away. The ever-so proper landlady blinked not one eyelash at Kate's story of a sister, recently arrived on an early train. She showed them to a cozy room with a double bed and a corner sink and left them alone. Lily and Kate sat on the bed, facing the room's only window. Monty lay curled in Kate's lap, blissfully unaware that he was the hero of the hour.

Kate told Lily about Mrs. Becker and showed her a letter from the lady. Mrs. Becker found Lily's child—now a five-year-old boy—at the City Workhouse. He'd been there since infancy, having been left there with a sizable bequest to ensure the staff's cooperation and silence. Because children younger than five were generally turned over to one of the city or-phanages, no one had thought to check the workhouse.

Tears streamed down Lily's face when she read the letter from Mrs. Becker saying she had the boy with her and they were waiting for his mother.

Eventually the sun rose high enough to send beams of winter sunshine through the room's only window. A ray of silvery light shown on Monty, revealing a scrap of navy blue wool wedged between his front teeth. He also had a smudge of blood on his muzzle and another on his chest. Kate picked the fabric from her dog's teeth, remembering the high-pitched scream that rode the air after Monty made his escape. Kate showed the fabric and blood to Lily and they laughed together for the last time.

Chapter 32

February 14, 1862
Washington City, District of Columbia

Kate kissed her way along Hazard's collarbone and up his neck, marveling the way his skin changed texture from silky smooth to rough stubble. The morning sunshine streamed through her bedroom window, lighting the room with a glow that matched how she felt. It was a soft, clear Washington light that made a welcome change from the thin winter light of the frozen north. She'd arrived home the night before last and spent most of yesterday sleeping. Charlotte let no one disturb her, not even Juba. Late yesterday afternoon Hazzard showed up at her bedroom door with a dinner tray. Having him all to herself for the next few hours made the Rochester mess almost worth it.

"Woman, you will be the death of me." Hazzard pulled Kate up on top of him and grinned at her, his teeth gleaming white against his black mustache.

Kate smiled back. "The first time I saw you I thought you looked like a pirate."

His chest rumbled with a chuckle. "Like Blackbeard?"

"Nooo. Less wife murdering fiend and more dashing lord of the high seas with a cutlass between your teeth."

"Hmmm." He nibbled at her ear lobe and whispered, "Cutlasses are heavier than you think. I'm not sure I could hold one in my teeth." He nipped her ear lobe for emphasis.

"In my imagination, you can hold a cutlass in your teeth."

"Your fevered imagination," he whispered into her ear. There was no talking for a while.

A while later Hazzard tipped himself up on his elbow and appraised Kate. "You never finished your Rochester story."

She smiled up at him and stretched like a contented cat. "You keep interrupting me." Kate felt a great sense of peace and belonging fill her. It was nice to be home with her make-shift family and her not-husband.

She smiled again. She couldn't seem to stop. "Where did I let off last night?"

"Where your Black Widow discovered Mr. Harcourt was the nefarious Reverend Bland."

Kate shook her head, but didn't correct him about the Black Widow thing. Instead, she told him about the trial. When she got to the bomb, Hazzard stopped her. "It was Harcourt, wasn't it? Or Bland? Whatever his name is."

Kate heaved a sigh. "There's no way to prove it. There never will be."

"That man needs a good thrashing," Hazzard growled. "And then a hanging."

Kate made a scoffing sound. "It gets worse." She finished her tale, starting with the Judge's jury tirade and ending at the boarding house.

Hazzard craned his neck to peer down at Monty, who was sleeping in his basket in the corner, his splinted leg sticking out in front of his muzzle. "That little dog kept the man from chasing and catching you?"

"Yep. You should have heard the man scream."

"We must take the little fellow to the butcher and let him pick out a bone."

Kate agreed. "The thing is, Lily was no Black Widow. I'd convinced myself she was. It's a box we put women into and I fell for it. Women are supposed to be all good or all bad. Woe betide the women who doesn't fit in a neat little box."

"No one's all good," Hazzard said. "I mean, except for me." He flashed a wicked smile.

"Weeeell," she drawled, earning herself a poke in the shoulder. "You're perfect for me, but not for other ladies. If you gave any other women used pocket watches and knives and guns, you would be in trouble." They beamed at each other. Kate thought it might be impossible to love a man more than she loved Hazzard. "Anyway, my Black Widow, as you call her, turned out to be just about the strongest woman I've ever met. I told her once she had an iron core running through her."

"No wonder you liked her. You've got that too."

"Not like Lily. I don't think I could survive what she did. When I was investigating, I'd find out something horrible in her past and I'd think it couldn't get worse. Then I'd find something even more horrible and then another thing and another. Somewhere between the parents, the first husband, the reverend and the second husband I would have given up."

He dropped a kiss on her forehead. "I disagree. You survived your parent's death, what you thought was Juba's death and marriage to a bad man. And still had the courage to march into Allan Pinkerton's office and ask him for a job. As a detective no less."

She sighed. "Maybe. At least I've always known my parents loved me. And Juba."

"And me," Hazzard said.

"Yes. You." Kate bit her lower lip. "Lily's never had anyone. But she kept fighting anyway, in a world that gives women like her precious little help."

"Well, she's got someone now, right?"

Kate grinned at Hazzard. "Her son. I never got to see him, but Mrs. Becker's letter said he has Lily's dark hair and her eyes."

Hazzard tapped Kate's nose with his forefinger. "I meant you. She has you."

"I owed her. My first investigation should have been better."

Hazzard dropped a light kiss on her nose. "First, you were new so don't blame yourself for not being as good as you are now. Second, it wouldn't have helped her. By the time you showed up she was already damaged."

"Maybe." Kate wasn't so sure. Hazzard hadn't met Lily, nor ever looked in her eyes.

"What will she do? Do you know?"

Kate pushed herself up until she was leaning against the headboard, pillows bunched behind her shoulders. Monty's head came up as soon as she moved, but when he saw she wasn't going anywhere, he put his head back down.

"I asked her if she had any plans. She was thinking of San Francisco. It makes sense. People go to California to start over."

"It would get her and her son away from the war too."

"Unlike us."

"I'm afraid we're in it until the bitter end, my dear." His stomach rumbled. "Speaking of the bitter end, did you see the news about Willie?"

"I found a newspaper on the train home." Her eyes welled with tears. "Poor Mr. Lincoln. He loved that boy so. He introduced both his sons to me once. They'd just let some turtles go in the canal."

"They say Mrs. Lincoln is lost to grief. She already had one son die, ten years ago and they say it nearly killed her."

"I don't know how any parent gets past the loss of a child. I met her once, back before the inauguration when we were trying to get Mr. Lincoln on the special train. Remember? She seemed nice though I know an awful lot of people don't like her. You could tell how much she loves her husband and sons."

Hazzard squeezed Kate's hand. "I spent a lot of time with her in Springfield after the election. She's a woman who speaks her mind and you're right. She'll say and do anything to protect her family."

Kate shook her head. "I can't even imagine. Lily never even met her child, she didn't know whether it was a girl or a boy, and it nearly broke her to lose it. Her real work was helping mothers of dead children. It's too bad she can't help the Lincolns. I suppose no one can." Kate paused for a thought. "Willie was how old?"

"He just turned twelve."

"Twelve. To have a child for twelve years and lose him. How do parents do it?" Kate looked over at Hazzard, the unspoken question hanging between them.

337

He cocked an eyebrow at her. "It is an argument for not having children. They're mighty perilous creatures."

"It seems so doesn't it?" She kissed him on the cheek. "And yet."

He nodded. "And yet,"

She looked him in the eye. "After the war, maybe?"

He nodded again. "After the war."

Kate's stomach growled, reminding her she hadn't eaten since late yesterday afternoon. "We should get dressed and see what Odetta has for breakfast."

Hazzard agreed and rolled out of bed. While he was pulling on his trousers he looked over at Kate. "Do you think you'll ever hear from her? Lily I mean."

Kate shook her head as she got out of bed. "She said she'd write, but I bet she doesn't. She's spent her life remaking herself. The key to reinventing yourself is not to drag anything from your old life into the new life. There's a man in Rochester who loves her, though he's a peculiar fellow." Kate smiled at the thought of Le Compte. "But I suspect Lily will never contact him. She'll try to forget Rochester. I know I would."

All the people Kate loved in world ended up in the F Street house kitchen, often all at once. She carried Monty down the stairs, then sat him down and pushed her way through the green baize door, into a myriad of voices and faces.

Juba hugged her first and longest. Afterwards she held him at arm's length and looked him over.

"Have you made progress on your network of Black Pinkertons?"

He grinned. "Oh, lots to report, but not now." Juba and Hazzard exchanged grins though Kate couldn't tell if they were both glad she was home or up to something and keeping it secret.

Charlotte took Kate into her arms and gave her a strong, fierce hug. "I missed you. With Hattie and you both gone, and my darn husband too, the house it just too quiet."

Kate squeezed Charlotte. "Next time I'll take you with me. You shouldn't have to stay home while everyone else has adventures."

Charlotte laughed. "No thank you. Taking care of you all is all the adventure I need."

Odetta interrupted them with her own hug and a kiss on the cheek before turning to pull a platter of pecan waffles out of the warming oven.

Louisa threw herself at Kate, nearly knocking her over. Kate laughed in joy. There was nothing as infectious as a fifteen-year-old girl's enthusiasm. Then Louisa saw Monty's cast and looked stricken.

"He's all right," Kate said in a rush. "He broke his leg but he'll be good as new in a month or two." She didn't think Louisa needed to know about the twenty hours he'd been unconscious, hovering in that grey space between life and death.

Louisa picked up the little dog and sat in a chair with him. Everyone pretended not to notice when she fed him a piece of ham.

Samuel hung back, watching the merriment from the far side of the table. As far as Kate could tell, Samuel never got real excited about anything. A lifetime of slavery had made him cautious. Kate moved around the table, leaned down and hugged him He reassured her that Excelsior and his stable

339

mate Lucy were in fine fettle and then tried to leave. Kate made him stay and eat breakfast.

"Where are Timothy and Hattie?" Kate asked once they were all seated and tucking into breakfast.

Charlotte answered. "He's to Richmond pretending to be a Confederate sympathizer. He was gone ten days on his first trip. Then eleven, no twelve days ago, he left again. This time with Hattie."

Juba spoke up. "Hattie's pretending to be his wife. She'll stay in Richmond for a while, while he comes and goes. He's carrying letters through the lines. The Union Army lets him through and the Rebs think he's a genius getting stuff back and forth."

Kate poured syrup on her waffle and snuck a glance at Charlotte. She didn't look worried so Kate let it go. They'd catch her up on the details soon enough..

Louisa bounced in her seat and looked at Charlotte. "Kin I show her now? Kin I?"

"Can, dear. You must enunciate," Charlotte said. "Even when Miss Hattie is not here."

Kate smiled. It was good to be home. "Can you show me what?"

Charlotte nodded at Louisa, who hopped up like a jack-in-the-box and grabbed a folded newspaper off the sideboard. She handed it to Kate.

Kate took the newspaper and looked at it. There, middle of the page, half way down, a short piece from the Rochester Dispatch.

Prominent Business Man Detained in Murder Case

Authorities arrested Mr. Abelard Lyon today in connection with the murder of his clerk Mr. Edwin Harcourt. Mr. Lyon claims Mr. Harcourt embezzled thousands of dollars from his business. Mr. Lyon is the same man who recently won a barratry suit against a noted spiritualist of this city. The lady has since been released pending appeal. Mr. Lyon alleges that his murdered clerk illegally used Lyon Enterprises funds to bribe Judge Townsend, who presided over the suit against the aforementioned lady spiritualist. In his statement to the press, Police Commissioner Peterman suggested that Mr. Lyon may have killed Mr. Harcourt in self defense. An investigation of Judge Townsend is also pending. It would be no exaggeration to say the entire city finds the news of this scandal most absorbing.

Kate handed the newspaper to Hazzard, who waved it away.

"I was downstairs before you, so I already saw it. All's well that ends well."

"I wish I could say 'poor Mr. Harcourt' but I can't. Still, if they're pretending they released Lily that means they won't be looking for her."

Kate laid the newspaper aside, wishing she could send it to Lily. She would if the lady ever contacted her. "I wondered how Harcourt got the money to bribe the judge. And buy the nitroglycerine. Now we know." She stuck a large bit of waffle into her mouth, savoring its buttery goodness.

Louisa bounced in her seat again. "We read your letters, so we know some of what you've been doing, but not all."

"The girl's right," Juba said around a mouthful of waffles. He swallowed. "You owe us a story."

Kate looked around the table. Odetta and Samuel watched her. Hazzard threw back his head and laughed.

"Go on then," Charlotte said with a wave in Kate's direction.

Kate swallowed her last bite of waffle and began her tale. It was a long time before anyone got up from the table.

The End

Real (and not so Real) Things

I found the premise for this story in a book written by Allan Pinkerton, *The Spiritualists and the Detective* (1876). I suspect he would recognize little of his book in mine. I wrote this book in a fever, mid-fall quarter, amidst a ruinous teaching schedule (6 classes at 2 colleges). I augmented, invented, prevaricated and otherwise made stuff up to create a substantially different story. Nonetheless, I owe Mr. Pinkerton a debt of gratitude for several story details. The lavender pants, for example, are from his book. I wouldn't have dared write such a daring bit of trouser fiction without Allan's encouragement.

Rose Greenhow entered the Old Capitol Prison on January 18th, but I moved up the date two weeks so this novel would end soon enough for the things that need to happen in the next volume of this series.

My fictional Kate Warne does not believe in spiritualism, nor in religion in general. Kate does not speak for me or you. A great number of nineteenth-century Americans were religious skeptics, but many were also fervent spiritualists.

Federal, state and local laws constrained nineteenth-century women of all colors and classes. These laws were based in the principle of coverture, which held that women were legally owned, first by their fathers and then their husbands. If this sounds suspiciously like slavery to you, congratulations, you understand coverture correctly. Indeed coverture is the legal basis for women's name change upon marriage. Women abused by fathers or husbands had no legal recourse because the law and social custom held that a woman's body did not belong to her. As repugnant as this idea

343

might be to most of us, it is one some modern Americana still believe.

Nineteenth-century women also had no right to property nor to their own children. They had few or no (depending on the state) rights to initiate a divorce, though they could be divorced if their husband wished it so. It was also extremely difficult for women to get an education. Most colleges didn't take women and most families wouldn't waste tuition money on daughters. The next time you hear someone refer to "the good old days" or bemoan the evils of modern feminists smack the speaker about the ears. You should thank your lucky stars that a bunch of women and men worked hard to make our lives (and the lives of our daughters) better than Lily's. And if you're still romantic about the past, consider these facts: no hot showers, no air conditioning, no wireless internet and no social media (OK, maybe not that last one).

Tic Tac Toe was invented in the mid-1800s, though not by a girl and a horse. Louisa would have known it as Tip Tap To. My beta readers kept thinking the "To" was a spelling error so I caved and used "Toe."

The Michigan Exchange Hotel in Detroit is real as is the Gibson House in Cincinnati and the Osborn House in Rochester. Peter Gibson financed the original hotel, but J. K. And D. V. Bennet first ran it. The Osborn House had steam heat and indoor plumbing. Alexander Gibson is a figment of my imagination, as are Pa Nettleton, Farmer Gosford and Reverend Bland, though the latter three are based on characters in Allan Pinkerton's book.

General George B. McClellan took command of the Union army as General-in-Chief on November 1, 1861, after General Winfield Scott's retirement. Before July 1861, McClellan made his headquartered in Cincinnati, where he oversaw the Department of the Ohio. Allan Pinkerton had his headquarters there because McClellan relied on him to provide him with intelligence. Allan would have left Cincinnati by January, but it suited the story to have him leave a little later. The bit about the King of Siam and the elephants is real. I use the lovely Long & Long, *The Civil War Day by Day*, to get the war stuff right.

The Arcade described in this book did exist as described. It was torn down and replaced with a newer version in 1930.

Civil War-era train schedules are difficult to read so I made up the train departure and arrival times though I tried to get the time train travel would take correct. The Ontario Ferry Company is real, but it did not operate until the early twentieth century. The Erie Railroad operated between Rochester and Dunkirk, New York before and during the Civil War. People wishing to travel to Detroit took steamboats across the lake, just as Kate did. The Detroit and Cleveland Navigation Company operated steamboats on the Great Lakes, including the side-wheeler State of New York, but the company did not exist until 1868. Lake Erie, being the shallowest of the Great Lakes, is the most likely to ice over, though not every winter. I don't know if it iced over the winter of 1862 or not. The Central Michigan Railroad operated between Detroit and Kalamazoo, beginning in the 1840s.

Here's a cool fact: Steel nibbed fountain pens were first mass-produced in the 1850s. Because they were affordable, they allowed many people who could not previously afford writing implements to buy and use pens. Thus this modest invention encouraged mass literacy. We can assume the vast majority of these pens were not used as illegal listening devices.

Barratry is an archaic legal charge, rarely used anymore, I assume because lawyers have agreed among themselves that there is no lawsuit too frivolous to not merit billing clients.

Liquid nitroglycerin was in wide use by 1862 and it did explode when jostled or dropped. This made it an unreliable explosive.

Amy Post was a committed nineteenth-century reformer as was her husband Isaac. In the late 1840s, the couple investigated the Fox sisters and declared their spiritual powers legitimate. In 1852 Isaac Post published a book in which he claimed that he and his wife had communicated with spirits of famous dead people like Benjamin Franklin. The book was well received and the Posts remained respected figures in reform politics. Years later the Fox sisters admitted that they'd faked their spirit rapping, though the Posts never repudiated them or spiritualism.

It suited me to put the Rochester courthouse, a bank, the Arcade and the Osborn House within walking distance of each other. In Allan Pinkerton's book about this case, the judge gave jury directions very much like the judge in chapter 30. This doesn't mean those directions were real or legally correct. Allan Pinkerton, like myself, was an unreliable narrator.

Violent Delights & Vampires
A Perils of Petronella Crabtree Journal

Petronella Crabtree's 1893 journal reveal a perilous world of monsters, some (but not all) more dangerous than a freshly sharpened parasol tip. Only the agents of the International Monster Hunter Organization & Thwarters of Evil Predators (IMHOTEP) stand between humanity and the rapacious fiends who delight in murder and mayhem. Petronella and her IMHOTEP agents disguise themselves as itinerant actors and travel to Elkhorn Montana to destroy a mysterious Giant Bat Monster. Shape shifter Petronella has help from a sword wielding vampire named Emma, Therese, a darkly mysterious Romani medium, Sierra, a six foot tall Fae woman whose second form is a unicorn and the Demon Botis, who masquerades as a mild mannered professor.

Can the Monster Hunters kill this ancient terror before it's too late? Or will the children of Elkhorn continue to die? In the shadow of the northern Rocky Mountains, the troupe must strap on their swords and parasols, don their night vision goggles and brave

Peg A. Lamphier

the lair of an ancient evil in order to end its plan to regain its lost power.

Peg A. Lamphier has a doctorate in American History she's used to write non-fiction monographs, encyclopedias and a small pile of novels. A native Montanan (go Bobcats!), she now lives in the mountains of Southern California with five dogs, six tortoises, a huge cat, two canaries, one daughter (who's away at college), one husband (who is around *all* the time) and a collection of vintage ukuleles that she plays with more enthusiasm than talent. When she's not writing fiction Peg teaches delightfully diverse young adults at California State Polytechnic, Pomona and Mount San Antonio Community College. For more about the Peg see www.peglamphier.com.

www.ingramcontent.com/pod-product-compliance
Lightning Source LLC
Chambersburg PA
CBHW021438240626
47153CB00001B/205